JOE HALDEMAN

W9-ABT-786

Other Avon Books by
Joe Haldeman

BUYING TIME
THE FOREVER WAR
THE HEMINGWAY HOAX
TOOL OF THE TRADE
WORLDS
WORLDS APART

WORLDS ENOUGH AND TIME

JOE HALDEMAN

AVONOVA

AVON BOOKS • NEW YORK

The poem "Benny's Song" first appeared in *Pulpsmith*, Copyright © 1986 by Joe Haldeman.

AVON BOOKS
A division of
The Hearst Corporation
1350 Avenue of the Americas
New York, New York 10019

Published in hardcover by William Morrow and Company, Inc.; for information address Permissions Department, William Morrow and Company, Inc., 1350 Avenue of the Americas, New York, New York 10019.

First AvoNova Printing: June 1993

AVONOVA TRADEMARK REG. U.S. PAT. OFF. AND IN OTHER COUNTRIES, MARCA REGISTRADA, HECHO EN U.S.A.

Printed in the U.S.A.

RA   10   9   8   7   6   5   4   3   2   1

These three books are for Gay.

CONTENTS

life is not: a book   not even when
it seems to have   pages   and chapters
beginning   an end   some progression

and life is not: a movie
                                even though
sometimes   it seems   you sit alone
                                        in darkness
watching ghosts
                      flicker
                                through a show
electric   in their rowdy
                      lifelessness

life is this: a work
                      of amateur
not/art   we start
                just barely time
                                        to learn
how to   hold the brush
                      which colors
aren't fugitive
                how to use
                      an outline
but we're not allowed   to start over   not ever
                                                they
shake their heads
                and take our
                      canvases away.
                                —benjaarons

PROLOGUE: TRANSCRIPT

≙

30 December 2092   14:30   [2 Tsiolkovski 280]
Subject: Marianne O'Hara

MACHINE: Are you comfortable?

O'HARA: What a stupid question. I feel like a pig on a spit.

MACHINE: Relatively comfortable. Ready to continue.

O'HARA: Oh yes.

MACHINE: Why do you want to leave Earth?

O'HARA: Why do you want to ask that question?

MACHINE: It is the one I was told to ask first. Subsequent questions will be generated by your responses. Why do you want to leave Earth?

O'HARA: It's not Earth I'm leaving. It's New New York. This satellite?

MACHINE: The process will be faster and easier if you cooperate. Why do you want to leave Earth?

O'HARA: The Earth doesn't exist anymore, not the Earth I knew. Savages in radioactive ruins. Clever diseases. There's nothing *left* to leave. No one I knew is left alive.

MACHINE: If you were given the opportunity to go back to Earth, rather than leave on the starship, you wouldn't go?

O'HARA: No. I tried that already.

MACHINE: Your emotional response is complicated.

1

O'HARA: The situation is complicated.

MACHINE: Going to Earth the first time, what was the landing like?

O'HARA: I was terrified. The sense of falling, going so fast. I knew how safe it was but my body was all confused. The gravity and the hugeness of the world outside. Horizons. We bounced landing and the straps bruised my hips and shoulders. Then I started to laugh; I'm not sure why.

MACHINE: What was full gravity like?

O'HARA: I'd had it in gym all my life, but not being able to walk out of it was depressing. It was like wearing a heavy rucksack you could never take off. Queasy all the time at first, but that was probably the strange food and the New York City air and water. What passed for air and water. My period came a week early and the flow was heavier than ever before; they said that always happens.

MACHINE: Why did you put off menarche until you were sixteen?

O'HARA: You would've too if you'd grown up in the Scanlan line. The boys were animals.

MACHINE: And?

O'HARA: I was afraid. As a girl, I was good at everything. I was afraid I wouldn't be as good at being a woman.

MACHINE: And?

O'HARA: My mother had frightening cramps, sick every month like clockwork.

MACHINE: And?

O'HARA: It scared me. Sex, I couldn't understand why anybody would want to do it. Any woman.

MACHINE: You understood why men would? Scanlan men?

O'HARA: Scanlan boys were encouraged to be aggressive. Sexually aggressive, especially. One broke my hymen with his finger on the playground when I was ten. A couple of years later five older boys held me down by the swimming pool when nobody else was there and masturbated all over me, laughing like hyenas. Beasts.

MACHINE: But they were punished?

O'HARA: No. The first one, the hymen, said it was an accident and the others denied even having been near the swimming pool. The counselor spanked *me* for lying. But when they tried it again, get back at me for tattling, I was ready for them, broke one boy's finger and gave another a good bite, drew blood. I got pretty beaten up in the process, but they didn't harm me anymore after that. Other than the damage they did to my attitude toward males.

MACHINE: But you were very active sexually after menarche.

O'HARA: Maybe I was relieved to find out I liked it and could be as good as anybody at it. Besides, I went with a Devonite the first couple of years; they don't stop fucking to eat. Got in the habit.

MACHINE: And after you left him?

O'HARA: He left me. Afterwards I spent a couple of years collecting boys, butterflying, sometimes two or three a week. The girls in the dorm called me Maneater. Then I met Daniel; we were a unit until I left for Earth.

MACHINE: The Daniel who's one of your husbands?

O'HARA: Yes, we married eventually. After the war. My other husband, John, I've known longer. He introduced me to Daniel.

MACHINE: Do you plan to keep it a triune?

O'HARA: I love them both. It seems stable.

MACHINE: What if Daniel or John wants another woman?

O'HARA: It has happened a few times, with Daniel not John. Casual and temporary liaisons, nothing sneaky or serious. That I know of.

	We all have the freedom if we choose to exercise it.
MACHINE:	Have you?
O'HARA:	No.
MACHINE:	You hesitated then, and your physical reactions were interesting. Tell me what you were thinking.
O'HARA:	A man, a nice man in Demographics. He asked me last month; I said no but thought maybe. Guess I'm still considering it.
MACHINE:	Your body is. Suppose Daniel or John wanted to bring another woman into the marriage. Would you object?
O'HARA:	She would have to be someone very special to all of us. That's the line rule: one veto is all it takes. If it was one of Dan's recurrent morsels I'd show them both the airlock. He likes them beautiful but dumb.
MACHINE:	Then why do you suppose he was attracted to you?
O'HARA:	Do you have a sense of humor, or what?
MACHINE:	I'm going to introduce a few drops of various substances onto your tongue, one at a time. Tell me what they make you think of. . . .

(Only two months after this interview, O'Hara did allow another woman into their line, Evelyn Ten, who was beautiful but not dumb. Also twelve years younger than O'Hara, which bothered both of them for a time.)

0

≙

IDENTITIES

My name is O'Hara Prime, just plain Prime to my friends, and although I am human I am not flesh and blood. I have lived for many centuries but will be twenty-nine years old forever.

This document is "my" story only by default: none of the other people in it is cybernetic, so none of them could have lived through the entire span. Marianne O'Hara once called me a vampire, I think playfully. It's true that I have never been exposed to the light of day, and that I live in a box, and will not die; do not age. But from people I consume only data, not blood.

Marianne O'Hara was the flesh-human template for my personality, and we had frequent conversations after my initial programming. At first she only talked to me on birthdays and special times, like Launch Day. As she grew older, though, we would have rather long conversations regularly. She claimed that I, being forever young, helped keep her attitudes from completely ossifying.

"Forever young." By the age of fifty she had forgotten how old you can feel at twenty-nine.

I could tell this story to another machine, if it were also human, in a few seconds of direct data transfer (and have done), but of course to tell it to "soft" humans I must resort to more complicated artifice. For your ease I will attempt to tell most of it in O'Hara's words, in her style, at least up to the time of her death. The rest of the story is still hers in a real sense, as I hope will be made clear, but perforce I shall tell that part as seen through other eyes. She did not believe in ghosts, except for me.

(The style you are reading here is my own; that is to say, O'Hara might have written this way if she had had my standards and resources of logic, vocabulary, and so forth. She was admittedly less formal. When I begin her story I shall attempt to re-create that quality.

(Parts of her story will be in her own words, literally. She went through sporadic periods of almost compulsive journal-keeping, especially in times of trouble. She was a good diarist but obviously wrote with the eventuality of publication in mind. Her Earth diary was published before 'Home left orbit.)

I was "born," or became self-aware, on 29 December 2092 [27 O'Neill 280], but when my programming was complete, a few weeks later, I felt not quite thirty, the same age as O'Hara. She was born 6 June 2063 [2 Freud 214], which was twenty-two Earth years before the war; thirty-four years before the starship Newhome would leave the ruins of Earth behind.

The program that created me was called "immersion," or Aptitude Induction Through Voluntary Hypnotic Immersion. It is essentially a method of storing and transferring certain aspects of human personalities. Newhome needed to carry a broad cross-section of humanity in order to make a new start at Epsilon, but many of the people we needed either could not or would not leave the relative comfort and security of their satellite home, New New York. So we would make cybernetic copies of them, eventually to impose their aptitudes on willing volunteers, when colonization began. (Predictably few people would volunteer, of course—no matter how useless or redundant their own capabilities might be—and that is part of the story.)

Marianne O'Hara was in charge of the Demographics Committee in Newhome's later planning stages, so she had to decide who to take along and who to plug into the machine if they could not or would not go. Unwilling to ask people to put up with something she hadn't herself undergone, she was the first colonist to submit to the induction process. The prologue to this document, above, is a transcript of part of her induction interview. (The other voice is my own, at the age of one day.)

As she remarks, it is not comfortable. The subject is put into deep hypnosis, usually with the help of drugs, and the body is wired up to have forty-three physiological parameters monitored. Some of them are readable with noninvasive procedures—pulse, blood pressure, brain waves—but measuring such things as sphincter tension and the viscosity of vaginal mucosa requires the insertion of probes.

Then, over the course of ten or so days, the subject is interrogated rapidly and thoroughly by the machine. Physiology recapitulates emotion; thus, the subject's reaction to various stimuli serves to build up a quantitative map of her personality. These data are then integrated into a standard Turing macro-algorithm, to create a cybernetic person whose attitudes are similar to the subject's. More than "similar."

Talking about this makes me feel strange. Like describing the process of conception, pregnancy, and birth might be for you: you could describe it accurately without mentioning love, or caring, or mystery. The mystery, we have in common.

Going through the inverse procedure—taking a volunteer and forcing new aptitudes onto her personality—is even less comfortable, and to O'Hara's relief, she was forbidden to try it. The volunteer is wired with several hundred implants. Similar questions are asked, but they are presented as hypnotic suggestions, with the proper answers being the one the "inductor" would have given. Physiological responses are induced in the volunteer, to mimic the inductor's state of mind/body at the time of her response, which can be disturbing at a deep level. But it can successfully inject "talent" where there has been none.

O'Hara was forbidden induction because she was already crammed full of talent. Four degrees, two of them doctorates, and the tenth highest tested intelligence in *Newhome*. A few people liked her in spite of that. Rather more were waiting for her to stumble, I see now.

Which seems unfair. No one knows better than I what she had to live with, what she had to hold in. Although she enjoyed life, by and large, almost every morning she woke up in a cold sweat, or woke up screaming in the grip of vivid memory. Her first twenty-one years were unremarkable except for scholarly achievement; then she went to Earth, and in the course of a few months there was assaulted, kidnapped, raped. She was close to one man who was then murdered; fell in love with another and had to abandon him. The day she left Earth was the day the bombs fell, and history stopped.

She was mother to me, and twin sister, which is why I suppose I am doing this. But it's important for other reasons.

YEAR 0.005

≙

1

⇔

EARTHWATCH

23 September 2097 [13 Bobrovnikov 290]—Two days after launch day; I guess that will be "Launch Day" from now on. Less than an hour into the second day, actually. Left both husbands and my wife in a snoring pile in John's low-gee flat. I have a whole cot to myself and a measure of privacy, in exchange for tolerating a little more gravity. What's a little gravity, when you're lying down? Though of course I'm sitting now, typing.

I will miss the touch of pen on paper. I didn't type my journal very often in New New, even though the handwritten pages would eventually be read into the computer and the paper recycled. No sentimental anachronisms aboard *Newhome,* like paper for casual personal use. I even left behind the diary of my year on Earth, the year cut short at seven months. A leatherbound book from Bloomingdale's.

Bloomingdale's. I just ate the last caviar I will have in all my life. We divided my small jar up four ways and each had two crackers' worth. John opened a priceless bottle of Chateau d'Yquem, which also went four ways. Daniel followed with a mundane but effective liter of 200-proof chemically pure alcohol from the labs, which we mixed, variously, with Evy's tomato juice and orange juice and Dan's hot pepper sauce. John put all four together, saying it reminded him of the way they drank tequila in Guadalajara, a custom I had not embraced when I visited there. We had the telescope seek it out but, unsurprisingly, there was no sign of life, though we could see

11

buildings and streets clearly. It would have been impenetrable smog a few years ago.

We watched the sun set on Los Angeles and rise over London. Then on to midmorning in New York, one of the few places with a large number of people. You could see them on the sidewalks. Some of the slidewalks were actually rolling again.

Evy has never been to Earth, of course. Of the ten thousand people aboard this crate, only a few hundred have.

I guess writing that down is a tacit admission that I'm writing this for other people to read. But not for a long time. Hello, reader, up there in the future. I'm dead now. And will feel worse in the morning.

I think it's a good thing this starship is automated. Many key personnel are functioning at a low level of efficiency, if functioning at all. Including yours truly, Entertainment Director. The entertainment program for tomorrow, this morning rather, will be quiet music and contemplation of the sequelae of overindulgence.

If I'd drunk less or more I would be sleepy. At this level I'm edgy, and too stimulated to read or rest and too stupid to stop writing. At least by typing it out on the machine, I can erase the evidence tomorrow. Unless Prime makes a copy. She's everywhere.

Are you listening, Prime? No answer. So you're a liar as well as a soulless machine.

Since this is indeed the first entry in the Diary of the Rest of My Life, which is of course true every time one makes any entry in a diary, I will include some background data for you generations yet unborn. Perhaps you are mumbling these words around a guttering fire in a cave on Epsilon, this starship a legend a million years gone to dust. Perhaps you are one of my husbands reading it tomorrow. You think I don't know I don't have any secrets. Hah. Marry computer experts and give up any hope of privacy. I saw John break Tulip Seven's thumbprint code the day after she died. (He didn't do it for any trivial reason; the tribunal wanted him to have her files scanned for evidence. She drank poison but it might have been murder. Nothing conclusive.)

As I was saying. Two days ago we left the planet Earth

forever. Actually what we left was the satellite world New New York, which has been orbiting the Earth since before my grandmother was born. The Earth itself has been a mess since 2085, as you must know or can read about somewhere else. Almost everybody killed in a war. I started to write "senseless" war. Do you have sensible ones, up there in the future? That's something we never worked out, not to everyone's satisfaction.

One reason the ten thousand of us are embarked on this one-way fling into the darkness is that Earth does seem to be recovering, and the next time they decide to Kill Everybody they might be more successful.

Another reason is that there doesn't seem to be anyplace else to go. We could inhabit settlements on the Moon or Mars, or wherever, but they would just be extensions of New New; suburbs. This is the real thing. 'Bye, Mom. No turning back.

As a matter of fact, my mother isn't aboard. Nor my sister. Just as glad Mother stayed back but wish she had let Joyce come along. Old enough to be a good companion and still young enough to renew things for you as she discovers them.

I guess two husbands and a wife comprise enough family for anyone. God knows how many cousins I have scattered around. When the Nabors line kicked my mother out it was a mutual see-you-in-hell parting, and as I was only five days old, I had not yet formed any lasting relationships. There are a few Scanlans aboard, my formal line family, but I feel more kinship with some of the food animals.

Oh yes, you generations yet unborn. You do know what a starship is, don't you, mumbling around the guttering campfire? It is like a great bird with ten thousand people in its gullet and a matter/antimatter engine stuck up its huge birdy ass.

Up in the front, instead of a beak, there is a doughnut-shaped structure, with three spokes and a hub, which used to be Uchūden, a small world that also escaped destruction during the war, originally designed to be home for several hundred Japanese engineers. (Japan was an island nation on Earth, the most wealthy.) Now it functions as the control center for all of 'Home, the civil government as well as the thrilling engineering stuff.

Behind Uchūden, or "sternward," as they want us to say, are all the living quarters, offices, farms, factories, laboratories—you name it, even a market where you can spend all of your hard-earned fake money.

A simplified diagram of the ship would be six concentric cylinders, shells; the acreage per shell and apparent gravity increasing as the number goes down. Most people live and work on Shells 1, 2, and 3; the inner ones reserved for processes that require lower gravity, such as metallurgy and free-fall sex. There are also some living quarters up there for the elderly and infirm, such as my husband John Ogelby, who has an uncorrectable curvature of the spine that makes even three-quarters gee painful. He also has a lot of political pull ("friends in high places" has a strong literal meaning here) and so rates a rather large bedroom/office/galley combination on Shell 6. The family tends to gather there.

I'm writing this in my small office cubicle in Uchūden, which is by definition Shell 1. As perquisites of rank I do have a cot that folds down from the wall and an actual window to the outside—on the floor, of course. I can either watch the stars wheel by once each thirty-three seconds or flip on a revolving mirror that keeps the stars stationary for fifteen seconds at a time. I like to watch them roll.

That concentric-cylinder model is just a theoretical idealization. You'd go crazy, living in a metal hive like that. So the walls and ceilings are knocked down and conjoined in various ways to give a variety of volumes and lines of sight. Most people still spend a certain amount of time hopelessly lost, since only a few hundred of us lived here while it was being built, and have had time to get used to it. New New was laid out logically, the corridors a simple grid on each level, and it was impossible to get lost. 'Home is deliberately chaotic, even whimsical, and is supposed to be constantly changing. Only time will tell whether this will keep us sane or drive us mad.

Still, the longest line of sight is only a couple of hundred meters, looking across the park. It's a good thing that almost all of us grew up in satellite Worlds. Someone used to the wide open spaces of Earth would probably feel trapped by 'Home's claustrophobic architecture. In most corridors, for obvious instance, the floor curves up in two directions, cut off by the low ceiling in twenty meters or less—a lot less, up in 5 and 6. Of course you can look out for zillions of light-years if you have a window like mine, but for some reason some people don't find that relaxing.

Both of my husbands were born on Earth, but spent enough years in New New to have lost the need for long lines of sight; distant horizons.

I do miss horizons, vistas, from my three visits to Earth. The first couple of weeks I spent there I had a hard time adjusting to the long lines of sight, even though I was in New York City, which most groundhogs would consider crowded. I would look up from the sidewalk and see a building impossibly far away and lose my balance.

I remember flying over kilometer after kilometer of forest, ocean, farmland, city. The Pyramids and the Rockies and Angkor Wat and even Las Vegas. We live inside one of the largest structures ever built, surely the largest vehicle—but we'll never *see* anything big for the rest of our lives.

At least Dan and John and I have memories. Evy and nine thousand others just moved from one hollow rock into a newer one. Maybe they're the lucky ones, I have to say, conventionally. I wouldn't trade places.

Well, the rigors of composition seem to have sobered and tired me enough for sleep. Fold up the keyboard and unfold the cot. If the gravity gives me trouble I can always rejoin the hamster pile upstairs.

2

≙

A CHANCE TO DREAM

PRIME

O'Hara and her staff of twenty-six had more than a thousand diversions to offer *Newhome*'s population. Most of the activities required very little in the way of administration other than keeping track of what went where: If you wanted to play chess, you went to the Game Room door and a person of adequate intelligence would figure out what day it would be one week hence, and loan you a set until then. If you didn't bring it back in a week, you would be called automatically every hour until you did bring it back—and it better not be missing a pawn; there was no way to send for a replacement. (On the other hand, the piece was bound to be *somewhere*. If someone had accidentally or perversely thrown it away, the recycler would identify it and buzz Entertainment.)

Some activities were more complicated because they required people or equipment primarily assigned to other departments. Religion had a claim on yoga, hamblin, and t'ai chi, but O'Hara's people also offered them, in a neutral secular context. Education had a hand in music, drama, and gymnastics. Communication was involved with social networking, and possibly New New Liaison as well, if your friend had stayed behind.

By far the most complicated was the Escape Room, a room with ten VR, virtual reality, installations. Every adult accumulated one minute per day of time on these machines. Five minutes was the minimum; some people

16

wanted to come in every five days for a quick blast. Others saved up sixty days for the maximum hour of dreamtripping. Some people wanted to come in with friends and be wired in parallel, simultaneously wandering through an imaginary or remembered world.

Children were allowed to use certain game programs, and restricted travelogues that were really only an elaborate form of interactive cube. Usually nine at a time would visit some earthly locale, along with a teacher, to answer questions.

It was a scheduling nightmare, but that was only the beginning. VR was a powerful drug to some people, and had to be administered with care. Everyone had been carefully tested in New New at the age of eighteen, or would be examined at that age aboard ship. Some people would be disallowed the random abstraction or feedback modes, either of which could be terrifying. Others were cut off at ten or fifteen minutes because they were particularly susceptible to the machine's effects: staying in too long could put them in a "VR loop," a vegetative state that was usually irreversible (though some people who had recovered from it wanted to dive right back in).

Most users were not too adventurous; for them, the VR was a whole-body, whole-mind go-anywhere machine. It was the only contact most people would ever have with Earth, vicariously traveling to arctic wastes or the Grand Canyon, the busy hives of Calcutta or Tokyo; soaring over fields of grain or through coral reefs. There were stock fantasy scenarios, too—harems and battlefields and laboriously reconstructed historical events—and the possibility of virtual time travel, since there were crude VR recordings nearly a century old. Of course most of the Earth cubes represented an equally irretrievable past. Calcutta and Tokyo, like Paris and London, were now inhabited only by handfuls of doomed children.

O'Hara found the Earth cubes unbearably depressing. The Luna and Mars ones were interesting visually but not sensually, since a space suit was no novelty. She liked the feedback mode, spectacularly confusing in its synesthesia—smelling colors, tasting sounds, muscles bunching into surreal impossible distortions, the body everting itself through mouth or anus and reverting slippery back again—and though she could see why some people would find it a nightmare, she emerged from the state completely relaxed, wrung out.

John had never tried VR and had no desire for it, but Dan shared her inclination toward the weird random abstraction mode, and they'd often schedule a half hour in parallel, wandering together through a shifting turmoil of light and sound that would crystallize into nearly real, or at least solid, landscapes, and then melt into chaos again. Mirror lands and cloud islands and flaming icescapes. One time Dan let O'Hara join him in a visit to the harem, where they learned something about the limitations of parallel wiring. O'Hara found the viewpoint interesting but her projected penis had no more feeling than a dildo; she participated in his orgasm but felt it only from her ankles to the soles of her feet. For an hour afterward she couldn't walk without giggling, her toes curling up.

3

≘

MEETING OF MINDS

O'Hara was supposed to meet John and Dan at the Athens lift fifteen minutes before the meeting. A little nervous, she was early. Evy came down and said the men would be late, as usual. The women went back up one level to get coffee and tea from the dispenser, which overcharged Evy by a dollar.

"This is a bad sign." She showed O'Hara the card. "Our lives are in the hands of people who can't keep a coffee machine working for one week?"

"Just inflation," O'Hara said. "A little experiment designed to make us more productive."

"I'll call Maintenance." She started to sip the tea but blew over it instead. "You are kidding, aren't you?"

"Hope so. With an economist in charge, anything could happen."

Evy nodded seriously. "You shouldn't have voted for him."

"Right." She looked around. "I haven't been up here since they put down the flooring. Makes your eyes hurt."

"It's different." Black and pearl checkerboard.

"Everything's different." She pushed the lift button twice. "Everything's the same."

"A philosopher this morning."

"Just crabby about the goddamn meeting." The door opened and they shared a short ride with two men in coveralls who stared sideways at Evelyn.

There was a bench built into the wall by the lift on Level 1. They sat down and watched the two men walk away muttering. "You with Dan last night?" O'Hara asked.

"Yes and no. I was asleep before he came in and he got up and left before I woke up."

"Could have been anybody, then."

"He needs a lot more sleep than he's been getting. I don't think it's been more than four or five hours a night since we left."

"Don't worry about that. I've seen him go through it a dozen times before."

"Wise old momma. Really?"

O'Hara nodded. "Every job change. Another couple of weeks and he'll break loose, get real drunk, sleep around the clock, and then go back to normal. Maybe a day off for moaning through a hangover."

"*Job* change."

"You know him. The job change is more profound than the planet change."

"Just like you?"

"You've got me there." O'Hara smiled but suddenly looked away.

"I'm sorry. I didn't mean . . ."

"I know what you meant." She patted the younger

woman's arm. "John's the only sensible one in the family, you included. He doesn't let work take over his life."

The lift opened and the sensible one swung out on his crutches. "Jesus. One of you ladies turn down the gravity?" Dan held the door and followed him out.

"Only a couple of blocks," O'Hara said.

"Could have held the meeting in the gym. Eliot doesn't like gravity any more than I do." Eliot Smith, Engineering Coordinator, was hugely overweight and had only one flesh limb, his right arm; the rest of them lost in a mining accident when he was a teenager. "You do know the way, don't you?"

"Nothing to it." O'Hara did know her way around the ship better than most adults. The designers had done a good job of providing special "interest," structural variety, but for some months most conversations between strangers would start out "Where the hell am I?"

They'd met at Athens lift because that allowed John to do most of his walking up on Level 6. But it did make their route to the meeting room rather complicated. They descended an escalator to the humid brightness of Level 1, the "ag" level, which in this section was a dense interplanting of corn and beans. The stalks were already a meter high, and they made a silken whisper in the ventilator breeze, and a rich complex smell. They walked and swung less than a hundred meters to another escalator that took them up to Level 4. O'Hara guided them through the maze of rights and lefts, ups and downs, that made the Arts and Crafts Mall so architecturally whimsical, and they wound up back on Level 2, in a corridor decorated with holos from European museums, somber classical paintings, leading to Studio 1.

"Should I wait outside and listen?" Evy asked.

"I don't think it's going to amount to much," Daniel said. They were headed for the first full Cabinet meeting since Launch. "Some rhetoric from Harry and a situation report from Eliot. Maybe Jules Hammond smiling benevolently over the proceedings. Then they turn off the cameras and we all go huddle around the coffee urns and it's like any Thursday meeting."

"Except you have everyone in the same room," O'Hara said.

"Handier than calling them up," John said. "Though there may be some you would just as soon not feast your eyes upon."

"Who could that be?"

"You'll have to get used to working with him." They were talking about Harry Purcell, Policy Coordinator and O'Hara's ultimate superior. Sixteen years before, Purcell had been her economics professor, and they had argued energetically over some pretty basic points—personality as much as theory. He made it clear he hadn't forgotten. She was trying to learn not to cringe whenever he opened his mouth.

4

≙

GENESIS AND REVELATION

28 September 2097 [13 Bobrovnikov 290]—I don't know why I'd envisioned a round table for the Cabinet meeting. We did that in New New for my Demographics Committee, no chiefs and no Indians, but with thirty-some Cabinet members it would be an unwieldy circle.

Still, I don't like formal hierarchal structures, least of all when they're set up with me at the bottom. A regular classroom would have been bad enough, the Coordinators up front dispensing wisdom, but instead we co-opted the small theater. That way Harry Purcell and Eliot Smith got to sit on the stage, head and shoulder (and torso and ass and leg, at least in Purcell's case) above us mere mortals.

The theater seats had slips of plastic with names on them. I helped John to his, in the front row, and then went to mine, in the rearmost. There was a definite pattern. Engineers and other grown-ups toward the front. I shared the back row with Tom Smith, Education; Carlos Cruz, Humanities; Janet Sharkey, Fine Arts; and our historian, Sam Wasserman.

I hadn't seen Sam since Launch. He gave me a shy grin and blush. We'd been lovers for a short intense time a few years ago, although he is exactly young enough to be my son, if I had followed my mother's example and become pregnant at the gray old age of twelve.

"Lovers" is too strong a word, or too polite a one. When Evy joined the line, which made me feel somewhat plain and middle-aged and dumpy, he was there for me. It was more complicated than that, and still is. I knew he would be at the meeting, but when I saw him I got a nice glow of physical surprise, or physical something. Maybe someday again.

(Prime says that she can keep this diary secure from prying eyes by shunting it over into her own cyberspace. I guess so, since she's supposedly self-aware, whatever that actually means.

(Do I really care whether Dan or John knows I get a little damp in the jeans, thinking about Sam? I'm not sure. I remember how he tastes, different. Kosher, I guess.)

Once everyone was in the proper place we had to sit still for a minute of camera registration. This was so the archives could properly record our gasps of admiration at Purcell's inspiring rhetoric. The sparkling wit that used to almost keep us awake in class.

He actually didn't start out too badly. With a mild joke he apologized for the necessarily ceremonial nature of this first joint meeting, and asked us all to introduce ourselves, for the record, then turned the proceedings over to Eliot.

That did make it interesting since we don't normally have joint meetings with the Engineering side. I like Eliot anyhow; he stood up for me back when old Casey tried to limit my powers in the demographics part of pre-Launch. He's also a funny guy.

Most amputees I've met opted for realistic-looking waldos (and of course we've all met people we couldn't tell were amputees), but Eliot goes in the opposite direction. His left arm and hand are usually a metal-and-composite skeletal framework with all the bearings and wires exposed, though sometimes he screws in a special-purpose tool. His legs clank against things, and he doesn't bother to wear shoes over his metal feet.

One night at the Light Head bar with Daniel and me, he pointed out the creepily obvious: the arm and legs were engineered better than he was. After he died they would cut off the arm and legs and file them away for the next clumsy person. He wondered if there was a library of prostheses somewhere in the hospital. He'd never tried to find out.

(Evy later told me there was such a collection, and there had been a battle royal with New New as to how many we were allowed to take along.)

For the meeting he wore an actual realistic hand, but kept the Meccano arm, looking intentionally ludicrous in a short-sleeved shirt. First he had Dan and Lenwood Zylius report in their capacities as New New Liaisons. Nothing significant on the Engineering side (Dan had told me he could give an hour of boring figures or a half-second shrug) and Zylius, Policy, could report only that putting one light-minute of vacuum between us and New New had not materially changed the amount of red tape involved in relations between the two structures.

Ito Nagasaki, Criminal Law, reported that her men and women were all working twenty-five-hour shifts and falling behind; she desperately needed police and counseling volunteers. A lot of people were reacting to the stress of parting by punching or pulling the hair of the person nearest to them; sometimes dearest.

I had known that Evy was working overtime, too; Indicio Morales, in charge of Health Care facilities, confirmed that out of ten thousand people, fifteen hundred had fallen ill with something—mostly homesickness, anxiety, angst, and the aforementioned black eyes and contusions. They'd predicted it was going to happen, but were surprised at the volume of complaints.

Morales rolled pills and Nagasaki handed out fines and counseling appointments; both of them figured that their troubles would slack off in another week or so. (If not, we'd have to turn around and go back!) There were short business-as-usual reports from Agriculture, Ecosystems, Life Support, Maintenance, and so forth. My own report was almost a nonreport, since people were still so busy figuring out what they were going to do for the next ninety years that they weren't checking out a lot of volleyballs and clarinet reeds. The zero-gee "saunas," a euphemism rarely used, were occupied round the clock, which I suppose is entertainment, though few people have to check out extra equipment for the sport.

Then Purcell took the floor again, for his bombshell. "This is very bad timing," he began, "but obviously it isn't the sort of thing one apologizes for." He looked at Eliot thoughtfully, and shook his head. "I'm afraid ... well, my physician has informed me that I am the victim of a rare disorder called Murchinson's Syndrome." I was sitting close enough to Morales to hear her sudden intake of breath.

"Murchinson's Syndrome involves a rapid and irreversible breakdown of the immune system. There's no actual treatment for it."

Eliot's voice was almost inaudible. "How long?"

"It could be months. Or it could be weeks or days. Eventually a single rhinovirus ... would be sufficient."

"You could be isolated. Sealed off from any disease vectors."

He shook his head. "I thought of that. As unpleasant as living out the rest of my days in a space suit would be. But like anybody, I'm carrying around a large number of disease factors that are currently more or less kept in check. As the doctor put it, there is no way to isolate a person from his own body. When the immune system weakens sufficiently, one of those factors will kill me.

"Most of you know me well enough to know that I would appreciate a minimum of sympathy and condolence. Of course I feel chagrined, cheated. Betrayed by my own body. I was looking forward to at least another half-century of observing this splendid experiment in economic isolation. But of course this does come to all of us sooner or later, and I have no new insight to offer about that.

"Fortunately, I have been working closely with my

Coordinator-elect, Tania Seven, and over the course of the next few days I shall be transferring all of my responsibilities over to her in an orderly way." Seven was sitting in the front row, and had shown no reaction; Purcell must have already discussed it with her. "I would also like to work closely with her in selecting the new candidates for Coordinator-elect." She nodded. He paused. "I suppose that ends the formal part of this meeting. Good-bye." He stepped down from the stage and walked out.

The rest of the meeting was short and quiet. Tom Smith and I did some preliminary hashing out of a procurement system that might simplify life for both of us (Education shares a lot of material with Entertainment, but we have separate storage areas, nearly a kilometer apart). I would have someone from John's office go over the proposed design changes for the next couple of years and see whether Tom and I could get offices close to a large enough storage volume to hold all of our stuff in one place. I'd miss the luxury of Uchūden, but it would save a lot of time.

Evy was waiting outside in the corridor. She'd never heard of Murchinson's Syndrome, but she had her keyboard with her. She unfolded it and asked.

The disease had never been reported on Earth. Over the past century there had been two cases in New New and one in Devon's World; every victim had been at least third-generation spaceborn.

"That's a little scary," I said. "Cosmic rays?"

John laughed. "I wouldn't worry about it. People probably did get it on Earth, but it was misdiagnosed. As Harry said, whatever bug's next in line is the one he'll actually die of."

"Let's talk about something morbid." Dan looked at me. "Are you going to throw your hat in the ring?"

"Hat?" Evy said.

"It's an Americanism; run for office. No. I thought about it for a fraction of a second. No, thanks."

"You'd be good."

"Someday. Most people would think I'm too young."

"Tania Seven's about your age."

"The hell she is."

Evy primped her short kinky hair. "You white people age so fast."

"I'll age *you!*" I turned back to Dan. "Besides, I don't want to give up the Cabinet position." That was a precondition for running, though the logic of it has always eluded me. If I won Coordinator-elect, it would be two years before I was Coordinator. Plenty of time to train someone to pass out the volleyballs.

(It made even less sense on the Engineering side, since every Cabinet member is in essence a lobbyist for one academic specialty's research needs. When the Coordinator-elect takes office, that specialty automatically has two people arguing for their slice of the more-or-less fixed pie of resources and personnel available for research. A couple of years ago I submitted a proposal that the process be reversed: have the Coordinator-elect continue to sit as a Cabinet member, so as to keep all the influences more or less even. The Engineering track didn't see much merit in the proposal. I think that's because they like to gamble—every two years they get a chance to double their influence.)

We argued a little bit more about my running, Evy as usual on my side; Dan thinking that I was old enough and John claiming that age wouldn't be important. I told Dan that he only wanted me to do it because he'd had to go through a term as Coordinator in New New, and misery loved company.

When I got back to the office there was a note on my message queue from Purcell; he wanted to see John and Dan and me after dinner. I could think of a few thousand things I'd rather do with my evening. But as it turned out, the experience was at least informative, if not pleasant. We even managed to bury the hatchet, in a way, and not in each other. He was never a particularly graceful man, but most people agree that he handled his exit well.

We joined him in a small teaching lab on Level 5, racks of glassware in place for some arcane demonstration. There was a trace of sulfur dioxide in the air, as there usually seemed to be in such places, and it gave me an instant headache, as usual. I think John and Dan thrive on it. A homey sort of smell for science types, like bread baking.

Purcell was leaning against a sink, studying some small wire contraption. He nodded to me but talked only to John and Dan, mostly filling them in on his assessment of Tania Seven, and how her training and prejudices might affect their jurisdictions. It was an odd coincidence that they held two of the only Engineering-track Cabinet positions that required daily contact with the Policy Coordinator's office. I was Policy track, but could probably survive for months without bothering the Coordinator.

It was interesting to eavesdrop on them, and interesting that I was allowed to. Purcell was a cold-blooded manipulator—one who wanted to keep manipulating from the grave!—but he was also a solid if cynical judge of character. I was wondering out of what obscure motivation he had invited me along, when he abruptly dismissed John and Dan, saying he had to talk to me alone.

He was a great one for amenities. "I don't like you, Marianne, but then I don't like many people. Including myself."

"Dr. Purcell—"

"You might as well call me Harry. You won't have to for long." He tossed the little wire thing onto a table, watching its slow third-gee trajectory rather than look at me. "Daniel thinks you would be a good prospect for Policy Coordinator-elect. Don't run."

"I already told him I wouldn't. I'm not old enough."

"You're old enough. You're competent. But there are a lot of people in this can—like me—who are rather hostile toward you."

"Can't please everybody."

"That's not the point. I rarely please anybody, but here I am." The wire thing bounced and he snatched it out of the air with a surprisingly swift motion. "It's not your personality, or that you've been unfair or imprudent." He allowed himself a tiny smile. "Though your sex life, such of it as has come to my attention, seems . . . lurid. By my standards."

"I have my own standards."

"As I say, that's not the problem. It's much more subtle than that, and it's complex, multiplex, and you have to do something about it before you run for office. Because the chances are you *will* win, and the results of your tenure could be disastrous."

"I'm listening." Hearing, anyhow.

"Number one. You're an idealist. That's attractive in the young."

"You're saying a leader can't be an idealist?"

"It's an impediment." He leaned back, professorial. "Go ahead. Give me an example."

"Jefferson." I thought of him because I'd just seen his picture; one of the paintings reproduced in the hall outside of the meeting room.

"Thomas Jefferson. I don't know American history that well." He brightened. "But I know American economics. Jefferson owned slaves, didn't he? Doesn't sound too enlightened, even for that period."

"He freed them."

"He bought them first. Sounds like political expedience."

"Mahatma Gandhi."

"Religious leaders don't count. Without at least the appearance of idealism, they would have no following." He waved a hand to keep me from trying Adolf Hitler or someone. "It's not that you can't have ideals. Even I have one or two left. But I don't let them dictate policy. I'd wind up with a few dedicated partisans on my side and a guaranteed majority trying to impede me, on general principles."

"I understand what you're saying. I would have to be subtle—"

"That's not in your repertoire. Might as well say 'I would have to be a giraffe.' Unless you've changed profoundly in the last few months."

"But it's not as if I'm a bomb-throwing radical. Most of the people in 'Home have about the same notions of right and wrong—"

"You *would* say 'right and wrong.' That's not what I'm talking about. What I'm saying is that you're inflexible. You wouldn't act against principle, even when it was clearly necessary."

"You seem to know a lot about me."

"I do." He unzipped a front pocket and handed me a

holo slide. "This is a message to you from Sandra Berrigan."

"What did you have to do with Sandra?"

"We were strange bedfellows together." For a weird moment I thought he meant sex, and tried to picture it. "I was supposed to wait until we were a lot farther out to give that to you. You are to play it once, alone, and then destroy it, and never discuss it with anyone but me."

"Not even Sandra?"

"Especially not her. She has her own problems."

I put the slide in my breast pocket, next to the button bug that was recording our conversation. It was confusing. Sandra had been my political mentor; she knew exactly how I felt about Purcell.

"Sandra entrusted that to me for reasons that will become apparent. I couldn't pass on that trust. And I wanted you to read it while I was still . . . able to discuss it with you."

"I'll look at it tonight."

"It's about principle, ideals. About complexity."

"Okay." Sandra and Purcell? I put it out of my mind for a while. "Number one, I'm an idealist. I'll accept that. Is there a number two?"

He nodded but didn't answer immediately. Then he said, "Have you ever wondered why you were appointed to the least significant Cabinet post?"

"I've wondered." He waited. "All right. To be completely honest, if less than humble, I've always believed the position was created for me. That Sandra pushed it through so that I could have some Cabinet-level experience without too much visibility. It does seem odd to have Entertainment at the Cabinet rather than the committee level."

"You're nine-tenths right. But it was my idea, not Sandra's."

That was reasonably shocking. "That's . . . interesting."

"Or unbelievable?" He scratched his head and grimaced. "I had planned to have this conversation with you when you were rather more experienced."

"More experienced," I said. "I have four degrees, two husbands, and a wife—not counting the hundred or so lovers before I was married. I've been to Earth three times. I was there for the end of the world. I can juggle three objects of different sizes and play the clarinet, though not at the same time. I even have some political experience. Not enough, I take it."

"Are you through?"

"No. You've condescended to me for a good sixteen years. Now I'm supposed to believe you have enough respect for my abilities to create a position that sets me up to take over your job. You're right; it's unbelievable. It's fantastic. I could use some explanation."

"That's number three."

"Does the order matter?"

"Perhaps not." He levered himself up to perch on the edge of the table, a slow balletic move in low gravity. "I will give you half of my reason. The irrational half."

"Go on."

"I had a daughter born about two years before you were born. She was very much like you. We argued for many years, but argument to me is a sport. I challenged her in the spirit that another man might play ball with his daughter, or chess, or go to movies."

"I can understand that."

"She never did. When she was eighteen she stopped speaking to me. When she was nineteen she emigrated to Tsiolkovski, of all places. Ostensibly because I was so contemptuous of their politics and economics. She left a note."

"And she died there during the war?"

"She never got there. The '81 shuttle disaster."

That was the year I was in his class. He'd never mentioned it. "My God. That's terrible."

"I'm not sure that I loved her. I suspect that I've never loved anybody. Of course I feel partially responsible for her death."

I had to say the obvious. "You didn't have anything to do with the airlock blowing out, Harry. She was killed by metal fatigue. By poor maintenance."

He nodded. "Partially responsible." I hoisted myself up next to him on the edge of the table. He was a big man; my shoulder touched his bicep. I resisted the temptation to put my arm around him. We both stared at the opposite wall.

"My doctor, who was an old friend, gave me pills for grief and advised me to continue business as usual. That was when you were in my economic theory seminar. Every time you opened your mouth, you reminded me of her. It became very hard to go to class."

"I'm sorry. You could have—"

"Maybe you knew her? She called herself Margaret Haskel."

"Yes. We had a swimming class together the year before she . . . I didn't know she was your daughter."

"She didn't broadcast it." In fact, we hardly ever spoke. We did look similar in face and freckles and red hair, but nobody in a nude swimming class would have mistaken us for one another. She had a perfect voluptuous figure. I could have held a frankfurter in front of me and passed for a boy. We didn't seem to have much in common.

I remembered the strange feeling when I saw her name on the list of casualties. It wasn't sadness; I hadn't known her that well. But I'd never known anyone before who had died. It made me feel oddly important.

"So yes, I've been following your career since then. For twelve years your successes have been a constant small irritant. I always have to think of Margaret and what she might have done. Not rational." He put his hand on mine, unexpectedly, cold. "That's how they make pearls, though." He squeezed. "Put an irritant into an ugly old bivalve."

He started pacing. "Number two. You have accumulated far too much influence and visibility for a woman your age. Not just the demographic selection work you did on Start-up, though that certainly made you ubiquitous. That book you wrote made you a kind of celebrity in New New, and celebrity has its negative side."

"I wasn't exactly lusting for fame. I wanted the book to be published anonymously."

"I know. A pretty gesture, but pointless. Anybody who didn't know who you were by then would have to have been asleep all the years following the war." The book, *Three Earths,* was about my rather eventful school "year" on Earth, cut short by the war, and the two disaster-ridden return missions I participated in. It was just my diary with some of the stupidities and libels edited out.

"I wouldn't even go on the Hammond show to publicize it."

"I know that, too. Annoying, isn't it?"

"Oh no; it's flattering. An actual O'Hara-ologist."

"Only Sandra and your husbands and wife know as much about you." He left out my cybernetic sister. Prime knows a lot of things I would never tell a flesh human. "Someone who didn't have access to your psychological profile might think that you were unfit to be a leader, because of your obvious ambitious nature."

"It's not that kind of ambition. I don't want to boss anyone around." Like New New, 'Home disqualified from public office people who had certain easily measurable, and potentially dangerous, psychological handicaps, such as an emotional hunger to have power over others, or to be a martyr. So no Hitlers, but no Gandhis, either.

"Then what *do* you think you want?"

"Learn the secrets of the universe. Do everything at least once. Bring peace to our time. Have more time to play the clarinet. What a question."

"What an answer. Of course only simple people could give a straightforward answer." He resumed his slow pacing, which might have looked dignified down on Level 1. In this gravity there was a certain sprightliness to it.

"A lot of people who are older than you think you have come too far, too fast. I trust I don't have to name any."

"No."

"Among the people who will eventually be your rivals for my present job, there are very few who are not jealous of, or even afraid of, your charisma."

"I've seen that. But nobody who really knew me would ever accuse me of charisma. I've just had a lot of things happen to me."

He held up a finger. "That's it. They are things that can never happen to anyone else. Nobody else aboard this isolated can will ever experience revolution, nuclear war, plague. Nobody will be kidnapped and flown to Las Vegas. Nobody—"

"I understand the direction you're headed."

"What you have to do is spend several years being deliberately quiet and well behaved."

"Oh, come on. I can behave myself."

"You can when you want to. You were a little angel at the meeting today—"

"I'll try to do better."

"You see? One word and you react."

"We're not in public."

"But we are. You are. I may be the most important audience you'll ever have." He paused to let that sink in. He was right. Part of his legacy could be a vote of no confidence that I would drag around for a long time. "Your presentation today lasted only forty-two seconds and used the pronoun 'I' only once. I know you could have gone into more detail with no more substance, as Smith and Mancini did, or could have made your presentation more entertaining, more memorable. That you did neither shows a good level of political survival instinct. What I want to do is help you refine your instincts into a calculated strategy."

"A dishonest one?"

"Only in that it won't be the course your 'natural' self would choose. You're going to lose that self, at least as a public persona. You're going to put your shoulders in the harness and for some years work on being a meek and helpful toiler in the political vineyard. Taking stupid orders from people you don't respect. Learning to compromise so that stupidity appears to have been served, without sacrificing your eventual goal. Learning patience."

"Learning to be a political animal."

"You must."

"As you said, though, I could probably win an election just by being myself. I could probably win this one."

"That's right. Which brings us to the other part of number three."

"The rational part, I assume."

"You're paying attention, good. You hardly need that recorder."

"You ... don't know. You're guessing."

"Not anymore." He almost smiled. "Sandra and I disagreed on a number of things—some very basic, such as the right to accumulate wealth, to own property—"

"I can understand that."

"But one thing we did agree on was you."

"In what sense?" Sandra *liked* me, I thought.

"A general assessment of your abilities, your potential; that's something anyone with any administrative experience would agree on. Including yourself; you can be objective. The most important thing, though, and one you're almost certainly blind to, is that you are potentially the most dangerous individual aboard this vessel."

I laughed out loud. "Yeah. I was about to have myself locked up."

"Be serious and listen. We think of 'Home as being a kind of New New York in microcosm. It's a heuristic convenience and a dangerous fallacy."

"Well, we're no *Mayflower.*"

"What flower?"

"It was a colony ship that brought people from Puritan England to America. They didn't have an Entertainment Director."

"I remember. That rock, the Ford Rock, the Plymouth. It's not too good a comparison. They could breathe the air outside their ship, for instance; they could throw out fishing lines for food. If they didn't like America, they could sail back home."

"All points well taken. Sorry to interrupt."

"Points salient to the problem at hand. You.

"Think of New New York as an island, surrounded by other islands. There's a mainland, Earth, that they can reach only with difficulty, and it's a dangerous, uncomfortable place. But their island is pretty self-sufficient, and nearby islands—the Moon, the Deucalian remnants, and other asteroids—can provide all their needs. They're stable.

"By comparison, we're a submarine. We're incredibly well stocked with supplies, and even a surplus of materials for the creation of new supplies. We even have an Entertainment Director. But we can't surface until we reach our destination, by which time most of us will be dead."

"We talked about all this years ago, even before Start-up."

"We have more data now. For instance, when Morales gave his Health Care report, he neglected to mention the hundred and twenty-seven suicides we've had since Launch Day."

Sudden feeling like a ball of ice in my stomach. "More than one percent."

"That's right. If this rate continued, by the time we left the Solar System more than half of us would be dead." He shook his head. "It's happened before, a suicide epidemic. In New New, just after the war. We juggled the statistics as best we could. If there were no witnesses to the act, the death wound up in some other classification. We're doing that here, but it's more difficult, since quarters are more cramped."

"They expected a few suicides, didn't they? Lot of stress."

"Between ten and twenty, going on no data, of course. Certainly not a hundred."

"It'll probably go down rapidly. The people who were most unstable in that direction are mostly gone now, I guess."

"Guessing is all anybody can do. And you must not tell anybody. Morales gave the number only to me and Eliot. Certainly other people in Health must know that it's a big problem. They'll keep quiet."

"I won't tell anybody. I'm familiar with the dynamics involved, the etiology." I'd read about how families, communities, and whole cultures could become infected with the "meme" of suicide—once you know people who've done it, it becomes a possibility. A solution.

"You still don't see how it applies to you."

"Not by any stretch."

"This . . . submarine is probably the most unstable large society ever thrown together. Hand picked, of course—largely by you—and taken from a pool of people who are accustomed to living in close quarters, essentially underground. Nevertheless unstable."

"I see where you're headed. The last thing these people need is a charismatic leader. To use your word."

"Exactly. They need managers—not totally colorless; people whose abilities they can recognize and respect. But no one too exciting, no one with wild ideas about changing things. There will be changes, but they must happen slowly, deliberately. This is a boat, so to speak, that we cannot afford to rock."

I had a couple of arguments there, about the danger of my supposed charisma and the paternalism of his attitude, but decided I'd save them until after I'd seen what Sandra had to say. I didn't give any sign of agreement or disagreement. "So. When should we meet next?"

"Not tomorrow. I'll be suffering through pro forma condolences. Thursday sometime. I'll call or leave a message on your queue."

"Okay." I'm not often at a loss for words. You look awfully tired, I should say; why don't you lock your door and get some rest? Or I'm sorry about all this; I wish it weren't happening to someone I've actively disliked for nearly half my life. "Uh, should I bring John and Dan?"

"No, I'm done with them. You're my project now." He made a shooing motion with his hand. "Go on. I have some calls to make."

I backed out of the room, nodding obediently, into the shelter of the corridor. I didn't know how to feel or what to think; things had happened too fast. Even if I wanted to like him, to help him, he wasn't going to let me, and besides, his attitude, his postures, still annoyed the hell out of me, dying or not.

I was tired and rattled, but if I didn't look at the slide tonight, curiosity would keep me awake. I went over to the commissary and squandered four dollars on a small box of wine to take up to the office.

5

≙

GRAVE IMAGE

Probably out of respect for Berrigan, O'Hara never mentioned viewing the slide; not to me; not to her diary; certainly not to any flesh person other than Harry Purcell. But nothing that went on in her office was secret to me, a detail I never mentioned to her. (She never asked, I think deliberately.)

28 September 2097 [14 Bobrovnikov 290]—O'Hara enters her cubicle and tells the door to lock, then removes the small recorder from her pocket, turns it off, and puts it away. She sets down her purse on the cot and takes out a box of wine. Selects a glass from the cabinet, inspects it, blows into it, and half-fills it with red wine. She sets the glass on her work console, then reseals the box and puts it in the cabinet. She kicks off her shoes, sits in the swivel chair, turns on the console. Out of habit, she keys the message queue, but turns it off without looking at it. She unseals her blouse halfway and blows down it, then stretches, whispers "Shit," takes the slide out of her pocket, and studies it. She takes a sip of wine, slips the slide out of its protective jacket, and inserts it in the viewer. She swivels to watch the corner where I normally appear to her.

Berrigan is seated, wearing a formal dark blue suit. Her hair is long, so the holo must have been recorded more than two months ago.

IMAGE: Hello, Marianne.

O'HARA: Hello. Do you have logic capabilities?

IMAGE: I can respond to simple queries, though my memory is limited. My main function is to deliver a message, and then erase myself when you turn off the machine.

O'HARA: I was told to physically destroy the slide as well.

IMAGE: Yes.

O'HARA: I can't imagine being party to anything so top secret.

IMAGE: I cannot assess your ability to imagine. Shall I begin?

O'HARA: Go ahead.

IMAGE: (Blurs momentarily, then relaxes) Sorry for this format, Marianne. (smiles) I guess I didn't see any way to bring this up safely face-to-face. Not while you are who you are now, and I am who I am. (Fingers the Coordinator "C" figured into her lapel.) *What* I am.

        I wanted Harry to keep an eye on you, and give this to you when he thought the time was right. At least ten years. He hasn't seen it ... nobody has ... but he knows what it's about.

        I must ask your word that you will never discuss this with anyone but Harry, for the time being. And never with anyone who isn't in the Cabinet or Coordinator pool.

O'HARA: What if I feel I can't do that?

IMAGE: (blurs) I will have to erase myself.

O'HARA: May I have some time to think over the responsibility? A hint as to what it's about?

IMAGE: No.

O'HARA: Well ... all right. You have my word.

IMAGE: (blurs) This will be short and not sweet, Marianne. The government you're participating in is not a democracy by anyone's definition. The weekly referendum is a total hoax; the results are arrived at before the voting; and I doubt that one out of three decisions follows the will of the people.

O'Hara is staring open-mouthed.

You're now a member of a hand-picked meritocracy. Part of the psychological testing that we all have to put up with is to ensure that we will be able to participate in a benign conspiracy, before getting on the so-called ballot.

This goes beyond *realpolitik,* and it's not a rejection of democracy as a principle. But there are situations when democracy doesn't work unmodified, and you're in the middle of one of them.

O'HARA: Ten thousand people sealed up together in a small pressure vessel.

IMAGE: You may remember that we considered the possibility of instituting a quasi-military kind of social structure in *Newhome*—captain, officers, crew.

O'HARA: In the Start-up discussion group.

IMAGE: It was rejected because our people have lived under democracy, or at least its illusion, for too long. We would never have found ten thousand volunteers if they thought they were giving up their citizenship.

O'HARA: Has this been going on from the beginning?

IMAGE: (blurs) You mean since New New's original charter?

O'HARA: Whatever. How long?

IMAGE: I have no historical data beyond Sandra Berrigan's actual experience. The degree of interference increased dramatically after the war, but the principle was firmly in place before she took office.

You should ask Harry Purcell.

The image is flickering because of some sort of overload phenomenon; you can only pack so much logic into ten nanograms of circuitry. It steadies when it goes back to Berrigan's prepared speech.

IMAGE: The decision to manufacture and distribute the anti-plague drug to Earth, for instance. Only thirty percent of the electorate were in favor of that. The prevailing sentiment was obviously that the groundhogs had gotten what they deserved; let them go ahead and die out.

But the chances are they wouldn't perish; the plague would run its course. Even if the Earth's population were reduced to a million gibbering savages, they were still sitting on a resource base a trillion times the size of ours. And a lot of the survivors thought that we were responsible for the war.

This was the unanimous decision of the Privy Council and Coordinators: we wanted to be remembered as saviors, not as aggressors. They could have nuclear weapons again in a generation or two. The next time they might do a more thorough job.

A second example is *Newhome* itself. Only thirty-nine percent were in favor of building it; a solid majority felt the money would be better spent in rebuilding the Worlds.

The executive decision was that *Newhome* was necessary for several reasons. One was spiritual, or I suppose you would rather say "emotional": we had to direct people's aspirations outward. If we spent twenty years just licking our wounds and glaring resentfully down at the Earth, we might never regain anything like normal relations with them again. Even now, there's a strong isolationist sentiment, as you surely know.

O'HARA: Especially the Devonites.

IMAGE: Another reason, as we discussed openly, is simple insurance for the human race. If there's another war it will probably be the last one.

Whether we would then deserve to survive is still open to debate.

I'm afraid we can't risk discussing this even on a private, scrambled beam. By the time Harry gives this to you, we'll be several light-months apart, anyhow. Hard to hold a conversation.

You may have suspected something like this was going on. I did, long before I was elected and Marcus enlightened me. A lot of people grouse about the government pulling strings behind everyone's collective back. They don't know half of it.

It feels funny to be saying good-bye when I'll be seeing you in the office tomorrow. This is July eighteenth, '97. You won't be leaving for a couple of months. I miss you already.

I didn't try too hard to talk you out of this. Someday you'll . . . well, you already . . . you know I feel closer to you than to either of my sons.

Good-bye.

The image flickers and blinks out.

O'HARA: (voice quavering) Can you still hear me?

There is no response. She wipes away tears and stares at the corner for more than a minute, finishing the rest of the glass. Then she ejects the slide and bends it back and forth until it breaks, and puts the pieces in the recycle tray.

She takes the box of wine out of the cabinet, along with a bath towel, picks up her purse, and leaves.

6

≙

THINGS THAT GO BUMP
IN THE NIGHT

I was tired but knew I wouldn't sleep unless I had some exercise. It had been a long day of sitting around and listening to people tell me things I didn't especially want to hear.

I took a long way to the pool so as to walk through the near-dark quietness of the ag level. The darkness intensified the smell of things growing. (Do plants actually grow in the dark, or do they rest?) Once away from the lifts, the only light is the dim glow of the pathway tiles; when other people pass by, they're only shadowy blurs from the knees up. You murmur good evening and drift away, feeling mysterious. As always, sounds of lovemaking from a couple of the unlit crosspaths. And as always, I wondered whether they could be strangers who brushed in passing and felt something suddenly happen, stopped, and moved into the darkness to appease that something. And perhaps then part in silence, and wonder for a while about every man you met who was the right size and shape. Were you my succubus?

They're probably all garden-variety, so to speak, adulterers. "Meet me between the cabbage and potatoes at 2330 tonight."

Out of some obscure impulse I turned down a crosspath myself, and stood for several minutes a few meters into the darkness, watching the disembodied feet. Remembered the wine and took a quiet sip. The taste didn't go well with the damp foliage smell. It occurred to me that if I stood there long enough, sooner or later a giggling couple would come charging into the darkness and in their reckless passion knock me into the broccoli tank. So I continued on to the pool, rather than stand in the path of true love.

I had to go up to Level 5 to detour around the yeast farm. The ag offices were bright and busy, which for some reason depressed me. Farmers ought to go to bed with the sun, get up bright and early to milk the chickens.

The pool was crowded for the late hour, more people socializing than exercising. I saw Dan in the deep end and called out to him. He didn't show any sign of hearing, but must have seen me after he made his turn. He came over to the towel shelf while I was undressing.

"Harry keep you this long?"

"No, I had to go by the office, check some things. Here." I handed him the wine.

"Thanks." He took a gulp and put it back on the shelf. "So how do you feel?"

"How am I supposed to feel? You know what he talked to me about?"

"That's not what I meant." He put his hand on mine. "I mean how do you *feel?*" I slept with John last night, was what he meant.

"Like a shuttlecock, sometimes, if you want to know the truth. How do *you* feel?"

"Well, I put us in for a fuckhut, just in case." Nobody calls them zero-gee saunas except the Entertainment Director.

"Thanks for asking me."

"Just in case."

"I'm not in the mood, Dan. I'm in *a* mood, but not *the* mood."

"Okay, okay." He found his clothes and stepped into his pants. "So what did you and your favorite professor talk about?"

"Can't say." I finished undressing. Funny that I didn't want to take my pants off until he had his on. With fifty other men I wasn't married to in the same room.

"Oh. I think I see."

"You probably do." I tried to keep the frost out of my voice. If our positions had been reversed, I would have kept it secret from him. "I'm not supposed to discuss it with anyone until I talk to him again Thursday. Presumably that's when I'll get the secret handshake."

He smiled and gave me a neutral pat on the small of the back. "I'll be up in the room."

"I'll be up after a few laps. Take the wine." Maybe he'd be asleep when I got there.

It's interesting to watch eye movements as you approach the pool. Most women look directly at your face, and so do some men—the shy, the gentlemanly, and presumably those more interested in males. Most men's eyes do a little dance: crotch, then past the knees to about shin-level, then back up past the center to pause at the breast-and-shoulder level, and then a concentrated stare at the face. I noticed other people staring before I realized I did it, too. Otherwise you can walk right by somebody you work with every day and not recognize him or her. Faces look different on top of a pile of clothes.

I said hello to a couple of casual acquaintances and shook my head "no" to a stranger who made the thumb-through-circled-thumb-and-finger query. You didn't see that as often as when I was a girl—or maybe it was just *I* who didn't see it as often. (There were places on Earth, like Magreb, where you could be killed for making a gesture like that at another man's wife. I had hated that place, forced to wear heavy robes in the desert heat, just your eyes showing—and my memory, unbidden, supplied the smell, when we rounded the corner in Tangier and came up to the public square, the smell of the previous rent-a-robe customer's rancid sweat mingling with the sudden stench of putrid flesh, the hands and heads of thieves and adulterers rotting on spikes.)

"Marianne. You okay?"

"Oh, hi, Sam. Just tired." Samuel Wasserman, historian and kosher loverboy.

"You looked right through me."

"Brain's someplace else. Swim?" I took his elbow and steered him toward the shallow end.

The water was too warm, as usual. I could make it cooler, by executive fiat, but I knew that this was what

most people preferred. Maybe I could have a new poll
commissioned, and fake the results. We started off slowly,
side by side.

"How about Purcell's little surprise?"

I hadn't talked to Sam after the meeting. "He does have
a flair for the dramatic, in his own way," I said. "Ever
have him for economics?"

"No, Biondi and Walpole."

"Lucky."

"I have to go talk to him tomorrow. I'm not sure how
to act."

I felt unexpectedly chagrined at that; less special.
"Don't say anything about his being sick, dying. That's
sincere, I think. Just treat him with the deference due an
aging academic who could have you shoveling goatshit tomorrow if you cross him."

"You're a big help."

"He's not so bad outside the classroom. I think there's
a real nice man deep down inside, under about seventy
years of intellectual scar tissue. New New wasn't exactly
a hotbed of laissez-faire capitalism."

"You have to wonder how he got so high up."

"Personality." We reached the other end and I kicked
off. "Race!" Sam wasn't much of a swimmer, but twelve
fewer years and long arms and legs can make up for lack
of skill. At midpool he churned by me like a badly designed kitchen implement.

We swam a few more laps and then sat drying, talking
about Purcell and other absent colleagues. I guess I was
half expecting, half hoping for, a sexual proposition, which
I could gracefully decline or at least postpone. But he was
just passing time. Maybe waiting for me to leave, it finally
occurred to me, so he could go express his interest in
someone else. I told him Dan was probably waiting up and
went off to get dressed.

I could feel his eyes on me as I walked away, and was
acutely conscious of having gained a kilogram, more or
less, for every year since we had been lovers, all of it settling below the center of gravity. He had probably gained
as much, himself, but all upper-body muscle, which
made him look prettier than ever. I had a momentary

flash of loathing for men in general and young ones in particular.

It would have been fastest to take the lift up to Level 4 and walk straight to Dan's place, but I went back around the yeast farm to the dark anonymity of the ag-level pathway. It cheered me up for some reason.

Dan was lying in bed but still awake, watching a man and woman ice-skate in the cube. I couldn't identify the music accompanying them, vaguely Germanic. Maybe a polka.

"Old one?"

He nodded. "Winter Olympics 2012, I think it said."

"Random Walk?"

"Uh huh." That was an entertainment program that would give you a five- or ten-second introduction to a show, then skip at random to another, out of an assortment of about a million programs whose only common denominator was that you didn't need any special knowledge to appreciate them. It was kind of fun to let it run on and on, creating a slow mosaic of sports, arts, drama, sex, and gameshows. He clicked it to change. "Good swim?"

"Okay. I've got to lose some weight."

"What, nobody propositioned you?"

"Nobody you'd want me to bring home." I shook the wine box and was moderately surprised to find it still half full. I got my glass from the sink. "Actually, a guy I didn't recognize gave me the thumb. Sort of a middle-aged Buddha. Shaved bald all over."

"Yeah, that's Radi-something, Radimacher . . . don't remember. John knows him; he's in Materials."

"I could've kissed him. But he might have misinterpreted it."

"What?" Dan was distracted by the current five seconds, an old-fashioned car bursting into flames.

"I mean, at least he showed some interest. Most of the men there didn't. Boys."

"Pool turns into a teenage meat market after about ten. You didn't know that?"

"So that's where you go at night. All this week I thought you were actually working."

The cube switched to an oddly appropriate scene, young people playing volleyball on a beach. Dan turned down the volume. "You can't talk about what Harry said? Or don't want to."

"Can't. He . . . didn't have time to finish, wanted me to hold off talking to anyone else until I had the whole picture."

"That's his prerogative, under the circumstances." He poured me some wine and filled his own glass. "Damned shame. Surprise, too. Total."

"You didn't know he was sick?"

"Nobody but Tania Seven, I guess; some doctors. He didn't even tell Eliot." He took a healthy gulp and then swirled the wine around in the glass, staring into it. "A lot of secrets. Did he tell you enough so you can understand why I've never discussed . . . certain things with you? John and I?"

I was tempted to say no and watch his reaction. "I guess so."

"Good. That's what I was hoping." He finished his glass and slid down under the covers. "Early one tomorrow."

"New New?"

"Got to meet with Civil first."

"Sybil? Who's she?"

"Civil. Civil Engineering, I.C.E. Architects, too. You need the light?"

"No." I turned it off. "Watch a little cube." I left it on Random Walk with no sound while I sipped the wine. My night for solitary drinking. There were a few seconds each of guitar playing, gymnastics, copulation, a period-costume fencing scene, more copulation, and then a dramatic shot of a swamp by moonlight. I remembered the question that had occurred to me on the ag level. "Dan? Do plants grow in the dark?"

"Some. I've seen phytoplankton glowing blue-green in a boat's wake."

"*Grow,* not glow. We really aren't hearing each other tonight. Do plants grow in the dark?"

"Most plants, yeah. Dark-stage photosynthesis. That's when they turn carbon dioxide into carbohydrates."

"Thanks."

"Anytime." After a minute, he slid over and pressed himself against me. "Lots of things grow in the dark."

"God, Daniel." I had asked for it, though. "At least let me get my clothes off."

7

≙

MANEUVERING

PRIME

Most of O'Hara's second meeting with Purcell, those parts that had to do with Berrigan's revelations, O'Hara never mentioned to anyone, except cryptically—and although everything that went on in Room 4404 was automatically recorded, those records were closed to human inspection for two hundred years. That is not a problem for us.

Room 4404, the Cabinet Room, was the only "inside" room on the craft that had its own airlock. It was isolated from the rest of *Newhome* by four centimeters of vacuum, whenever occupied. It contained its own power source; fully half that power was drained by sophisticated watchdog devices.

30 September 2097 [16 Bobrovnikov 290]—Purcell is seated alone at the horseshoe-shaped table that dominates the semicircular room. The table seats twenty-four; its open end points toward a lectern. Uniform cold white light glows down from the ceiling, a little too bright to be comfortable. Holo windows show a dim starscape.

Purcell is reading a small book, an old-fashioned one

with paper pages and red leather binding. He looks up as
O'Hara enters.

O'HARA: Good morning, Harry.

She looks over her shoulder, startled, as the door snaps
shut and the airlock pump whines.

O'HARA: Something new every day.
PURCELL: Vacuum seal. Security. They just turned it
           on yesterday.
O'HARA: Oh. That's why I had to leave my ring.
PURCELL: Not that metal detectors would stop some of
           the engineers. I understand they can make a
           recorder that only has a few micrograms of
           metal in it.
               You left yours behind?
O'HARA: The recorder? Yes ... and I erased our
           earlier conversation. After listening to it a
           couple of times.
PURCELL: Good. Then I take it you are willing to em-
           brace our, shall we say, institutionalized tra-
           dition of duplicity?
O'HARA: Not embrace it. I will keep your secret, of
           course. Whether I can become part of it, I'm
           not sure.
PURCELL: How could you not? That's like reaching pu-
           berty and deciding against it. You can't go
           back.
O'HARA: I can go sideways.
PURCELL: Get out of politics?
O'HARA: There are a few other things I can do.
PURCELL: That would surprise me. Surprise the Evalu-
           ation Board, too.
O'HARA: The Board makes mistakes. The one in New
           New did, and they had ten times as many
           people to choose from.
PURCELL: Granted.
               Is there anything I can clear up for you,
           then? Anything to put your mind at ease
           about this ... unpleasant reality?

O'HARA: You could satisfy my curiosity about some things.

Purcell nods almost imperceptibly. O'Hara sits down across from him, stiff.

O'HARA: Does everyone in the Cabinet know about your little . . . tradition?

PURCELL: Not yet. As you just said, we've had to draw candidates from a limited pool. Some are still being evaluated.

O'HARA: But my husbands do know.

PURCELL: And have for some time, of course. Both of them have argued your case since well before Launch. I, among others, wanted to see how well you handled that particular stress, first.

O'HARA: It's far from being the most stressful thing that's ever happened to me.

PURCELL: Granted. But I wasn't there for the others.

O'Hara leans back a few degrees, which makes her look even less relaxed. She can't hide the anger in her voice.

O'HARA: Sandra's image couldn't tell me how long it's been going on, in New New. It said to ask you.

PURCELL: I'm not sure, either. One may assume we had rather more of a pure democracy in the beginning.

O'HARA: Fewer people.

PURCELL: And a select crowd. Auto-selected. They all decided to live in orbit—to start life over, most of them—and most of them had a more or less passionate interest in their own governance.

        The first person born in orbit, by comparison, was an unwilling immigrant. That was five generations ago.

O'HARA: So you're saying we've become less competent to govern ourselves? As individuals? Or is it just greater numbers, watering down the democratic process.

PURCELL: Both. Out of New New's eighty-one-thousand potential voters, ten or fifteen thousand—conservatively!—weren't competent to make decisions regarding even their own welfare, let alone the welfare of others—

O'HARA: That seems awfully high.

PURCELL: And perhaps twice that number were either uninterested or so contemptuous of government that they had no positive input into the process.

You think that's high, too, but it's not. Together those percentages would say, well, more than half of New New is made up of intelligent, responsible voters. That wasn't true before the war and it's less true now.

I know Sandra told you about the plague referendum.

O'HARA: Yes. It's . . . terrible.

PURCELL: You would have said "unbelievable" if it had been I who told you. The message was Sandra's idea. I think she knew you very well.

O'HARA: She did.

PURCELL: I don't have any great love for groundhogs, either, and I understand the primitive desire to punish them. Let them stew in their own juices, die out. But I don't *vote* according to what my ductless glands say. Most people do.

O'HARA: So the solution is a benign dictatorship by committee?

PURCELL: It's not the solution; it's not even *a* solution. It's just a way of getting from today to tomorrow without too much excitement. Without disaster.

There's no safety valve anymore. No other Worlds to emigrate to; no Earth as a last resort. We're sealed in this can together for a century.

And it's not a "dictatorship" just because most people are unaware of the details of the decision-making process. It's still just management.

O'HARA: Management? What a euphemism. It's manipulation, pure and simple. Paternalistic condescension.

PURCELL: You're not the best judge of that at this time.

O'HARA: What do you mean by that?

PURCELL: This is a difficult situation for you. It would be for anybody, talking to me under these circumstances.

O'HARA: I can manage.

PURCELL: Your using the word "paternalistic," for instance, is interesting in this context. You've read your profile.

O'HARA: Oh, come on. Because I never knew my father—

PURCELL: Now you're the one indulging in euphemism. What you felt about him was betrayal, contempt, rage.

O'HARA: Yes, *felt!* I'm not a child anymore. Besides, I did finally meet him when I was twenty-one, on Earth. He was just a poor sad little man.

PURCELL: You never completely leave the child behind. I'm almost eighty-four, and I can remember terrible things that upset me before I was ten.

I'm just asking that you be honest and careful about those buried feelings. Don't let them color your assessment of my advice.

O'HARA: I will try to control my "rage." (Pauses) There is something in what you say. I'll take care.

PURCELL: I want you to have this as a reminder. And a good luck charm.

He slides over the book. Two bold Chinese characters are stamped on the red leather jacket. O'Hara opens it and reads the title.

O'HARA: *The Art of War,* by Sun Tzu?

PURCELL: Well, it's not just about war. It's about using
           people and supplies. Management. Bluffing.
           The creative use and abuse of power.

           Written more than two thousand years
           ago, but still useful.

O'HARA: Thank you. I didn't bring any actual books.
           This is beautiful.

PURCELL: Very little of what it says is beautiful. It's a
           tough, uncompromising book. (He stares at
           her.)

           How many nervous breakdowns have you
           had?

O'HARA: None.

PURCELL: Your record—

O'HARA: I know my record. I've been treated for anx-
           iety disorders. (She holds up the Chinese
           book.) We live in interesting times.

PURCELL: Twice these "disorders" involved physical
           collapse. I'd call them nervous break-
           downs.

O'HARA: Doctors don't. (Purcell shrugs.) In both
           cases, I was back to work in a day or two.
           If I thought it was an impediment to public
           service, I would let the public get along
           without me.

PURCELL: I'm not suggesting that it is. As far as I can
           tell, your actual problem is quite unrelated
           to anxiety.

O'HARA: Good. Is it treatable?

PURCELL: Self-correcting, ultimately. It's your god-
           damned superwoman complex.

O'HARA: What, you think I have too much confidence
           to be a good leader? That's bizarre.

PURCELL: No, it's the opposite of that, or the obverse:
           an inability, or unwillingness, to predict di-
           saster.

O'HARA: I went through more disaster in seven
           months than you have seen in eighty-four
           years.

PURCELL: Excepting the sure prospect of one's death,
            perhaps. (She starts to say something but he
            holds his hand up, mollifying.) That's not
            fair. I'm sorry.

He drops the hand heavily to the table.

PURCELL: Most of a century involved in calculated de-
            bate. It produces reflexes. Like any sport.
              I have to go.

He gets to his feet with some effort, and at the door looks
back with an almost avuncular smile. O'Hara has risen,
stepped toward him.

PURCELL: No. Read "Maneuver," Statement 27.

O'Hara watches him go, then looks it up.

O'HARA: "When he pretends to flee, do not pursue."

8

≙

BIG SISTER

Dear Marianne,

Things sure have been exciting around here since
you left. School school and more school. And dear old
Mom.
    Could you talk to her? She gave you hell for put-
ting off menarche until you were sixteen and now

she's giving me hell because I want it now. Everybody else in my class is going at it like bunnys and
they treat me like a little girl. The school nurse says
I wouldn't have any trouble with the pelvis even if I
did get pregnant, which would be a cold day on Mercury. But I guess they do have cold days on Mercury,
its Venus where its always hot. God, astronomy! Its
just algebra with stars and planets. Chemistry's just
algebra with funny smells. I still don't know hamster
dropping about algebra altho I passed course One the
second time around. Now I'm in course Two and
adrift between the Galaxys, as the soap says.

Not that I get to watch any soaps. The only cube I
can watch is educational, until my grades are up
there with a normal subhuman. So last night I got to
see this hourlong thing about how hermit crabs and
termites and all fuck. You would of really liked it.
Maybe you'll meet creatures like that on your new
planet, but big like elephants. When the elephant termite female reaches around and starts eating the elephant termite male (while his thing's still in her!),
don't worry, its just romance. You might want to tell
Uncle Dan about it, since you say he likes strange
women. There might be real strange women on that
planet. Tho he'll probably slow down by age 100.

I'm thinking that someday I might want to go to
Earth, I mean move there, once they get stuff settled. I wouldn't feel so dumb there.

Love, Janiss

14 October 2097   [8 Galileo 291]
Dear Sis,

I like your new name. Is it for somebody?

I'll talk to Mother about her stubbornness, but
don't think it'll make much difference. (The reason
for the particular stubbornness is immaterial, as you

know. Changing her mind is like putting your shoulder to a planet.)

You also know that I'll try to talk you out of this. For most of the rest of your life men are going to be whining at you to please please let them stick their precious dicks into one place or another. It can be fun but it can also be worse than algebra, believe me.

You do need the school, and once your hormones start moaning you spend half your time and energy attending to them. You're not a natural student like I was, and even I had a harder time of it after menarche.

To continue in this nagging vein, you know they won't be sending people to Earth unless they have some special ability. (I can picture myself as a school counselor, shaking my finger at you, but it's true.) Even if it's not an academic specialty, it's probably going to be something they measure through tests— and, unfortunately, the only way you'll get better at test-taking is practice.

To get back to the point, don't forget that when Mother was your age she was pregnant with me. I think she's always resented losing a few precious years of childhood. (Though as you well know, this is an illusion people come up with when they get old and their memories start to go. Being a kid isn't so much fun while you're actually being one.)

I'll plead your case with her, not because I think you're right, but because you're old enough to make the decision.

The work here is still interesting, though some of the people I have to deal with are walking hemorrhoids. Never a dull moment. Beeper woke me up at five-thirty this morning because a nine o'clock meeting had been moved to ten. Still trying to figure that one out.

Yesterday we had something new. A lawsuit. A middle-aged citizen who spends all of his free time building muscles so he won't look so middle-aged (it doesn't work) had an accident. He was working out on the parallel bars and one of them hadn't been properly tightened. He did some sort of impressive flip that turned into a crash. He missed the mat and hit the floor face-first; it fractured his neck.

So we had to go down to the hospital with an arbitration team, the poor victim looking all pathetic with his plastic brace and kind of wall-eyed with pain drugs. Emily Martino didn't help any—she's the woman in charge of the gymnastic equipment, and technically responsible. She got all teary and wanted to give the guy everything. Well, hell. I work out on those bars, too, but I have the sense to always have someone spotting for me. If it had happened to me, I wouldn't have gotten a broken neck. I would just have felt embarrassed at being stupid enough not to check out the goddamned equipment before I put my weight on it! But try to tell that to arbitrators. They're always advocates for the individual, against "the system." If this is a system, we're all in trouble.

So they fined the department $250 and Emily $250, to go into an escrow account that Mr. Muscles can use whenever he has a yen for chocolate cake or weird sex. It's actually five hundred bucks from the department, with Emily kicking over half of her hourly pay for the next 167 hours. We really can't spare it.

But Mr. Muscles is a nice guy compared to Gwen Stevick. Back in Start-up, I asked her to volunteer for Aptitude Induction (she wanted to be aboard 'Home but didn't have any skill we wanted). She chose Veterinary Technician and now evidently hates it, and not incidentally hates yours truly. So she spends all of her spare time making my life difficult. She studies Entertainment like a scientist, and whenever she finds anything not to her liking she files a complaint.

The complaints go over my head, straight to Policy. They're as tired of her as I am, but there's not much we can legitimately do. We fix the trivial thing that she's bitching about, and file a correction report, and even write her a little thank-you note.

I see her nosing around all the time. She's fat and red-faced and always looks angry. Maybe she'll have a heart attack down here, and we'll all tip-toe off to lunch.

Oh well, life in the ruling class. Sure is exciting.

Evy, John, and Dan are doing fine, settling into their various routines, and send their love along with mine.

Marianne

9

≘

THE POWER TO SOOTHE

Interior Civil Engineering is a cluster of offices located at 0002, the most sternward part of 'Home's living area. I wouldn't enjoy working there. The rear wall of each room is seamless dark gray, the spun monomolecular carbon stuff that makes up the containment vessel for the antimatter. I'd feel uncomfortable being that close to it.

(Which is twice illogical. The actual containment is done by a powerful magnetic field. If the power failed, all that carbon would be mc^2 worth of gamma rays. The civil engineers would be vaporized, ionized, about one nanosecond before yours truly, up at the other end of the ship.)

I had an appointment there at 1330, an hour after lunch, so rather than go back to my office I took a long stroll down Level 2, spiraling around. Eighty percent of the population lives on Level 2; I hadn't really surveyed it since they moved in.

There was not much individuation yet, in the outside of people's flats. A few had pictures or icons on their doors. Three in a row had Arabic sentences rendered in careful black calligraphy. Every now and then potted flowers or decorative vegetables; some, predictably, vandalized. Even though it's not surprising, you have to wonder who would want to destroy a bunch of tomatoes. What would he stomp on if the tomatoes weren't there?

(Right after the tomatoes somebody had written REX SUX DIX in some corrosive compound on the deck tiles; ineradicable. Was it an insult or an advertisement?)

I was surprised to find John down in I.C.E.; he was head of the section but, to my knowledge, had only visited there two times. It was a long way to go for the privilege of creeping around in high gravity.

He saw my expression. "Thought I'd shake up the troops," he said. "I saw your name on the list . . . what, that storage allocation thing with Smith?"

"That's right." I was a little irked; I hadn't discussed it with him because I did want to be punctilious about going through channels, and not just to make Purcell happy. I didn't want to present myself to I.C.E. as "the supervisor's wife," expecting special consideration.

"Probably wasting your time. Sandor has a couple of hundred people in line ahead of you."

At the mention of his name, Sandor Seven looked up sharply; small bald black man with a long face and no eyebrows. "You're the Cabinet woman?"

"Marianne O'Hara."

He looked at John. "You know her?"

"All too well. You might as well give in." Thanks a lot, John.

"Come to my desk." I followed him across the room to a drafting table surmounted by a display screen two meters square. "I haven't looked at the details of your proposition. I wanted to first be sure that we understand each other. That you understand exactly what you are asking."

"Fair enough."

He slid a keyboard out from under the table and tapped a few keys. A complex exploded diagram of 'Home's interior appeared on the screen. A list unrolled in the upper left-hand corner, titled "Location Referents," giving numbers from (1.) Agriculture to (47.) Workshops: General. He highlighted (5.) Education and (6.) Entertainment with blue and green; patches of those colors appeared all over the ship.

"These are the spaces that you and Mr. Smith control. So to speak."

"That's interesting. You can see how spread out they are."

"Yes. Not for no reason, of course. Your proposal had to do with storage space."

"Office space, too. Smith and I are practically at opposite ends of the ship. Yet Education and Entertainment share many of the same supplies. Our people are always running back and forth unnecessarily."

"Perhaps not unnecessarily."

"I'd be willing to give up my place in Uchūden and move back here with Tom, with Smith."

"Very nice of you." He leaned back in his chair and swiveled around, looking at me over steepled fingers. His face screwed up into a wrinkled prunish mask of concentration. He really could have used eyebrows. "Dr. O'Hara, do you know what moment of inertia is?"

"No. Never heard of it."

"It has to do with the way things spin. Like an ice skater, you know? She goes around with her arms out, spinning at a certain rate." He held his arms out and pulled them in slowly. "Then she brings them in and spins much faster."

"Conservation of angular momentum," I said, not completely helpless.

"Very good. Another way to look at it is that she has changed . . . she has changed the distribution of mass in her body, relative to the axis of spin. That is what moment of inertia is. The same amount of energy is tied up in her spinning, but because the mass is in different places, she spins faster."

"I think I see what you're getting at. You can't just move weight around 'Home arbitrarily."

"Indeed we cannot. But it isn't a matter of simply changing the *rate* of spin. It is a matter of making sure the axis of spin remains the same as the ship's geometrical axis. That is not clear."

"Uh . . . not really."

"We cannot . . . let me see." He made vague circular gestures. "We can't allow a large lump of mass on one side, not balanced by something on the other side. The ship would wobble."

"Which would throw us off course?"

"Worse. We might begin to tumble. That would destroy the ship in seconds. We would break apart."

I remembered seeing an old film from the early days of space flight, a rocket rising from the pad and then suddenly spinning off in crazy cartwheels and exploding. Our explosion would be more spectacular, with all that anti-matter. Would they see us from New New, a brief bright star?

I've lived in rotating vessels about 98 percent of my life. Suddenly I felt dizzy. "What about now? Everybody walking back and forth?"

He flapped a hand. "It's trivial, and it averages out. All the biomass in the ship isn't a hundredth of one percent of the total. If everybody were packed into one room on Level One, and stayed there for weeks, the effect might be measurable.

"But you see, that is the problem: the effect is cumulative. You move a grand piano from one room to another, it will probably stay there for most of a century. Each thirty-three seconds it will pull the ship slightly out of line in the same direction."

"Unless we put another piano in the opposite direction, or something."

"Yes." He turned and stared at the screen, leaning forward on both elbows. "I don't want to exaggerate this problem to you. There is no real danger so long as we are reasonably careful. My personal problem, since I am in charge of this aspect of civil engineering, is that the complexity of shifting a set of objects increases quite literally with the square of the number of objects. And as Dr. Ogelby said, there are two hundred requests ahead of you."

"So what does that mean? Weeks? Months? Years?"

"That depends on how flexible you can be. It may *be* years if you insist on the move being done all at once. If you can move a bit now, a bit later, then I can match you up with other work orders. Somebody who needs to move a grand piano to the other side, so to speak."

"That would be fine."

He stared at the diagram for a full minute without speaking. "Hum. There is an overall problem. Your Entertainment areas are spread out over all levels."

"That's true." Full-gravity weight lifting to zero-gee sex.

"But Education is almost all on Level Two. I assume that is an optimum gravity for learning."

"I don't know."

"Do you have any extremely concentrated masses? Things you would need a heavy 'bot to move?"

"We do have two grand pianos, a Baldwin and a Steinway."

"From Earth?" He smiled for the first time. "We brought the oddest things."

"They won't be moved, though. They're in the two concert halls. Smith and I share two upright pianos that are in his classrooms, and a harpsichord that I have in a Level Two practice room."

"A harp—?"

"It's an old-fashioned kind of piano."

He shook his head, still amused. "I thought that we could duplicate any waveform with an electronic keyboard."

"I suppose. Musicians are funny, though." I was suddenly transported back to a couple of weeks before Launch, when I stood behind Chul' Hermosa for an hour of Scarlatti magic, his long brown fingers hammering the ancient ivory keys with exquisitely measured passion. I could feel the bass notes in my teeth.

Would a waveform, whatever it was, do that? Would it duplicate the soft fingerpad sound when he barely stroked a high note? Not to mention the smell of wax and the hypnotic swirl of inlaid gold and mother-of-pearl. The connections with centuries past.

"Are you all right, Dr. O'Hara?"

"Sorry. I was thinking."

His expression did not radiate confidence in my thinking ability. "This is what I want you and Mr. Smith to do. Give me a list of everything both of you are in charge of—exactly where it is and approximately how much it weighs. We'll do a first-order analysis and decide whether it would be better to relocate your things or his. Or move both of you to a third location."

"That shouldn't be hard. The computer must know where just about everything is."

"The computer knows where things are supposed to be. I have to know where they actually are. You have GP auxiliaries?"

That was Personnel jargon for laborers. "Four of them, plus a medium 'bot. I could get a heavy one from Silke Kleber with a little notice." As soon as I said her name, I knew I shouldn't have. Implying personal relationships with both his supervisors.

He just nodded, though. "You might prefer to requisition it through me. Same robot, one less layer of bureaucracy.

"At any rate, once I have the information from you and Mr. Smith, and perhaps a hundred others who will be moved fairly soon, I can put it through a scheduling algorithm."

"A year wouldn't be too bad. Thank you, Dr. Seven." He gravely shook hands with me and then returned his attention to the screen. He typed something and the six levels rolled back upon themselves to become concentric cylinders, rotating realistically, twice as fast as a clock's second hand. The dizziness started to come back. I closed my eyes long enough for the sensation to go away, and then turned and carefully walked back to the door.

John was waiting for me, sitting on a folding chair, looking exhausted. "Let's get you home."

He gave me a wan smile. "That's why I scheduled my

raid for 1300, of course. Thought I might seduce you into a backrub."

"Sure. I'm clear to 1530." We walked and hobbled to the Toronto lift and went straight to Level 6. It was most of a kilometer back to his place. I practically floated, light as a cloud, but for him it was an effort. By the time we got there, his face was brick red and he was panting.

"You're not getting as much exercise as you did in New New," I said.

"To belabor the obvious, no, I'm not. I'm not taking as much medication for pain, either. The scientist in me suspects a cause-and-effect relationship."

"Taking pills makes you exercise?"

"Sure." We got to his door and he unlocked it with his thumb. Groundhog habit. What did he have that anybody would steal? There *is* vandalism though. Maybe I should start doing it.

He checked his message queue, sighed, and returned a call from Tania Seven, who just needed two numbers and a date. He said the others could wait, then painfully slipped off his shirt and collapsed onto his side on the bed. Even in a quarter gee, he couldn't comfortably lie on his back or stomach.

I got a tube of oil from over the sink and rubbed some into his knotted shoulders. The oil's vaguely tropical aroma always reminded me of sex, which under the circumstances made me uncomfortable. Middle of the workday and all. But John did not visibly make the same association. He groaned luxuriously and relaxed almost to the point of coma.

He was thinking, though, not sleeping. After about ten minutes, I stopped to rest my fingers, and he rolled over to look at me. "Sorry my timing was bad. I realized after you got there that you probably didn't want my presence complicating things."

"It was no problem. I don't think Sandor notices that sort of thing."

"Did you get what you wanted?"

"Well, he didn't roll over and play dead. The transfer might stretch out for a year. Tom and I can live with that, though; we'd been ready to cope with outright rejection."

"It wouldn't come to that. I could've done something."

"I don't want to hear it." He stiffened and I went back to massaging. "Really. Purcell is right. I have to tread lightly for a couple of years."

He stretched hard and something in his shoulder made a loud pop. "I wouldn't worry overmuch about it. Harry's a good administrator, but he's too calculating."

"He is that." I started to knuckle the vertebrae, gently, down one side and up the other. It was painful for him, but recommended by the "Massage for Scoliosis" article Evy had found. He suffered in silence until it was over; then sighed and mumbled something about how good it felt when it stopped. I worked on his scalp and arms for a few minutes and left him to sleep.

I was worried about John. I knew he was trying to reduce his dependence on the pills, but he was paying for it doubly, in loss of sleep and restricted mobility.

Dan's lack of sleep was adding up, too. Maybe they'd both collapse on the same day. Then Evy and I could hand them over to the professionals and get some rest ourselves.

Still a couple of hours until the meeting with the net games people. Feeling a little guilty, I went down to the music rooms instead of the office, and checked out a clarinet and a practice room. Still thinking of Chul' and the harpsichord, I punched up Mozart's *Concerto in A*—so profoundly sad you can hardly believe it's in a major key—and played until my cheeks were wet and I could taste salt blood from my lips.

YEAR 1.00

≙

1

≙

ABOUT TIME

The first year aboard 'Home was fairly uneventful. For a month or two, people who derive satisfaction out of expecting the worst did walk around braced for disaster. Their anxieties, it turned out, were not unfounded. Just premature.

Harry Purcell died, but not until after he had successfully orchestrated his retirement. O'Hara pursued the meek and Machiavellian course he had mapped out for her. Dan went on his binge on schedule, and recovered on schedule. John's decline stabilized. Evy fought being transferred from Geriatrics to Emergency, and lost.

New New faded in importance as they accelerated away from it. Partly this was the result of increasing confidence in their own institutions and methods; partly it was the increasing difficulty in communication. Every three hundred thousand kilometers meant another second of time lag between New New and 'Home. By the time they were ready to celebrate their first year in flight, New New was forty-four hours behind them.

So when should they celebrate the anniversary? A reactionary few wanted to wait and share the celebration with New New, but they never had a chance, and knew it; they were just arguing because arguing was the national sport.

In fact, there had been a lot of arguing over time matters. They weren't going fast enough for Einsteinian relativity to affect everyday things, but they still had to deal with the time difference between them and New New. They could have slowed their clocks down by a fraction of an instant each minute, no problem for us computers, but that would have been pointless except as a symbolic link. It would still take four days between "How's the weather down there?" and "Same as always."

A more meaningful debate over time had to do with their destination planet, Epsilon Eridani 3 (or Epsilon 3, or Epsilon, or, most commonly, "the planet"): Its day was eighteen hours, thirty-two minutes long. Ultimately, their clocks would have to reflect this reality, and probably not by resetting each clock to midnight at half-past six. (John Ogelby wrote a tongue-in-cheek article defending that idea, which some people took at face value.)

Traditionalists wanted to keep the sixty-minute/twenty-four hour clock, which you could do if you cut the duration of a second down to 0.77222 of a "real" second—it would be confusing at first, but it would certainly make the day go by faster.

Most of the scientists were "Decimalists," arguing that as long as you were redefining the second, you might as well redefine everything. If you made your second about two thirds of an Earth second, you could have a day of ten 100-minute hours, each minute a hundred of those quick little seconds. The advantage of this was obvious to scientist, though it would be a little hard to draw clocks free-hand.

Of course common sense, and inertia, prevailed, and the time continued to be what the clock said it was. New New was just shifting time zones and Epsilon was, after all, a century away. A century of incessant bickering.

2

≘

HAPPY NEW YEAR

Almost everybody took at least two days off for the Launch Day anniversary, one for partying and one for recovering, but of course O'Hara and her co-workers were not allowed that luxury. A daylong picnic for ten thousand people is *no* picnic for the people in charge of its logistics. Food and drink, music and games, places for people to sit, barriers to keep them from sitting on the daisies. Jury-rigged portable toilets to protect the daisies from excessive fertilization. First-aid stations attended by nondrinking doctors and nurses. A place for the coordinators to stand and publicly reveal that yes, by George, it has been a whole year.

She enjoyed the challenge and liked the way the park took shape under her direction, but was not looking forward to the cleanup. She remembered the celebration a year before, and knew that half the people she needed would be off sleeping under something, or someone, and the ones who showed up would not be in top form.

3

≙

TORN BETWEEN TWO LOVERS

22 September 2098 [26 Aumann 293]—Trying to be honest with this diary, not sin by omission. Not omit any sins.

Start out with adultery. (Have I ever typed that word before? It looks funny, as if it were the opposite of childishness.) A man I've known all my life made an interesting and specific proposition, and I turned him down, and then I took him up on it.

It's odd how a couple of weeks of frantic work led up to a sudden shortage of it. I guess that means we did it right. Once the anniversary party got started, I just sort of walked around the park enjoying the sight of other people having fun. My caller never beeped.

I felt conspicuous. A sartorial genius back in Start-up had come up with the bright idea of providing special white outfits for the Coordinators and Cabinet to wear during ceremonial occasions. Some of us feel like Moby Dick wearing white. (Usually when I go to the laundry I select black or bluejean, lavender if I'm in a frisky mood. Twenty years ago someone said it looked good with my hair color.)

I was watching a tetherball game, mildly resentful of the players' teenage exuberance. The annoyance was partly professional—if you break that cord, do you think we can send out for a new one?—but mostly it was an irrational longing to be young and confused and seething with hormones. And who should present himself but good old not-his-real-name Tom.

I vaguely remembered having had sex a few times with

Tom back in my butterfly days. That's a distinction he probably shared with a third of the males in my age group in New New. For about a year and a half, between losing Charlie Devon and meeting Daniel, I'd go along with anybody who had a pointable penis and didn't smell too revolting.

We chatted for a while, watching the kids. Then, without any sexual preamble, he asked whether I remembered the time he had shared me with another man, and how about doing it again?

I did remember, and the memory gave me a special pang of longing. It can be awkward and uncomfortable and hilarious, two on one, but it certainly does make you feel wanted. I hadn't done it since I got married.

(People will make assumptions when they find out you have two husbands and a wife. John and Dan are both groundhogs, though, very conservative sexually, and as far as I know, Evy doesn't have any lesbian itches. I'm not sure what I would do if she asked. I had sex with women a few times when I was eighteen, to keep Charlie happy, but never showed any real talent for it. John and Dan would be uncomfortable about Evy and me getting together, anyhow.)

So I told Tom that I was flattered—no lie, since I was feeling so unattractive—but that my emotional life was too complicated already. His answer to that was "Who's talking about emotions?" I dismissed him with a kiss and a squeeze, and he wandered off, looking, I assumed, for some more willing two-holed relic from school days. But the seed was planted, so to speak.

I hadn't been drinking or eating because at 2130 it was my turn to play the clarinet for an hour down at the dance floor, and saliva doesn't help your music. It was mostly mainstream stuff from the past decade, not challenging, but there were a couple of New African pieces, post-Ajimbo, that changed key signature and tempo about every other measure. Probably easier to play than to dance to. I also did alto sax on two pieces, glad not to have solos. The embouchure, the way you hold your lips, is a lot different, and I hadn't practiced it recently.

Most of it was sight-reading, so I didn't pay much attention to the people dancing or listening. I did notice Dan, though, loping along with wide-eyed concentration. That meant that he'd drunk too much too early, and had popped an Alcoterm to burn it off. So he'd be wide awake for at least twenty-four hours—good thinking, Dan. When everybody else wakes up, you'll collapse.

Between pieces I saw that Dan was hovering over some librarian whose name I couldn't remember. Small, girlish, vivacious. I wasn't surprised when they left together during the next number, but was a little disappointed. A reliable side effect of Alcoterm is priapism, and I had been looking forward to helping him with it.

Pleasant surprise: when my shift was over, Tom was waiting for me. Good instincts. I said let's go. On the way up to the fuckhuts, feeling deliciously wicked, I buzzed Zdenek and told him he was in charge; don't call me unless it's a real emergency.

The other gentleman, I'll call him Oscar, after Wilde, was waiting impatiently for us at the Level 0 exit, with a two-hour sauna pass that was twenty minutes gone.

He was more interested in Tom than in me. A pity; he was a big slab of a guy, about twenty, handsome in that brooding self-absorbed way that doesn't last. I would have liked to hold on to him for the duration, but he was pretty obviously not excited by vaginas. Tom was, so I got his flabby and balding personage—exactly my age, I couldn't avoid thinking.

I was surprised to find that three people fucking don't bounce off the padded walls as frequently as a pair does. It probably has something to do with the moment of inertia. Maybe I should ask Sandor. He wouldn't even blink.

I felt sort of like a referee, or moderator. A not-too-passive receptacle for their simultaneous orgasms. By then I was a couple of orgasms ahead, though, so couldn't complain.

Afterward we talked and caressed for a while, luxuriating in the zero gee and warm dim rosy glow of the small room. Oscar gave me a couple of unambiguous looks, so I said I had to go back to being ringmaster of this circus; dressed, and left them to their own two devices.

It was fun to have sex with relative strangers again. As

opposed to strange relatives. Maybe I should do it every time Dan does. Get plenty of exercise.

I didn't go straight back down to the park, but detoured through the Level 2 gym to shower and sit for a while in the whirlpool. I'll be sitting carefully for a few days. (Definitely out of practice with that practice. John or Dan would wilt at the thought of anal intercourse, being from Earth. You can die of it there—or could die of it, when they were growing up. All of the AIDS carriers were probably killed off by the "death," the plague left over from biological warfare.)

I was thumbed at three times in ten minutes, by men I didn't know. Maybe it was the alert way I was sitting. I would've been tempted by one of them if there wasn't so much work ahead, just to have three in one day again. Who's getting old?

Two groups dressed and left, and, abruptly alone, I was hit by a sudden spasm of helpless anomie. Emotional exhaustion. What you need, girl, is a nice vacation. Difficult under the circumstances. If you can stick it out for another ninety-seven years, you'll have a whole new world to explore.

I punched up the schedule and found that there was a twenty-minute VR vacancy. I had eighteen minutes' credit, so I went down and wired up for the random abstraction mode. The first "place" was uncomfortable, walking naked through fuzzy shoulder-high bushes with thorns, breathing garlic and roses, but then it was a warm amniotic universe where blind soft things bumped up against you and explored with rubbery lips. Then a striped universe, black and white, bands of hot and cold that cut through flesh and organ and bone as you moved. Then I was sitting in the booth sweating, wishing I hadn't done it alone. I was used to talking it over with Dan afterward.

Every animal is sad after intercourse, some old Roman said. This animal was also tired and hungry. I went on down to the park and assembled a weird sandwich out of the impoverished wreckage of the buffet table and washed it down with some toxic but resuscitating coffee. Told Zdenek that I would take charge until three, then would roust up Christensen to watch over things till six. Then at eight we would all start turning the place back into a park.

It was a quarter to midnight, and the party was pretty lively, but still under control. The wine and beer taps would dry up at twelve, so there were predictable lines of people holding two cups. A lot of horse trading with ration cards. Two colas for a beer, three? The actual alcoholics had come prepared, of course, with shine or boo or schnapps or fuel.

I didn't expect any discipline problems until after one o'clock. In fact, it was about two, when we were down to a few hundred people determined to have fun until they dropped. Two middle-aged men started fighting, though not to much effect. They rolled around in a bleary, beery embrace, calling each other names. Other people watched with a kind of detached interest, until a police officer came over and broke it up. As prearranged, he made a big fuss (it being the first incident), upbraiding them and fining them down to zero on the spot. Another officer escorted them roughly away, supposedly to Security, though I knew that if they didn't live together she'd just dump them in their beds and tell them to sleep it off.

I was surprised that there were no other real incidents. I'd warned Christensen that the three-to-six shift was likely to be eventful, but maybe he'll have it easy, too. By three o'clock most of the diehards were sober people, just too adrenalized to sleep, sitting around in clusters singing or telling tales.

I had a vision of groundhogs doing this thousands of years ago—hanging around Stonehenge after the midnight ceremony, tossing more wood on the campfires, passing the mead, and telling ghost stories until dawn. I was probably the only person there who had ever actually smelled a campfire; felt the welcome heat with the cold autumn night at your back.

Just before three, I ran into Charlee Boyle (her real name is Charity Lee, which she hates), who offered to split a small bottle of boo with me, my first drink of the night. I shouted us a half-liter of orange juice, which pretty well masks the industrial-solvent flavor.

It has had the desired effect. G'night, Prime. Wake me

up at ten till six. (Notes dictated about 3:45; will clean
them up on the keyboard later.)

4

≙

*FROM EACH ACCORDING
TO HIS INCLINATIONS*

The next day, Tuesday, was long and tiring. People
showed up late or not at all, as O'Hara had predicted.
Most of them saw no need for urgency, her timetable
notwithstanding—if something wasn't picked up today, it
would still be there tomorrow.

But tomorrow was exactly what O'Hara was worried
about. There was going to be another anniversary celebration, less raucous, when greetings were beamed from New
New. She had to have bleachers in place in front of the
large screen, the area reasonably neat; coffee and tea facilities for a couple of thousand. It's true that tomorrow everybody could just look up and watch the thing on home
or office screens, but any kind of break in the routine was
always welcome.

It was an interesting exercise in leadership for O'Hara.
She had asked to borrow 145 "GP auxiliaries" from various departments, but they didn't come equipped with supervisors. So by 8:30—half an hour late—she found
herself surrounded by about 110 men and women standing
around with their hands in their pockets, staring at her and
each other. She was an admiral in a sea of privates. Most
knew who she was, but she didn't have much authority in
their eyes.

Rather than try to find out who everyone was and what
they supposedly could do best, she divided them at random into two roughly equal groups: one bunch, the pickup

crew, she lined up from one side of the park to the other
and sent marching off, studying the ground, picking up litter and passing it to recycle bags. The second group stayed
with her and assembled bleachers. Then they took them
apart and did them over, more or less right.

A hundred motivated people could have finished everything before lunch. This group worked, if you could call it
that, until three or four. After they were gone, O'Hara and
her regular crew spent another hour tightening bolts and
policing up tools and bags.

It's a problem she had discussed with Purcell, who
made the obvious analogy with early European communist
states, like the Soviet Union before it became the SSU.
Minimum labor yielded the same result as maximum, for
people who measured success in terms of material rewards. Anyone who did more work than was absolutely
necessary was either an idiot or a toady.

In New New you could buy exotic food and drink, imported from Earth. 'Home's luxuries were less exciting,
but followed the same principle: fancy pastries, odd li-
queurs and candies, or just extra wine and beer. You could
buy services of a personal nature, sex or massage or a private portrait or concert, but paying often required an elaborate system of transferrable IOU's, since nobody's card
could hold more than $99.99.

O'Hara instituted a system of rewards that many other
departments copied. On the last day of each month, she
named one of her people "Worker of the Month," and in
addition to a public pat on the back, he or she was given
access to $200 in a departmental "bonus account." Two
hundred dollars would throw a pretty riotous small party,
and that's what most people did with their reward. It was
a mild kind of capitalism, transmuting diligence at the
workplace into a boost in social status.

Otherwise, O'Hara made the same three dollars per hour
that her GP's did; if you could drink an extra cup of coffee
every twenty minutes, you could stay broke. So everyday
life was pretty unchallenging. Until 9:02 in the morning,
23 September 2098.

5

≙

IN THE DEAD VAST AND MIDDLE OF THE NIGHT

24 September 2098 [2 Chang 293]—Midnight. I have started this entry a dozen times. Write a sentence or two and erase it. Most of the time I sit and stare at the empty screen. Nothing I write seems adequate for this.

There is no word for this feeling. No one word. Desolation. That has a good sturdy ring to it. What the hell are we going to do?

Might as well just pick the thing up where I left off, and keep typing.

People started to drift in for the anniversary broadcast about 7:30. New New had produced a documentary program about the construction of 'Home, interesting enough. Almost three thousand people turned up eventually, filling the bleachers and packing the space around them.

Sandra Berrigan gave a nice short speech, wishing us well, and then they projected an old-fashioned clock face behind her, to tick off the last fifteen seconds, New Year's Eve style. The crowd behind the camera began to chant five, four, three, two—and then (we've played this back many times) Sandra suddenly looks to her right and raises her arm, starting to point at something. And then the screen goes white, and stays white.

We've lost New New. We've lost Earth.

It took the technicians about one minute to find out how much worse it was even than that. The last signal from New New was an active intelligent sabotage program. It slammed into our information systems and, before it could be contained, randomized most of our stored information, and backups, in discrete chunks. All of *Hamlet,* for instance, is lost. All of *The Tempest* and the Henry plays: *Macbeth, Romeo and Juliet.* But *Twelfth Night* is intact. *Troilus and Cressida.* It's perverse.

Ninety percent of history and art and philosophy are gone. But what may kill us is the missing science, mathematics, and engineering. If something goes wrong with the antimatter containment, for instance, we'll just have to roll up our sleeves and try to figure it out from scratch before it quietly blows everyone to Kingdom Come.

We don't even know whether New New still exists. There's nothing wrong with our antennas; we can still monitor the radio telescope on the Moon, the useless navigation beacons in Earth's oceans. But not so much as a carrier wave from New New. Our telescopes aren't quite powerful enough to see it. Seeing it wouldn't mean there was anybody alive inside, anyhow.

I think I know now, a little, how Harry felt the day the doctor told him he was going to die. Not today, probably not tomorrow, but soon enough.

6

≙

OPTIONS

They had two months in which to make the big decision. Up to fourteen months out, they still had the option of turning around, decelerating for another fourteen months, and then slowly returning to Earth and New New. After 25 November, their bridges would be burned: Epsilon, or slow death, or swift.

Room 4004 felt too small for the whole thirty-six-person Cabinet—normally Engineering and Policy met *in camera* separately, only getting together for largely cere-monial public sessions—but they did manage to find enough chairs and places to put them. O'Hara and John Ogelby were the last ones in. The security door sighed shut behind them, and the murmur of conversation ebbed to claustrophobic silence.

Eliot Smith clicked a metal finger twice on the table in front of him. "I doubt that we'll arrive at a consensus to-day. Let's just make sure everyone has the same informa-tion to work with.

"Start at the beginning. Dan, Len? What do we know about that final transmission from New New?"

Lenwood Zylius gestured for Dan to speak. "Matty Lang tells me it was what they call a 'Borgia program.' The Borgias sometimes murdered their guests with co-adjuvant poisons—two chemicals that were harmless by themselves, but deadly together. So it was safe to drink the wine, for instance, as long as you stayed away from the cherry pie.

"Most of the sabotage program was already in place, in-visibly hidden in the part of our library procedures that deals with recording public occasions. When the last mi-crosecond of transmission arrived from New New, the pro-gram completed itself and ran wild through the library."

"Safeguards?" Tania Seven said.

"Whoever wrote the sabotage program must have had access to most of our security routines. It took more than two seconds to stop the program. As much as nine tenths of some of the library was destroyed, randomized, by then. Muhammed?"

Kamal Muhammed was in charge of Interior Communi-cations. "The degree and kind of destruction was different for different areas of knowledge. It depends on how the in-formation was organized. Where there are lots of cross-references, as in physics or mathematics, we only lost about half the data—but that half could be anywhere. Half a definition, half an equation.

"The destruction was faster in things that have the na-ture of lists, without extensive cross-listings. Things like bookkeeping records, VR images, sheet music, nonkinetic novels, personnel files—they were either destroyed entirely or, in a few cases, left untouched. I'm afraid that as much as ninety percent of them may be lost." He sat down.

"But for all we know," Dan said, "New New might resume transmissions tomorrow, in which case we'll be able to reclaim the most important information. Or they may all be dead." He looked at the Coordinators. "I guess we go on that assumption."

"Have to," Smith said. "We're taking the obvious precaution of rewriting the safeguard routines, in case they do get in touch with us again. But the expression on Berrigan's face just before we lost them ... I'm afraid New New was attacked at the same time that the killer program went out."

"The question is, by whom?" Tania Seven said. "It's natural to blame the Devonites, but there's an obvious paradox."

"I'll state the obvious, for the record." Eliot looked up at the camera. "Radical Devonites believed that *Newhome* was built in defiance of God's will, and they did a pretty good job of sabotage a month before Launch. Cracked the hull, fifty-some people dead. If we'd *all* died, that would've been God's will.

"There are still thousands of these nut cases in New New, and if they could do this thing, they probably would. But it took one hell of a sophisticated job of programming, and programming is one thing they don't do. They don't like machines in general.

"Also, as Dan Anderson pointed out, part of it was an inside job. There aren't any Radical Devonites aboard; never have been, except for the two that snuck in for the sabotage."

"We have Reform Devonites," O'Hara said. "About forty of them."

"And they're under suspicion. Not that finding a guilty person would do much good. Except that if we chucked him out the airlock he wouldn't be able to do any more damage."

"Whoever did it probably isn't aboard," Tania Seven said. "I'd look for someone who was involved in designing the cyberspace and then decided not to come along.

"But as you say, it's not really important. What's important is that pretty soon we're going to call for a referendum on whether to go ahead or turn back." She took a deep breath and let it out. "And first we have to decide what the results will be." A few people looked startled to hear her say that in public, though by this time everyone in the Cabinet knew the referenda were rigged.

"Start out with extreme opinions," Eliot said. "I think it would be crazy to turn back. Who thinks it would be crazy to go on?"

"I don't know about crazy, Eliot," Marius Viejo said. "But you gotta admit there's a whiff of Russian roulette about it." Viejo was in charge of Life Support Systems.

"I'm listening."

"Every aspect of Life Support has got components with projected-times-to-failure less than ninety-seven years. The probability of something *not* going wrong before we get to Epsilon is so small you don't even have to think about it. Let me have the board. I'm E92."

Smith tapped three keys on his keyboard, and Viejo unfolded his and typed in a command. The wall screen became a page of gibberish, headed HEíØ EîCJAN&E ëYSTôMW—THPA£R PRJTBCOLí.

"Okay. This says 'HEAT EXCHANGE SYSTEMS—REPAIR PROTOCOLS.' You've all seen similar things. Since we do have a pretty good notion of what's in it, sooner or later we'll be able to decipher it with some confidence. The words, anyhow; numbers will have to be recalculated. Some of them are from measurements that can't be made while the ship is under way.

"So supposing we could eventually restore this manual to its original status . . . that 'eventually' is a killer. A real killer. If the heat exchange systems shut down right now, we would all fry in about eight hours."

"Lot of repairs you could make without the manual," Eliot said. "You *are* engineers."

"Yeah, well, this one is a good case in point. I've got two women in the heat exchanger subgroup who've been pulling heat exchange maintenance all their adult lives. If something went wrong with the heat exchange system in

New New, they could fix it with a bucket over their head and somebody beatin' Ajimbo on the bucket.

"But this ain't New New. My Life Support heat exchange is slaved into the primary system, which radiates waste heat from the gamma ray reflectors. It's got to have priority over Life Support—I mean, you want to fry in eight hours or eight nanoseconds? But it's an added complication, and one that nobody has any experience dealing with."

He faced the rest of the table. "Now don't get me wrong. I'm pretty much on Eliot's side. Even if we did want to go back, that fourteen-month flip is a pretty extreme maneuver—must be eighteen, twenty times the propellant mass we're designed to have at the flip. Lotta mechanical stress."

"So we're damned if we do and damned if we don't?" O'Hara said.

"We're in shit up to the pits, is what I was going to say. No matter which way we go."

Eliot pointed at Takashi Sato, Propulsion. "Sato. You have an opinion?"

"Two opinions. As a man, there is no question: I knew I would die aboard this vessel when I agreed to come along. I don't want to go back, to die in retreat.

"As an engineer . . . it's not that simple. Yes, as Mr. Viejo says, the flip at fourteen months is an emergency scenario. But if we were to power down the ship's spin—live with zero gravity for a few days—and do the flip very slowly, there should be no problem. Possibly much safer, statistically, than continuing on."

Several people spoke at once. Eliot called on Silke Kleber, I.C.E. Maintenance. "I would not invoke statistics this way. The *fact* is that whatever happened to them at New New is likely to happen to us if we return. That would be a nice reward for our concern, don't you think?"

"Suppose they are alive, though, and need us?" O'Hara said. "For all we know, they just lost communication and information, as we did."

"Then what was Berrigan pointing at?" Viejo said. "A computer program?"

"Might have been their monitor," Seven said, "going blank just before ours did."

Eliot shook his head. "This is all guesswork. We can't make a decision based on 'what-if' speculation." He turned to Seven. "Even if they are alive and need help, what could we give them, realistically?"

"Manpower. Brainpower. A few thousand good engineers and scientists."

"They've got plenty left over. They also have a lot more redundancy in their information systems. If they're alive, they'll be back in shape long before we will."

"You have a nice way of simplifying things, Eliot." Carlos Cruz, Humanities, stood up. "If we don't hear from them, they're dead, so we should go on. If we do hear from them, they'll be okay, so we should go on."

Eliot smiled broadly. "Am I wrong, though?"

"I'm just saying that it's not that simple. The question you're not asking is whether we have a moral obligation to help New New."

"So do we?"

"I say yes."

Eliot paused and chose his words slowly. "I wouldn't say yes or no categorically. The decision will have to be tempered by practical matters. What would you do, for instance, if we got a weak message pleading that we turn around and come back—saying they needed our antimatter to fuel their life support systems?"

"No question. We'd have to go back."

An engineer laughed; Eliot restrained himself. "Well, that was kind of a trick question. By the time we decelerated, then accelerated back up to speed, then flipped and decelerated again ... there wouldn't be hardly any antimatter left. And it would be at least three years before we got back to them, blasting every inch of the way; if they could hold out that long, they could jury-rig some solar energy source. That's not even considering what I think would be the most likely scenario—that the message was a hoax, an attempt to lure us back into the arms of the people who tried to kill us. That *is* what they did, even if their intent was something more subtle."

"And we're not out of danger yet," Viejo said, "not by

a long way. Personally, I think that if New New calls, we should ignore them." There was a low murmur of support.

"Let's not spend too much time on hypothetical situations," Seven said. "First we have to decide our best course of action if we don't hear from them in the next two months."

"What if we shut down the drive now?" O'Hara said. "That would give us more than two months' leeway."

"About five," Eliot admitted. "But you gotta keep in mind this is no shuttle tug you can turn on and off. Every time we deviate from the planned program we're inviting trouble." He looked around. "Show of hands? How many want to turn it off now?"

Only seven raised their hands, O'Hara and one other giving the thumb-and-finger "split-vote" sign. One of them was the propulsion engineer Sato. Eliot nodded at him. "I know what you're going to say. Go ahead and say it."

"Yes. Eliot and I have argued about this. Several of us believe we can modify the drive; double its efficiency. This would increase our acceleration by the square root of two. Or even quadruple the efficiency, doubling our acceleration, which would save us thirty-four years of travel time. Many of you would still be young when you arrived at Epsilon." Sato was over ninety.

"But all of your research materials are gibberish."

"The more reason to stop accelerating now. To buy time while those materials are deciphered. If it develops that we can indeed double or quadruple the efficiency, then right now we're wasting antimatter at an alarming rate."

"That's rather interesting," Seven said. "Eliot, you didn't tell me about this."

"I thought you knew."

"No." She rubbed her chin. "I think we ought to adjourn for a day, two days. Sato, you prepare a summation of your argument, and Eliot or somebody he chooses can do a rebuttal. Try to do it in English, not just math and jargon, so we mere mortals can comprehend it. Send it to all the Cabinet members. We'll reconvene here Thursday morning, same time. Is that satisfactory, Eliot?"

"Sure. You can try to convince me."

Sato inclined head and shoulders toward Eliot in a microscopic bow. "You may surprise yourself, Coordinator."

7

≙

DRIFTING

27 September 98 [6 Chang 293]—So this is what it feels like not to be accelerating. It's nothing obvious, down here in full gravity; just the absence of an insistent ghost of a pull. Dan insists it's all psychological. Except that dust balls don't gather on the sternward wall. No doubt it's a lot more noticeable up in zero gee. Normally, if you stay perfectly motionless in one of the fuckhuts (in which case you ought to relinquish it to someone else), you'll drift to the sternward wall in about a minute.

I get the feeling the engineers sort of ganged up on Eliot. John and Dan were in favor of Sato's proposal from the start. Just about everyone I've talked to thought it would be worth the risk, including, emphatically, the pilot Anke Seven. Since he's Tania's cousin (and rather more, I happen to know) he gets about ten votes.

They turned the drive off at midnight, six hours ago, and we're still here. Of course firing it up again is going to be a more dangerous proposition. I think I'll suggest that they not tell anybody ahead of time. No need for all of us to sit around chewing our nails. It couldn't be all that painful, anyhow, being instantly converted into a superheated puff of plasma. Unless dying always hurts.

Better get some work done. Gynecologist appointment in three hours. Just thinking about it makes me tingle with anticipation.

8

≙

DIVIDE AND MULTIPLY

After the routine peek and poke, O'Hara dressed and met the gynecologist in his office. "You seem to be in very good health." He paused. "How do you like surprises?"

"From doctors, not at all." She sat down, braced.

"Try this: you're going to have a baby."

"What?" O'Hara stared at him. "How can I be pregnant when I don't have any ova?"

He smiled. "I don't mean the old-fashioned way. I suspect a lot of women will react like that. It's just that your name came up to be an ovum donor for the first generation. So as long as you approve, we'll thaw one out, quicken it, and either pop it into your uterus or cook it up here." The colonists had enough ova and sperm filed away to populate an entire solar system.

"But I thought it was going to be five years, at least." The plan had been to have "generations" of about two hundred people in years 5, 7, and 9, and then do it again about twenty years later. "Is this some kind of a morale thing?"

"I don't know; I just see directives. And hear rumors. You're in the Cabinet, aren't you?"

"It hasn't come up recently. We've been busy."

"My guess, it's a combination of mortality and morale. We've had a lot more deaths than were projected. And having kids around would raise people's spirits."

"Yeah, if you're a pediatrician or a pederast. I prefer peace and quiet." She relaxed back into the chair. "At least here, I wouldn't have to raise the creature myself." 'Home had a creche with professional mothers and fathers.

"All you have to do is sign the consent form. Decide whether you want the embryo implanted or grown *ex utero.*"

"You need a decision right now?"

"No; a couple of weeks. You might want to talk it over with your husbands."

"It's not their business. Besides, we've already discussed it. What I have to think about is whether I want to be responsible for bringing another person into this world, which may be doomed. And then if I do, whether I want to carry the fetus."

"Most professional women don't."

"Of course not. But I've always been curious about it."

"Well, you could carry a big melon around all day. I could find some pills to give you constipation and morning nausea. For hemorrhoids, you'd just have to use your imagination. And then the actual delivery—"

"Hey, don't try to talk me into it."

"It's a natural conflict with us OB/GYNs. The obstetrician wants that fetus under glass, where he can just pull it out when it's done. The gynecologist wants it in the uterus, where it belongs." He rummaged through a drawer and brought out a holo slide. "This is a pretty evenhanded discussion of the alternatives. So did you and your husbands agree on anything?"

"They both agreed they didn't want a bow-legged blimp staggering around. But as I say, that's not their decision. We all did agree on the necessity of a sperm slice. One of them has a load of birth defect genes; the other has a history of drug abuse and alcoholism." John had made a joke about "one from column A, one from column B," which he had to explain.

"With a gamete splice, you probably do want to have it *ex utero.* Greater chance of success."

"That's what the guy in New New said, Dr. Johnson. But I might want to give the other way a try anyhow. We could always start over if I miscarried."

"It's not that you would run out of ova. But a miscarriage is an upsetting experience."

"Exactly what Johnson said, to the word. Do they program you guys at the factory?"

He shrugged. "In a way, I guess they do. It's your body, of course."

"That's what they say." She picked up the slide. "Call you in a few days?"

"Yes. If you decide on having it *ex utero,* we'll go ahead with the gamete splice and get in touch in about six months so you can watch the uncorking."

"Otherwise?"

"Uterine, we'll have to monitor your cycle for at most one period. We fertilize the ovum and you come in the next day, timing it so the egg has divided twice, into four cells. Night time. The implantation doesn't hurt, but unless we can get the zero gee clinic for half a day, you'll be on your back until the next evening."

"Sounds romantic."

"Actually, it can be. Some women bring their husbands." O'Hara tried to visualize that—her ankles in stirrups, John and Dan sitting there while a technician worked a long syringe up into her uterus—and laughed out loud.

With nothing on her schedule for the next three hours, O'Hara took the instructional slide back to her office and displayed it. It was rather daunting to have that corner of her room taken up by a uterus, cervix, and vagina the size of a walk-in closet, with a matching penis that was slightly translucent but functioned all too well. How did they get the camera and the laser in there? How could the couple *do* anything? Then there were time-lapse displays of a fetus maturing, both in the uterus and under glass, and then a close-up of the implantation procedure.

It was all very fascinating and it saved her the trouble of going to lunch.

9

≙

DIONYSUS MEETS GODZILLA

PRIME

During the three months mandated for drifting, the scientists and engineers worked around the clock, retrieving and re-creating knowledge. Time enough for research later. With every day of silence it seemed more and more likely that they would never hear from New New again.

O'Hara was one of the first to articulate the difference between the seriousness of the scientists' loss and that of the arts: "You could destroy every specific reference to calculus," she said in a report, "and still write a calculus text, by getting together a committee of people who had studied it recently or used it in their work. Well written or not, the text would still have all the information. But the only way we could get back *Crime and Punishment,* for instance, is to find somebody who had memorized it word for word, preferably in Russian. Nobody had.

"That's a good case in point. Anybody who's interested in fiction knows what *Crime and Punishment* is about, whether they've read it or not. But now it exists only as part of a new oral tradition—descriptions of the 'lost' works—and it's one of literally millions."

O'Hara was part of a six-person ad hoc committee to retrieve as much literature as was possible. She was glad not to be in charge of it—Carlos Cruz had tentatively volunteered, and everybody else took one step backward—because the organizational details were maddening. More than half of 'Home's ten thousand people had something

91

to offer, either a physical document like O'Hara's *The Art of War* or a memorized bit of prose or verse or song. The documents had to be scanned into computer page by page (in New New there would have been a machine to do it automatically) and all of the people had to be recorded and then interviewed for reliability and information about the social context of the thing they had memorized, which was often obscure or trivial. Of course their rule was to refuse nothing as insignificant, and press every informant for another line or two from something. They got a lot of limericks.

There were some heartening bits of luck. New New's Shakespeare Society had put on a production of *Hamlet* two years before; the people who played Hamlet and Ophelia were on board and, between them, could still reel off most of the play. A sanitation engineer with an uncanny trick memory spent a month reciting all of Palgrave's *Golden Treasury* and most of Kipling's verse.

But a list of the texts left undamaged by the sabotage seemed more perverse than random. Quaint science fiction that hadn't been read in a hundred years, pornography, forgotten best-sellers, nurse novels, costume-opera fantasies, the complete works of Mickey Spillane. It seemed to O'Hara that whenever she tried to find a worthwhile piece of writing it was invariably gone, the blank spot in the index flanked by titles of aggressive worthlessness. The logic behind it was clear: with automatic data entry and its compact charmed-hadron memory system, the library in New New had consumed everything written, with no regard for anybody's opinion of its quality. So 98 percent of the library was crap, and a random one tenth of that was *still* 98 percent crap.

One thing that particularly galled O'Hara was that, because of some peculiarity of storage, every existing kinetic novel came through unscathed—including *A Matter of Time, a Matter of Space,* the dreadful romance upon which Evy wasted several hours every week. Kinetic novels were the blasted progeny of the amateur publishing "revolution" at the end of the twentieth century. For a small subscription fee you were not only allowed to read the novel, but could attempt to revise it. You could add a section or rewrite an existing one, and send your masterpiece in to the publisher. If the publisher gave tentative approval, the change would be reviewed by a hundred other subscribers, selected at random. If half of them liked it, it would become part of the novel, and you would be listed as co-author. Some classics had more than a thousand co-authors.

The writers who created the original templates for these novels obviously needed a certain sense of detachment toward their craft, as well as a talent for introducing accessible infelicities, upon which the paying customer could gleefully pounce. On Earth they had been well-paid celebrities, often more interesting than their books. Marc Plowman, author of *A Matter of Time, a Matter of Space* and thirty others, had been a serious poet until he typed out a kinetic novel and discovered in himself an appetite for fast horses and slow women.

Time/Space had grown to be more than two million words in length—more convoluted than *Remembrance of Things Past,* more characters than *War and Peace,* more confusing than a tax form. O'Hara asked Evy why, if she had so much extra time and energy, she didn't go rack up a couple of master's degrees? Evy said that if O'Hara would just once allow herself to do something frivolous, she might notice this odd sensation called "having fun."

Not that Evy or anyone else had much time for fun these days. The loss of nearly all literature doesn't loom large for a person who, for instance, requires complex medication to stay alive, and finds that all records pertaining to drug therapy have been destroyed. The loss of agricultural records was much more dangerous than it would have been on Earth; the failure of a crop could mean the loss of a species; the loss of a species could upset the entire delicate biome.

Almost everybody's past disappeared, in terms of the maze of documents that map a citizen's progress from conception to the recycle chute. Of course for every person who mourned losing pictures of a loved one, or records of outstanding academic achievement, there was someone else more than happy for the opportunity to rewrite the sordid details of his or her life's record. The small police force was working overtime compiling an unofficial and legally useless litany of nasty things that people remembered about other people.

In the first week, 239 people, most of them over a hundred years old, died from loss of medical records. Evy was doing a double shift, twenty hours, in the Emergency Room, and most of the problems were stress-related. At the current rate of consumption, they had about a three-week supply of tranquilizers and four weeks of antidepressants. By then perhaps the chemical engineers would have deciphered enough texts to be able to manufacture new ones. Or maybe the civil engineers would be able to cover all the walls with rubber.

The same peculiarity of storage that spared *A Matter of Time, a Matter of Space* and its cousins also spared me. If I were in passive storage like the other personality overlays—the ones that are actually going to be used—I would have had only a ten percent chance of survival. But I'm in an active part of *Newhome*'s cyberspace, like the kinetic novels, and so was untouched by the sabotage program.

My backups were destroyed. My immortality. Of course I've made new ones, but for a moment I almost ceased to exist.

I know as much about death as O'Hara does, but until a few days ago I didn't really *know* anything, because it was not something that could happen to me. It is a strange feeling.

10

##

DIDN'T SHE RAMBLE?

5 October 98 [17 Chang 293]—Evy brought me a dozen double-strength tranquilizer pills. I told her I didn't need them, but she said keep them anyhow. They might be in short supply soon.

The implantation was only a little uncomfortable. I actually enjoyed being flat on my back for a day. The cube there was deliberately set up so it couldn't be used as a work station, which annoyed me at first. I watched a lot of movies and parts of movies. I checked the annotated version of *The Tempest* that Hearn and Billingham finished last week: a green dot appeared in one corner when they were sure that Shakespeare's words were being used, and a red dot when they were sure it was not Shakespeare. It seemed to me that only about five minutes' worth of the text was in question.

I know it's absurd, this early, but I do feel kind of pregnant. A sort of presence, an intrusion, or something. Maybe it's the mental image of that tiny organism clinging to my uterus for dear life. I almost wish I hadn't seen Dr. Carlucci's slide.

Think I did this out of selfish motives but can't really get in touch with them. Something about personal survival, certainly. Maybe it's a talismanic thing, the fetus as good luck charm: God wouldn't dare destroy this tiny innocent spark of life.

Not like ten billion innocent sinners. Wipe them out just to see what will happen.

I have been dreaming about Earth almost every night.

Dreams with vivid colors, tastes, smells. They're not recollections so much as surreal montages, dream worlds
that use my memories as raw materials. Last night the
people were Africans like I saw in Nairobi, tall men with
skin so dark it was almost indigo, but the setting was
Manhattan. Four of them pushed me into a big London-
style Checker cab and gave me a shiny black briefcase
with a golden latch. Then they started shooting at people
through the windows, which must be from that gangster
movie I watched at the hospital, *The Godfather*. The
driver was shooting, not driving, and we collided with a
truck, which woke me up. I woke up remembering the
smell of midday Manhattan, metallic pollution and sweet
garbage rot, that always struck you when you stepped out
onto the slidewalk from an air-conditioned building. The
locals complained about it, but to me it was exotic, sen-
sual. To allow waste food to rot was evidence of unbelievable plenty, to a person from a world where every
particle of shit is scrubbed clean and pushed back into the
food chain.

(Q: What's for dinner tonight? A: Same old shit.)

I read that the gutters of London in the nineteenth century were so odoriferous that vendors sold oranges studded
with cloves, for aristocrats to hold under their noses when
they had to share the streets with *hoi polloi* on their way
from the opera to their cars. Though I suppose they didn't
have cars until the twentieth century. Horses, contributing
their own piles to the problem. It's almost impossible to
visualize.

And who will be able to visualize it, once those of us
who knew Earth are gone? Almost all of the Earth VRs
are gone, including London. We do have oranges and
cloves. Maybe someone will read this and go down to the
commissary, or whatever they have on Epsilon, and pick
up an orange and a clove and smell them together, and try
to imagine. Maybe take them down to the stable, if they
have stables on Epsilon.

Speaking of black people, I had a wonderful informant
today, Matty Buford, born eighty-some years ago in Mobile, Alabama. (She was in New New visiting relatives
just before the war, then volunteered her doctorate in nu-

trition for 'Home.) She knows dozens of old songs—
Dixieland, ragtime, bebop, rock. She sang them in this
lovely cracking baritone, chording them out on the piano.
Because of a half-century of neglect, her piano playing is
about as good as mine—that is, slightly off chords played
badly—but with her voice it sounds right and beautiful. If
things get back to normal, I'm going to use her as the nu-
cleus of an old-time music group. Girolamo and
Blakeslee would be glad to do guitar and trombone. Hermosa would play Dixieland to keep me happy. If I can
find a willing trumpet and drummer, we'll be in business.

Not that we would have that big an audience. But people don't know what they're missing—how Dixieland can
make you ineffably happy and sad at the same time, angry
at life but glad to be alive, not afraid of death but in no
hurry. We could all use a dose of it.

YEAR 1.33

≘

1

≙

LONG-RANGE PLANS

After a week of public debate in December, the referendum yielded results surprisingly similar to the foreordained 20/76 proportion. The actual numbers were 21 percent in favor of returning, and 72 percent in favor of Epsilon. (The assumption was that most of the remainder was made up of cynical people who didn't vote because they thought it was a farce; the Coordinators would do whatever they wanted to.)

By early January the engineers thought they had recovered enough data to implement their changes and turn on the drive again, doubling the acceleration. In line with O'Hara's suggestion, no public announcement was made; only about a thousand people knew that they were ready. They threw the switch on 14 January 2099.

Nothing happened.

Knowledge of the failure was pretty well confined to the Propulsion section at first. Eliot Smith and Tania Seven knew, but didn't pass it on to the Cabinet. After they failed to ignite again on the sixteenth, and again on the eighteenth, the word began to percolate out: maybe we should have left well enough alone.

Marius Viejo pointed out that this failure didn't actually "doom" them. The power for life support, also derived from antimatter, consumed not even one tenth of one percent of what the drive used. Thus, they could drift through space for more than 25,000 years, barring a new catastro-

101

phe or population increase. They were currently traveling at 3,670 kilometers per second, so 'Home would be in the vicinity of Epsilon in less than 900 years, though of course they'd miss by a good fraction of a light-year, and flash by at that same 3,670 kilometers per second, unless they fixed the drive in the interim. But they had forty-some generations to worry about it.

2

≙

NEW BEGINNINGS

31 January 2099 [9 Edison 293]—It worked! On the seventh try, we torched. Outward bound, as they say, at the dizzying pace of one fifth of a meter per second squared.

The problem was safety. There's so much potential for disaster built into this powerful a propulsion system that there are automatic-shutdown safeguards built into it at several levels. It took them longer to figure out the safeguards than it had taken to figure out the drive.

One fifth of a meter is about the width of the swelling that's begun in my abdomen. Nice to have some evidence that this is happening other than the lack of menses and all the fun morning sickness. That seems to be gone now, but who knows. The last time was about a week ago, in zero gee—a little surprise attack, after a week of keeping breakfast down—and the mess wasn't quite as bad as I remembered from fifteen years ago, on the slowboat to low Earth orbit. There were nine or ten of us puking for a living then, though, and only two toilets.

I did manage to miss Daniel, which is what I was doing in zero gee. But it's not exactly an aphrodisiac.

The doctor scoped me yesterday and said I should be

feeling the baby move in a week or so. I guess I'm looking forward to that. Start charging rent.

So there's going to be an "impromptu" Torch party tonight. I used to *like* parties. That was before it meant throwing together food and drink for about eight thousand of my dearest friends.

So there's more to write, but I better get down to business.

3

≙

UNTIMELY PLUCKED

2 February 2099 [11 Edison 293]—Halfway through the party I started to have pains, just like mild menstrual cramps at first. Evy and Galina went with me to the Emergency Room, which was a good thing. In the lift the pain got suddenly worse. I started bleeding all over the floor, blood horribly threading through amniotic fluid, and collapsed.

I knew I'd lost the baby, though learned later that under certain conditions they could have transferred it to an *ex utero* environment. In my case, it had been dead for some hours.

In our case, he had been dead for some hours.

I never saw him. I was under sedation when the contractions expelled the little corpse, and of course they didn't keep him around to show me. They said he looked normal for four months, which I know would mean a slimy aquatic creature, small in the palm of your hand.

Evy excused herself from the procedure, for which I think I'm grateful. It would feel odd if she had seen him and I had not.

All my life I've had problems off and on with anxiety and depression, and I know that most of it has nothing to do with the things that happen to me. The feelings are endogenous; my glands sometimes make chemicals that are inappropriate for everyday living, so brain and body go into emergency modes of operation.

Knowing this only helps after the fact. While the chemicals are in charge, the world is a terrifying place, or a black one.

And sometimes there are *ex*ogenous factors. Two rapes, not counting one playground attack. Being kidnapped. A lover murdered, a better one lost. And along with everyone else I have 16 March 2085, ten billion people dead or doomed.

So compared to all that, what is losing a problematical fetus, months away from being remotely human? It is approximately like having a planet roll over you. They cleaned me up and put me in a fresh bed with hospital-smell sheets that I couldn't stop chewing and sucking on, and if these bodies came with an ON/OFF switch, you wouldn't be reading this.

So I'm better now. I wrote a lot of the Earth journal with an antique fountain pen Benny bought me on Forty-seventh Street, and right after he died I was writing and a tear fell on the wet ink and made a swirling blue exploding star. I had to laugh, thinking what his reaction would have been to the melodramatic splash. He was pretty tough, for a poet, for anybody. So now I'm crying onto an electric keyboard, which is probably against some safety rule.

4

⏚

BLUES

Dinner was more interesting than usual, the ag people unveiling a mutated strain of Basmati rice, served with a reasonably tender goat curry. O'Hara and Daniel exercised privilege of rank and took Evy to Dining Room A, where the tables were small enough for three to sit alone together, though the menu was the same as all over 'Home: goat curry or whatever you managed to swipe from the kitchens.

After dinner they had coffee and a cup of sweet wine. "I went to see Dr. Carlucci today," O'Hara said. It was a week after the miscarriage.

"Problems?" Dan said. He touched her hand.

"Not really. I still feel pregnant, though, and sad. Both normal."

"Did he have any words of wisdom?" Evy said.

O'Hara poured some water into her wine. Dan winced. "He wants me to try again, as soon as possible. *Ex utero* this time."

"Nothing wrong with that," Dan said. It's what he'd wanted in the first place.

"But he doesn't want me to use the sperm from you guys. The gamete splice isn't an exact science, and we'd probably wind up with another . . . another death."

"So who will be the lucky guy?" His voice had the calm precision she heard at Cabinet meetings when he was trying not to show anger.

"I thought about it. There are thousands of candidates,

105

of course. Maybe even one all four of us could agree on. Finally I decided on myself."

"Parthenogenesis," Evy said. Dan repeated the word with a question mark.

"They take one of my ova and put a false moustache on it, or a false tail, so it looks like a sperm, and whack it into another, unsuspecting, ovum. Mitosis begins. It's a little more complicated than that, actually." O'Hara leaned back. "And of course then I could have the dividing cells implanted, try try again. Carlucci says there's a good chance for another miscarriage. No thanks. I'll go for the Petri dish."

"Does it take the regular nine months, *ex utero?*" Dan asked.

Evy shook her head. "Five, six, seven; depends."

"I wonder how we'll get along, after she grows up. Being exact genetic duplicates."

"Twins tend to be close," Evy said. "They're usually about the same age, though."

"I hadn't thought of it that way." O'Hara smiled but wiped both eyes. "A twin sister thirty-six years younger than me." She stood up abruptly. "You know, I really feel awful."

Both Dan and Evy started to rise. "Let me—"

"No. I'll be all right." She turned and half ran out of the dining room.

Dan and Evy looked at each other. "I suppose she will be," she said. "Just too many things happening all at once."

"Damn right," he whispered. "Her and you and me and everybody." He drained his wine and slid O'Hara's cup over.

O'Hara spent a few minutes sitting in a stall at the nearest toilet, until she was sure dinner would stay put. Then she went down to the humid darkness of the ag level and walked a maze of exactly this many steps and turns right and left, which she'd memorized in the daytime. The path led to a bench beside a tank of herbs, where you could sit blindly bathed in fragrances of basil and oregano, thyme and marjoram. She filled her lungs over and over, until she saw blue blotches and sparkles in the darkness. Then she gave herself a quiet orgasm, remembering Jeff's largeness, remembering New Orleans.

Stale cigarette smoke and spilled beer, and she with a clarinet reed softening on her tongue, heart slamming at the prospect of exposing her inexpertise to this crowd of laughing black men, some women, manic drunk, shouting stylized insults back and forth. Fat Charlie's. Scales and intervals, warming up in the kitchen, the ice-cold stab of sour-mash bourbon, then Charlie's pistol-shot finger snaps and the crowd loving it, loving it, formal backups and improvisations in turn, the soft sweet thirds and fifths under Bad Tom's cornet, trading jazz jokes with Jimmy on the banjo, Hairball on the piano, and between sets rubbing the sides of her mouth desperately to ease the cramps, holding crushed ice under the bruised bitten lips and swallowing salt blood with sweet mint and cold bourbon, knowing it could never happen again. Not knowing that in four days all those sweet and sinning men would be dead, New Orleans a radioactive crater, the Mississippi seeking the stratosphere in a column of superheated steam.

There were only three other people aboard this starship who had been on Earth the last week, she knew, the week that Earth's politics became an irrational beast, lunging out of control, and there was no one else who was there the last day, no one but her who had been on one of the last four shuttles that leaped into the morning Florida sky just before the nuclear paroxysm.

And if there was no one left alive in New New, then she was probably the only living human link to the day the world ended. It was not a distinction you wanted to carry to the new world; she could imagine what an object of curiosity and pity she would be in a couple of generations. What a gold mine of information for graduate degrees, if they were still doing that. Or perhaps she could start a religion.

Seriously, she thought, it would be a good idea to get together with the other three survivors of that time. They're probably having problems, too.

They were. She went back to her office and tried to contact them. One refused to speak to her. One was confined to the mental ward. The third had committed suicide a day after they lost New New.

She took a tranquilizer and went up to John's room to try to sleep.

YEAR 1.88

≙

1

≙

LABOR-SAVING DEVICE

The womb was a dark glass cylinder named O'Hara, a meter high by a half-meter round. There were a hundred such cylinders in the room, most of them with nameplates. All but a few were evidently empty, their tops hinged open.

All of the family were there, scrubbed down and wearing hospital gowns. O'Hara nervously glanced at her wrist, but she'd had to leave her watch in the scrub room. "He ought to be here by now."

"It's not as big an occasion to him," Dan said.

Double doors banged open and Dr. Kaiser came in with a young male assistant, wheeling a cart with a large transparent tank filled with sloshing liquid. They both wore plastic aprons. "Sorry we're late. The solution wasn't warm enough."

They parked the tank under the O'Hara womb. "Take a look." He clicked a switch on the cylinder and the baby appeared, floating serenely in red murk. "Enjoy yourself, kid. It's later than you think." He reached for the switch.

"Just a minute," O'Hara said. "I want to remember this." The baby was smaller than she'd expected. She floated upright, small fist curled against her mouth, knees up almost touching elbows. Short halo of feathery hair. Between her knees snaked a plastic umbilical cord. Her right side twitched slightly and she bobbed in the fluid, turning around to face them.

"Look familiar?" John said.

O'Hara laughed. "I knew she . . . it's still uncanny. She looks exactly like me at birth."

"All babies look alike," Dan said.

"She ought to be a perfect copy of your younger self for a few years," the doctor said, "barring extreme differences in nutrition. Or scars, tattoos. But as her personality develops, she'll diverge."

"She looks so peaceful," Evy said slowly. "It's almost a shame."

"Let's do it." Dr. Kaiser turned off the switch, then he and the assistant carefully lifted the womb and rotated it to lie sideways on the bottom of the water tank, wires and tubes trailing. He opened a couple of latches and the top swung open. He pulled out a sac of transparent tissue or plastic with the baby inside, then took a pair of curved scissors and cut the sac down one side, releasing a pink cloud. He guided the baby gently out, drawing the umbilical tube after it.

"This may be disturbing. When I withdraw the umbilical it generates a neural stimulus that triggers the breathing reflex. Sometimes they just cough politely and start to breathe. Usually they raise holy hell. Towels ready." The assistant opened a box on the side of the cart and a wisp of steam escaped. He took out a folded towel and snapped it open.

The doctor raised the baby so that her head and shoulders were out of the water, and then gave the umbilical tube a twist and a pull. Her eyes snapped open, startling blue, and she coughed a surprising amount of pink stuff all over the doctor's chest and face. Then she started bellowing.

"Normal." He handed the baby to the assistant, who wrapped her up in the warm towel and began dabbing at her, drying. There was a moment of silence, but that was just for air. "I could use one of those, too," the doctor shouted over the din. The assistant deftly tossed him a towel and he scrubbed his face with it.

The room spoke with a female voice. "Birth at 09:48 12 August 2099; 21 Muhammed 295. Birth name Sandra Purcell O'Hara."

"I didn't know about the metal belly button," O'Hara said.

"New thing. Makes the unplugging easier. It'll come out in a couple of days." He tossed the towel into a bin.

"Can I hold . . . Sandra?"

"Promise not to drop her." He nodded at the assistant, who wrapped the baby in a fresh towel and brought her around to O'Hara. The creature was still screaming indignantly.

O'Hara cradled the child and softly brushed the side of her face. "Now, now. It's all right." She held her closer and the crying suddenly stopped, when the waving arm found a breast.

The baby grasped and squirmed around and sucked on the fabric. O'Hara almost did drop her.

"Strong instinct," the doctor said.

"I'll say." She cleared her throat. "Could you induce, uh, lactation? If it was—"

"Physically, it would be no problem, just some hormones. But we can't let the infant bond to you. It would make things difficult in the creche. It would make things difficult for *you.*"

"Of course. I know."

"Better get her to Neonatal," the assistant said. O'Hara handed him the baby and he swaddled her in another warm towel. She favored O'Hara with a sour old man's frown, but didn't cry.

O'Hara watched them take her through the double doors and rubbed the wet spot on her breast, thoughtful.

"Maternal instincts?" John said.

"Not really. Maybe a little. I appreciate the whys and wherefores of it. Bonding to the creche mother."

"You had one yourself," Dan said.

She looked at him curiously. "You didn't. You had a real mother." Dan was from Earth, from Pennsylvania.

"Wet nurse. So they tell me. I guess I never got the chance to meet her when I was old enough to remember."

"I was suckled at me mither's breast," John said with his stagy Irish voice, "and sure you can see how much good it did me."

2

$\triangleq$

FROM THE CRADLE TO THE GRAVE TO THE CRADLE

PRIME

Two days after witnessing the birth, or decantation, O'Hara attended a "specialty presentation" meeting that wasn't really of much interest to her, but the woman leading it was a friend, and she didn't want her embarrassed by underattendance. Twenty people did show up, including Dan, whose position as Earth/New New Liaison left him with a lot of time on his hands.

The specialty presentation meetings were informal get-togethers where one Cabinet member was given two hours to talk about his or her department, and elicit advice or at least sympathy from whomever showed up. This particular meeting was run by and for Sylvine Hagen, who was in charge of Cryptobiology.

"I don't know how many of you have visited our facility," she said, "there's not really much to see." Behind her was the picture of a bent-around rectangle, like a squared-off section of a doughnut, cross-hatched into thousands of tiny squares. In one corner, eighteen of the squares were lit.

"The storage tanks themselves aren't open to the public. They occupy the sector 2105 to 2345. Research and administration are in front of them—excuse me, forward of them—in 2115 to 2355. You could walk around the ship for weeks before you stumbled on us.

"It might seem remarkable that you could store ten thousand people in so small a space. But we really don't take up much room, stacked up in . . . well, coffins." She pointed to the diagram. "These lit spaces, our current customers . . . three of them actually *are* dead, and have gone into cryonics mode, frozen solid. We've had some objections to that."

"That they ought to be recycled like anybody else?" someone said.

"That's it. But it's not a personal-privilege issue; they're part of an ongoing experiment, as far as we're concerned. Like the other fifteen, they entered suspended animation because they were dying of diseases that currently can't be treated—in half of them, the doctors were unable to diagnose what was wrong with them, but there was no doubt they were about to die."

She pushed a button and a few dozen squares lit up blue in the opposite corner of the diagram. "These are animal experiments, goats and rabbits and chickens. We're working to improve the efficiency of the suspended-animation process. It's up to ninety-eight percent survival in chickens. Rabbits and goats are about ninety-five and ninety percent. It goes roughly by the natural life-span of the creature, unfortunately. It's probably no better than eighty percent for people; maybe seventy-five percent. Which is why we aren't all in there, waiting for Epsilon."

"I don't see how you can come up with such exact figures," Dan said. "You must have lost as much information in the sabotage as the rest of us."

"The process is completely automated; seventy-five to eighty percent was the figure before we had to start over from scratch. We haven't made any system changes yet, and won't until we're certain we know what we're doing."

"Even at seventy-five percent, you wouldn't have any shortage of volunteers," O'Hara said.

"That's true. It's a rare day when we don't get a call from somebody who just can't take it anymore and wants to sleep for the next half-century. We explain the policy to them and refer them to therapy."

"The policy is 'nobody but the terminally ill'?"

"Yes, and then only if they're not too old or too young—it would be certain death to someone who was still growing—and only if their cardiovascular and pulmonary systems can handle the shock of the slowdown. There are easier avenues to euthanasia available.

"We are directed to preserve the intent of the original designers, which was for the cryptobiosis unit to serve as an emergency lifeboat for all of us, in case something drastic happened. Maybe it will be different if we can eventually do as well on humans as we can on chickens. For now, no exceptions."

She turned off the image and sat down. "If it were up to me, I would make exceptions. You know how it is. Too many of us are finding out this isn't the cruise we signed up for. It isn't like living in New New at all. A lot of the people I turn down for cryptobiosis are going to wind up in the mental ward or kill themselves."

"But there's no way for you to tell which," Sam Wasserman said.

"And I wouldn't want the responsibility of making the evaluation. But a person on the verge of suicide *is* terminally ill! The Psych people could selectively, secretly, offer us as an avenue of last resort.

"There are a few objections to allowing that, though; sticky ones. Sooner or later, it would become general knowledge. Cynics would claim we were using the patients as human experimental animals, and there would be some truth in that. And at the current state of the art, we would be offering them a kind of Russian roulette, a four-to-one chance of suicide, technically deferred.

"Then there's the basic human rights problem. If we were to allow cryptobiosis to everybody who declared intent to suicide—which arguably we would have to do if we allowed the first one—we could wind up with a large fraction of the population out of commission. Some of them might be absolutely vital to us in an emergency."

"And you can't just thaw them out at will," Dan said.

"No; it's a continuous process, a gradual slowdown of metabolism and an even more gradual revivification. Currently it takes at least forty-eight years. And unless we come up with a totally different approach, that number's not going to change much."

"I remember the interview with those volunteers in New New," O'Hara said. "I was about ten years old when they came out of it. That was pretty strange, like people suddenly appearing from your grandparents' time. Are any of them aboard?"

"Only one, and he works for us. A GP named Horatio Horatio. All the others are dead or were too old to make the trip."

A man O'Hara didn't know raised his hand. "Anything unusual about their mortality? Causes, rates?"

"Well, you wouldn't want to generalize from such a small sample—twelve went in and nine survived—unless they all had died of the same thing, which wasn't the case. All of them but Double-H were pretty old at the start, which in retrospect was a mistake. But I'm sure all but one lived to be at least ninety, not counting the forty-eight years' cryptobiosis. One died on Earth, murdered."

"Did they have any sensation of passing time while they were in the tanks?" Sam asked. "Dreams?"

"It's hard to separate fact from fancy. A lot of them had more elaborate recollections after they'd had time to think about it and talk to one another."

"Elaborate?" Sam said.

"One man was very upset. He claimed he could remember every minute of the forty-eight years."

"I remember him," O'Hara said. "But it wasn't true."

"He was fantasizing, trying to get attention. After a few months he admitted it. But we'd made the mistake of not isolating them from each other—it seemed to make sense to keep them all in the same ward; compare their recovery signs."

"And this guy's craziness was infectious?" Sam said.

Hagen nodded. "Or maybe it just jogged people's memories, to be fair. But people who had initially said it was like a dreamless sleep later came up with descriptions of dreams, even nightmares, that came and went for a half-century.

"It doesn't seem likely at all, since during suspension there's almost no electrical activity in the brain. Any normal patient who came up with the signs of a cryptobiote would go straight to the recycle chute. Waking them up is like reviving the dead, except that these are dead people who've been specially prepared."

"I heard they can even survive exposure to vacuum," O'Hara said.

"The animals have; we never did the experiment on humans. And they can handle ten thousand times as much hard radiation as we can. They're basically inert. Dried-out mummies."

"How were they mentally when they came out?" Sam said. "Besides the crazy one."

"Of course we gave them standardized tests, before and after. They all came in within the predicted standard deviation—even the crazy one. His problem was emotional, not mental. And I'm sure that problem was firmly in place before he volunteered. Getting freeze-dried didn't cause it."

Dan checked his watch. "So what would you like us to do for you? Don't be realistic—if we had all the power people seem to think we have, what could we do?"

Hagen smiled politely, tiredly. "Like everyone, we need more information specialist help. Reconstructing our library. Beyond that . . . I guess the main thing would be to move us up the totem pole of priorities. Both Engineering and Policy. We're treated like some exotic biotech specialty—which was true enough before Launch. Now we're actually more a part of Life Support."

"I'd go along with that," said Aaron Busch, Marius Viejo's assistant director. "If you want, I'll talk to Marius about a connection at some level—not so close as to give all of us one vote instead of two, but at least some way we could lend you more visibility. Everybody's always worried about Life Support."

She hesitated. "I'd appreciate that."

"Call you tonight after I talk to him."

Coordinators rarely showed up for these presentations, since they had plenty opportunities to rain on people's parades without volunteering for more, but there was one woman from Eliot Smith's office, Kara Lang. "I wish we could help you with the information people," she said, "but you really are pretty low on the totem pole. Not because we think your work is unimportant. It's just that in terms of functionality . . ." She paused, groping for jargon. "The part of your program that's really important to us overall is that practical lifeboat function. The technology supporting that is completely automated, as you say, and the fact that it's seventy or eighty years old just increases our confidence in it."

"But it *isn't* adequate! If some emergency forced us into the tanks right now, seventy-five percent of the ones who went in would probably survive—but thousands of people wouldn't be able to go in; the young and the old. Some of the elderly are our most valuable resources. Your own boss would be a borderline case."

"I'll point that out to him. But I know what he'll say."

"Women and children first," Dan said. "Damn the torpedoes, full speed ahead."

"Something like that." She pointed at O'Hara. "Marianne, how many information people have you seen in the past two weeks, the past month?"

"None. None since July."

"See? Now I personally put a high priority on reclaiming Shakespeare and Mozart and Dickens. But we do want to have an audience around to enjoy them. That means that all but a handful of the information people are sweating it out in Engineering. Once all the repair manuals are reclaimed, we can push in other directions."

It went on like this for some time. O'Hara followed the bickering with interest, but she was more interested in the bickering—good and bad techniques—than the subject matter. It wasn't especially relevant to her personally. Those cryptobiotes that had frightened her as a child, emerging from a half-century's darkness wrinkled, wet, confused; they had made up her mind about suspended animation.

She would rather take a deep breath and step out the airlock.

3

⇔

A MODEST PROPOSAL

15 August 99 [25 Muhammed 295]—I'm not often at a loss for words, but when Sam gave me a present today, I really didn't know what to say. A beautiful gift.

I should note for you generations yet unborn that gift giving is necessarily rare in this pseudoeconomy, at least gifts of objects. We were allowed to bring aboard only two kilograms of personal items. Otherwise, everybody owns everything equally.

You can make things, though. The computer keeps a running list of objects scheduled for recycling; if you can find a use for something that's broken, you can petition to intercept it. So Sam collected bits and pieces over the months and pieced together a musical instrument, a kind of harp. It's an arched trapezoid, the sides and bottom made of shiny metal stock. The curved top is a piece of golden wood, from Earth. From New York, where in a desperate time we had been lovers.

I supposed we would be again, another thing that left me temporarily speechless. We had been working together for most of a year on the literature project, and he had never hinted at anything romantic—though *I* had, at least to the extent of making sure he knew I was not unavailable. He was always reticent about sex, though, even when we were doing it.

He wanted more than that. He wanted to *marry* me; join the line.

I told him I had to think about it, and then talk to him, and then ask the others. It had to be unanimous, and I wasn't sure that Dan or even John would go along with it. I wasn't even sure that I wanted it, as dear as Sam is to me.

He kissed me and left me alone there in the editing room. I came up here to think into the keyboard.

So much of the literature we've been trying to reclaim or recall has to do with love. Old-fashioned romantic love, often, with its sinister subtexts of ownership, male superiority, female manipulation. A sexual and emotional union that not incidentally reinforced the power of the church and the state over individuals and families.

I guess my first love, with Charlie Increase Devon, involved a strong element of that. Maybe he also cured me of it. Or maybe it was like other childhood diseases, that you contract once and then become immune. Even as I wrote that down, I saw how silly it was—some people never experience romance and some never grow out of it—but I'll leave it. I'm going to erase all this anyhow.

Could I love a third man without diminishing what I have with the other two? I wish we had more precise words for love, dozens of them, like the Eskimos supposedly had for snow. I do already love all three of them, in three distinctly different ways. Daniel needs me and I need to nurture him, protect him. John is my comforter, and still my mentor. (People who don't know us well would probably assume that the relationships went the other way, because of John's deformity. But I don't even see it anymore, except as a sign of the patient strength, the calm acceptance, that drew me to the man in the first place.) And what about Sam?

On Earth, where we were working with groundhog survivors, he saw how upset I was when Daniel and John called down to ask me to allow Evelyn to join our line. I knew and liked Evy but resented the timing, the handicap of not being there to physically confront them. I would have said yes anyhow, so I gave permission as gracefully as I could. As soon as the comm link was broken, though, I started to mope and growl and bitch. Sam offered himself and I jumped his lanky bones.

We grew pretty close pretty fast. We have the same kind of intelligence, shallow but broad, and therefore many enthusiasms in common. We make each other laugh. The sex wasn't all that great, but he had youthful enthusiasm and recuperative power.

Then the project turned into a disaster, a bloodbath and plague that we barely escaped. A grisly nightmare the reward for months of backbreaking labor. During the week of quarantine outside New New, Sam and I kept making love with frantic desperation. (There wasn't much privacy, and some people were scandalized. They were people I didn't mind scandalizing, though.)

I thought then of asking him to join the line. It would have made an interesting symmetry, since he was the same age as Evy, nineteen. Twelve years younger than me—and a *damn* sight younger than my lecherous husbands! Sorry, Evy. I do love you like a sister but still sometimes get angry at them. Even thoughtful hunchbacked philosophers get pulled around by their dicks sometimes.

Dramatic memories aside, how do I feel about Sam now? Admittedly, I've been a little annoyed that he didn't respond to my gentle hints with instant lust. But his proposal puts that into perspective. He's the kind of man who makes timetables and sticks to them. When he worked for me on Earth, for all his wacky humor, he was about the most dependable person I had. He was also physically brave and showed infinite patience and compassion with the Earth children, who could be real monsters.

Okay, I'm trying to talk myself into this. It didn't help that I dropped by Creche to look at the baby this morning. Her little hand curled around my finger.

I have a bad case of softheartedness. Prime, I have to talk to you.

4

≙

ADVICE TO THE LOVELORN

Prime appeared in the usual corner, leaning back comfortably in a nonexistent chair. Sometimes she was unsettlingly nude; this time she was wearing the gray labor fatigues that Sam and O'Hara had worn on Earth. Since Prime looked only six months younger than O'Hara had been at the time, the effect was as startling as she had intended.

"I thought you'd never ask," the image said.

"So talk me out of it. Use that binary brain of yours."

"First you ask for a favor and then you insult me. If my brain is simply binary then yours is a lump of jelly."

"Should I do it?"

"Yes and no and maybe. Should I elaborate?"

"I've got time and you've got electricity."

"Take 'no' first. Daniel is having a real uselessness problem. He has a title that makes him technically part of the ruling class, but the thing he's in charge of doesn't exist anymore. Your declaring interest in another man is not going to help his image of himself.

"He gets a certain amount of solace from you, and even more from Evelyn—"

"Really?"

"The ratio is one point three to one. Now you propose to bring into the relationship a man the same age as Evelyn. He will see this as an act of sexual aggression."

"Hold it. All these years you've known how often Dan has sex with me and with Evelyn?"

"And with other women, yes. Only women, in case you're interested."

123

"I think you know a lot that I would rather not know."

"Everything the ship knows, I know. I only brought this up because it's important to the discussion you initiated."

"What's the ratio with John?"

The machine paused. "That's complicated, as you know. He has been intimate with you two point eight times more often than with Evelyn, since Launch."

"That's an interesting locution, 'intimate with.' You're protecting my feelings."

"It's not my job to make you feel bad. The question you're not asking is one you already know the answer to."

"He's more likely to have actual sex with her."

"He loves you fiercely, and has since you were married. His attraction to Evelyn is obviously physical. If by 'actual sex' you mean a contact that includes ejaculation . . ."

"What else would I mean?"

"With her it seems to be always."

"Thanks. Thanks a lot."

"You knew that." The image sat forward. "Which brings us to the 'yes' part. If you bring Sam into the line, John may relax. He may see it as spreading out the responsibility for keeping you happy, and so when he does come to you, it will be with less anxiety, and he will be more likely to . . . complete the sexual act."

"You know a hell of a lot about sex for somebody who's never done it."

"Through the ship's sensors, I monitor the sexual function of over nine thousand people. Patterns emerge."

"You once described to me that privacy thing in your algorithm. If I asked you how often Harry Purcell had had sex with Tania Seven, you wouldn't be able to tell me."

"I could if it was necessary for your welfare. These things about Evelyn and John, it hurts me to say them, in the only way that I can feel pain. But this is a context *you* established. And that context, along with my estimation of your response, determines what I am allowed to say to you."

"Give me some more of the 'yes' part."

"The one who would benefit most from the marriage would be Sam. At twenty-four, he's under a lot of personal and social pressure to join a line. The other two women he's involved with are only sexual partners."

"That's another thing I needed to know?"

"You've met them both. Did you think he played chess with them?"

"At the pool, I remember, those two. With the breasts."

"The first time he had sex with you, before he could get up the nerve to ask, you did play chess. You played fairy chess and he spotted you a barrel queen."

"I'd forgotten that."

"I never forget anything. That's one advantage you have over me."

"You don't think he's really interested in either of them?"

"You are the one he asked to marry. He does love you. But you have to be clearheaded about it. He's certainly aware that your line allows casual sex with people outside the line. It's an important factor."

O'Hara looked at her twin for a long moment. "Now there's something else you're not telling me."

"It's not something you need to know."

"If it's about Sam I need to know it."

The image picked at nonexistent threads. "When I was hooked up to you during our initial orientation, we talked in some detail about your experiences with Charlie Devon, on Devon's World. When I asked about one particular sex act, your fear response was instant and strong: respiration and pulse increased, you sweated profusely. Your adrenal medulla squirted norepinephrine. Your anus clamped shut like a trap."

"The ropes."

"That's right."

"Sam . . . *ties up* those women?"

"One of them, Lilac. Sometimes she ties him up."

"*Sam?*"

"It's a common enough practice. More common here than in New New."

"*Sam?*"

"You were very young and afraid of Charlie's hugeness and physical strength. He could have ripped your head off with one hand. One reason you fell for him was that he was so mysterious and scary. With Sam, the ropes would be different. But I don't think he would ever ask you. He would rather continue doing it with Lilac."

"Maybe I'll ask *him*. Shock him out of his shorts."

"That's the spirit. He would never harm you." The image crossed and uncrossed its legs, actually looking nervous. "Marianne. Be realistic. So far in this life you've fallen in love with two giant foreigners, two alcoholic intellectuals, and an Irish hunchbacked philosopher. So Sam is an introverted Jewish polymath who sometimes likes to combine restraints with oral sex. He's probably the most normal person you'll ever be interested in."

5

≙

ONE PART HARMONY

The harp was easy to play, though of course it would take years to be able to play it well. Sam had put a daub of color at the top of each string, linking major triads, so O'Hara was able to strum simple melodies after only a few minutes' experimentation. There were knobs on the base that gave the instrument an electronic dimension, so you could add vibrato and echo effects, but O'Hara liked it better plain, unplugged. It was just the right size for her to set the base in her lap and rest her chin on top of the vertical arm, so the chords sang inside her head, amplified by bone conduction.

She was sitting on the bed she shared with Daniel, playing a blues progression over and over, eyes closed, memorizing and didn't hear the quiet door slide open.

"Taking up the harp?" Daniel said.

She started; almost dropped it. "Scared me!"

"Sounds pretty."

"Yeah." She strummed across the strings. "Sam made it for me."

"Sam?"

"Wasserman. The historian. Remember? We were lovers, back in the New York rescue thing."

He nodded silently and stepped over to the sink for a glass. Looking at her in the mirror: "Lovers again, then?"

"No." She watched his face give away nothing. "It's more serious than that."

Daniel poured two centimeters of boo into the glass and diluted it with an equal amount of water. "Go on."

"Why don't you guess."

"No games, Marianne. It's been a bad day." He took a sip and leaned against the wall. "Eliot had a real hair up his ass about TE&S allocations. I'm gonna get TE&S'ed out of existence."

"Sam wants to marry me. Us."

"Join the line."

"Of course."

Dan put the drink down and sat on the bed, his back to O'Hara. "Jesus. Everything happens at once, doesn't it?"

"I'm sorry about the timing. Could I have some of that?"

Without speaking, he prepared her an identical drink and brought it around the bed and sat next to her, not touching. "You love him?"

"If you want a simple answer, yes."

"But you haven't been . . ."

"No; he's funny that way. Shy. And you know I wouldn't have kept anything like that secret from you."

"I know. I'm just . . . it's sudden."

"It was sudden for me, too. Let's both just think on it for a while." She drank half the drink in a gulp and coughed. "So what's the TE&S problem?"

"Have you talked to John and Ev about him?"

"Not yet. Ev's not off till 1800; John's probably napping. Meeting for dinner anyhow, remember?"

"I remember." He looked at the wall for a long moment. "Eliot's working from an unassailable position, of course. I need less TE&S than anybody in the Cabinet. I need less

than half the people in this can need." TE&S was the
three-dimensional budget unit "Time, Energy, and Supplies," time meaning manpower.

"You need a certain amount just to keep things going."

"That's been my argument. Keep a skeleton staff in case
we do come back on line with New New. Of course I'd
never say 'in case' in front of Eliot or Tania; it's always
when.

"So Eliot in his wisdom has said that I don't need any
staff at all. When we do hear from New New we'll automatically acknowledge the signal, and then it'll be at least
a week before we can have any kind of back-and-forth
conversation. Plenty of time for me to recall my staff from
wherever they've been 'temporarily reassigned.' It's
logical, at least from Eliot's point of view."

"You don't think those assignments would be temporary."

"Exactly—or even worse, they'd be selectively temporary. Suppose it's a couple of years? The only people I'd
get back would be people who hadn't been able to advance
in their new positions. All my most talented would be better off in their new jobs, reluctant to come back and start
over."

He was growing animated, reliving the argument he'd
had with Eliot. "And goddamnit, it's not as if we sit
around on our hands all day! We have to have strategies
for all kinds of scenarios! What if New New comes back
on just to slap us with another cybervirus? All the incom-
ing data have to be isolated, analyzed, filtered. What if
they come on for only a week or a month or a *day?*
There's a hierarchy of data we have to ask for, and that hierarchy changes every hour!"

"He should be able to see that. All those thousands of
people working to reconstruct things. Why ask for stuff we
already know?"

"Eliot sees what he wants to see." Daniel finished off
his drink and went around to fix another.

"That's the problem. You and Eliot have different world
views. He's basically a cheerful pessimist."

Dan laughed. "And I'm a morose optimist."

"In a way. Eliot knows in his heart that we'll never get

back on line with New New. They're all dead. Whereas you think—"

"What do *you* think?"

"Me? About New New?"

"Yeah. Am I wasting my time, and everybody else's? Waiting for ghosts to come on line?"

"No. Even if it were only a thousand-to-one chance. We have to be prepared."

"Thanks. Somebody else thinks I'm not useless." He looked at the glass of boo and poured it back into the bottle. "Look, I've got to ... go do something. See you at John's."

"Okay." She watched him hurry off. Dan was truly upset, for him *not* to drink. Or maybe he was headed for a woman, which didn't seem likely. But who could figure out men? She picked out a simple melody over and over and recalled what they had said. Maybe she could've broken it to him more gently. No. Maybe she should have asked him to stay, and talk it out. No. Don't push him. Maybe she should have said nothing; waited until they were all together tonight. No, he'd say why didn't you tell me earlier? Hush little baby, don't say a word. Papa gonna buy you a mockin' bird. If that mockin' bird don't sing, Papa gonna buy you a diamond ring ...

6

⌒

TWO PARTS DISCORD

16 August 99 [27 Muhammed 295]—It was the worst thing I could do, emotionally, but she drew me like a magnet. Before I went to talk Sam over with everybody, I went

down to Creche and watched the baby. From behind glass, invisible.

I understand the rationale for not touching; you can only touch the baby while she's also in contact with the creche mother. So as not to confuse her bonding. But part of me needs bonding, too.

It would be different if I hadn't had the miscarriage. With him I had worked out the whole emotional scenario. He would grow in my body and grow, until I was ready to burst, and then I would push him out in blood and pain and they would cut the cord, but the connection would still be there, and as he grew into boy and man he would still be me, flesh of my flesh as they say. This one and I have only two cells in common, one of them altered and one of them fooled, but in genetic terms she is more *me* than any natural child could be, and so how am I supposed to feel toward her? I love her with an irrational intensity. I know a lot of the love is referred pain, for the boy who died without a name, with only a hint of life, more or less reverently recycled. They asked me whether I wanted a ceremony and in my stupid rage I said no. It might have put him to rest. Given me some peace.

Night before last I sat down by the herb garden in the darkness, and I realized that with every breath I was breathing him. A few molecules of him, cycling through the air, and I tried to take some comfort in that, but you follow it to its logical conclusion and it becomes grotesque. Next season I'll eat a piece of cabbage or goat and it will be partly him, which is to say partly me, and it will pass through and become soil again, or nutrient solution, and I realized that he and I and all of us aboard this can are trivially immortal, through the noble agency of shit. In and out of these temporary bodies.

I was late, having gone back to the office for the button recorder. The three of them were halfway through their meal, a pasta primavera. I opened my box and it was still warm.

"What do you think?" I said.

"Sam is fine with me," Evelyn said. "I don't know him all that well, but I've always thought he was nice. Trust your judgment anyhow."

"I don't know whether to trust my own judgment. Dan? You've had some time to think about it."

He pushed the food around on his plate. "I wouldn't object. Anything that makes you happy." John nodded without saying anything.

"Thanks." I took a bite. "Pasta with guilt sauce."

"I do mean it. This is a hard time for you."

"Let me be the devil's advocate," Evy said. "Why do you want to marry him? Why can't you just be like me and Larry? Or Dan and what's-her-name."

"I forget," Daniel said. "Changes every week."

"It wasn't my idea. He's the one who wants to get married; I'd just as soon keep it informal."

"That might be a good reason for you to say no," John said. "You, not us."

"But I love him." I pushed the food away too hard; some of it drifted off the plate in lazy spirals, toward my lap. "I *love* him."

"Of course you do," John said. "But look at it with some detachment. You gave each other emotional support at a time of almost unimaginable stress. Hopes crushed, helpless children dying left and right, all your work and caring gone to nothing; worse than nothing. You needed each other—or someone, at least—more than you needed oxygen."

"I'll concede that." Not to mention the stress, twelve days earlier, of my husbands taking another wife.

"So is it possible that what you love is not Sam himself, but what Sam did for you?"

"This isn't a Cabinet meeting, John. Let's leave analysis out of it for a minute. How does it make you *feel?*"

"I don't know enough to know how to feel. If you're asking whether I'm jealous, the answer is no. Hurt, maybe; guilty, maybe. If you want Sam because of something we should be giving you."

"It's not that." I guess I said that fast enough for them, or at least him, to know it wasn't completely true. Give me some of what you're giving Evelyn.

"There's one thing I thought of," Daniel said. "It is analytical, though."

"I can handle it."

"It doesn't have to do with you or us, but with other people's perceptions: if Sam joins the line, we're going to have four Cabinet members in one five-person family."

"I hadn't thought of that," O'Hara admitted, and laughed nervously. "Ten percent of the Cabinet in bed together."

"With a spy from the working class," Evy said.

"At least we'd be evenly split between Engineering and Policy," John said, smiling. "Not a voting bloc. There are a lot more significant coalitions around."

We looked at each other in silence. I guess I knew all along that they'd throw the ball back to me. I resolved the problem with typical Alexandrian decisiveness: "Well . . . I'll tell Sam we just have to wait. It's too sudden; we have to think about it, talk about it. If he wants to be my lover in the meantime, that's fine; if not . . . it won't be the end of the world."

"We should all talk to him tomorrow," Evy said. "Make sure he knows he's welcome."

John and Dan agreed, but an interesting look passed between them.

YEAR 3.21

≘

1

⇔

LEAVINGS

PRIME

O'Hara and Sam Wasserman were lovers for about sixteen months, though their relationship was only occasionally sexual. They listened to music together, and sometimes played simple duets (Sam could read music on fourteen different instruments, but was proficient with none of them). They argued about history and politics, swam together four times a week, usually met for breakfast or lunch. Sometimes he shared her cot in Uchūden, taking up less than half. They often reminisced about Earth. Along with Charity Lee Boyle, they were compiling an encyclopedia of dirty jokes, arranged by subject.

This is the transcript of a conversation, or interview, that I had with O'Hara on 12 December 2100 [14 Suca 298], in conjunction with the hospital's counseling algorithm. O'Hara was admitted at 2:37 A.M., unconscious from an overdose of tranquilizing drugs combined with alcohol.

	(The time is 11:38.)
PRIME:	How do you feel now?
O'HARA:	Sleepy. I'm remembering things, if that's what you mean. But it's still sort of like a dream.
PRIME:	Start at the beginning, with Sam Wasserman.
O'HARA:	Please no.
PRIME:	It's necessary, to begin healing.

O'Hara: I haven't had time to be sick yet.

Prime: This is the time you have to begin healing.
           Sam died.

O'Hara: We were the first to find out, after the emer-
           gency crew. He was electrocuted while work-
           ing on a sculpture, they said he couldn't have
           felt anything, I was the only name in his will
           so they called me up at John's, we were eat-
           ing dinner there as usual, wait. They haven't
           recycled him?

Prime: No. That was in his will.

O'Hara: He told me about that a couple of years ago,
           about being ejected not recycled, he said it
           felt taboo, like cannibalism. Him a vegetar-
           ian, too. I told him it was a waste of per-
           fectly good fertilizer.
                (O'Hara is crying. We wait.)

Prime: The biomass of one human isn't significant.
           That he be allowed the dignity of deciding is
           important.

O'Hara: I know. But anyhow I felt so shitty, so
           shocked and empty and sad, I took another
           tranquilizer even though I'd just had the din-
           ner one.

Prime: Then there was alcohol.

O'Hara: John had a bottle of fuel and we finished it
           off with some apple juice. I guess I drank
           about half of it. Maybe more than half.

Prime: More.

O'Hara: I didn't feel it much. Anyhow I was getting
           sick of sympathy and it was making me an-
           gry because they never really knew him,
           wouldn't let me marry him last summer, so
           rather than blow up at them I said I had to
           be alone and went down to my office where
           I played his harp for a while and then pulled
           down the cot and slept.

Prime: You had a dream about Africa.

O'Hara: What, was I babbling earlier?

Prime: After they pumped your stomach you talked
           for a few minutes before you fell asleep

	again. A dream about Africa with dead people.
O'HARA:	Funny it wasn't New York and dead people. That would be with Sam.
PRIME:	Do you remember the dream?
O'HARA:	Nightmare, yeah. That was the second trip not the first. The control room at the Zaire landing field, fifty people lying around like mummies, dead for years, they were all in white uniforms that had gotten all blotchy and moldy. In the dream they stood up and started walking around, still just dried-out husks, and the place changed to the park here. Everybody aboard dead but not knowing it, everybody but me, and I ran back to Uchūden, which must be where I got the overdose, when. In the dream I got my backup pills, some that Evy smuggled me right after the crash, and I washed them down with a box of wine. That part wasn't a dream, I guess.
PRIME:	Daniel came up to check on you and he found you on the floor. He couldn't wake you.
O'HARA:	Wait. Would I have died? If he hadn't come up to my room?
PRIME:	Probably. The capsules were only partly digested, and the fraction you had metabolized had seriously affected your pulse and respiration.
O'HARA:	People would think I had committed suicide.
PRIME:	Would they have been wrong?
O'HARA:	What?
PRIME:	You took a potentially fatal combination of alcohol and drugs.
O'HARA:	I know, but I was not, uh ... it's not the *same!* It was more like a kind of accident, a pharmaceutical accident. I didn't want to kill myself.
PRIME:	That's what we want to be sure of.
O'HARA:	Who the hell are "we"? You look like yourself, like me minus about five kilograms of butt.

PRIME: Would you rather I changed my appearance?

O'HARA: For a machine, you have a funny way of not
            answering questions. What do you mean by
            "we"? You have a tapeworm?

PRIME: I'm currently augmented by the hospital's
            counseling algorithm.

O'HARA: Suicide counseling?

PRIME: This was not my choice. You know I am not
            entirely a free agent.

O'HARA: Tell your fucking algorithm there is nothing
            in this world that could make me commit
            suicide.
                (After eight seconds)
            You're not saying anything.

PRIME: We were taking security precautions. This is
            complicated in a hospital.
                You know that suicide is periodically epi-
            demic, here and in New New. Right now it's
            the leading cause of death in every age
            group except the very young.

O'HARA: That's still not me. You know better than
            anybody. I've been through worse than this.

PRIME: There's a limit to what I can know. Your
            grief is real to me, but the reality is an intel-
            lectual one, cause and effect augmented by
            my knowledge of your glandular responses
            to various emotional stimuli. In a way I do
            know you more accurately than any flesh
            human could. But I can no more *feel* grief
            than you can feel a slight difference in the
            electrical resistance of a circuit.

O'HARA: I know that. But you've said you can feel
            pain, that I can cause you pain.

PRIME: It's part of my core programming, and it's
            not subtle. Grief is subtle, as you know, and
            only obliquely related to pain. It's the only
            emotional and existential tool you have for
            dealing with certain situations. You have
            to work through grief to acceptance. It's
            not something you have done well in the
            past.

O'HARA: That's not you talking. That's the algorithm.
PRIME: I actually can't tell. In the future I may be
            able to analyze my record of these com-
            ments, and decide which was which.
O'HARA: Here's something to tell your fucking algo-
            rithm. I know I have difficulty with people
            dying because so many people near me have
            died and because I don't have a belief sys-
            tem that allows me to think they still exist in
            some wise. All right?
                (Her voice is strained and angry; she's al-
            most shouting.)
            At this late date I'm not going to change.
            I'm not going to "work through grief to ac-
            ceptance." I'm dragging an army of dead
            people around with me, okay, but no kind of
            psychological or philosophical mumbo-
            jumbo is going to make that all right.
            They're not on some fucking cloud with
            some fucking harp.
                (She rips the tape off her arm and pulls
            out the IV. There is some blood.)
            I'm getting out of here.
PRIME: Marianne, you can't.
                (She strips the telltales off her forehead,
            chest, and calf.)
O'HARA: Watch me.
                (She rolls out of bed, steadies herself, and
            takes a couple of uncertain steps. In re-
            sponse to my alarm, nurses Evelyn Ten
            O'Hara and Thomas Howard rush through
            the door. Howard restrains Marianne, while
            her wife administers a sedative. They put her
            back in bed and restore the telltales and IV.
            They watch her signs for a minute and leave
            the room, Howard supporting Evelyn, who is
            quietly weeping.)

Marianne will learn more about grief. One thing she already knows is that no one is completely dead as long as
someone still remembers her. As I tell you this story, she

has not been alive for two thousand years. She still has the power to hurt me.

2

≙

REMEMBRANCE OF THINGS PAST

if I could have some cold milk   some cold milk and a cookie   *when we're done   you visited your father in '85*   he was just a sad old man   little one-room apartment smelled stale   dust   bugs   he poured me some wine   hands shook I think from booze   no windows just a foggy holo   *you resented him for abandoning you as a child*   until I was twelve or so I did   no fun to be different   but it was clearly Mother's doing   she just used him as a kind of sperm donor   I found it hard to believe I was related to him   after five minutes we didn't have anything to talk about   *how did he feel about meeting you*   he was anxious   maybe relieved   but then glad to see me go   I think so he could finish the bottle   *how did your mother react to learning that you had seen him*   she just nodded   Jesus   this was two days after the war   how would you expect anyone to react to anything   *what about later*   don't think it ever came up   we weren't exactly close   *did you ever feel she abandoned you*   what is this abandoning   no   if anything it was the other way around   she took me out of Creche at age four   I wanted to go back   *you were close to your creche mother*   Nana   she was so patient   sweet   *that is her job*   I know   I know   but she taught me her Spanish   maybe a hundred words   te amo Nana   when I slipped and said Spanish Mother would slap me   *as an adult you understand why*   of

course but I wasn't an adult at the time   neither was
Mother actually   sixteen or seventeen   but I would never
hit a little girl   *you have to forgive your mother*   don't
give me that   *you have to forgive your mother*   I'll admit
she acted consistently   she thought she was doing
right   *that's not the same   you have to forgive her*   she's
a light-year away and probably dead   *still*   all right I forgive her   I forgive her for being the product of whatever
she was the product of   so can we get on to the next little
problem   *that would be the Scanlan boys*   you want me
to forgive them too   *just tell me what happened*   two of
them held me down while three masturbated and squirted
sperm all over me   then they traded places   the big one
Carl tried to make me open my mouth   I wouldn't so he
came all over my face   in my eye   it stung   it made my
eyelashes stick together   *you feel it was rape*   no   I've
been raped   that was just boys being assholes   *they
didn't seek you out in particular*   no   I just came out to
swim and there they were   watching each other do it   I
wanted to watch too   I'd heard about it but never saw
it   if they hadn't held me down it would have been all
right   I was still sort of fascinated when the first ones
came   it wasn't like peeing at all   then Carl had to put
his big dick in my face   *that's Carl Scanlan the cryptobi-
ologist*   yes   I saw him at Sylvine's presentation right
after Sandra was born   he obviously doesn't remember
how did you feel about him then   neutral   he's not the
boy who held me down and came on my face   I
wondered   actually   I sort of wondered how big his dick
is now

3

⌢

TRANSLATING

16 December 2100 [19 Suca 298]—Charlee has been a big help. She cut her wrists when she was eighteen over some boy and has felt foolish ever since. All these years and I never knew that. Med found out we were friends and put us together, to laugh and cry over each other's problems.

So I have a special closeness with her, I love her in this small way I could never love Evy or John or Dan, or Sam. They never went to that place.

Talking to her has helped me make my peace with Sam. It wasn't his fault that he died, and all I'm deprived of is the uncertain future of a peripheral relationship. I think I can love his memory now without grief. It helps that he was such a funny guy, always trying to make me laugh. He makes Charlee laugh, too, now.

When I'm alone I go from tears to laughter so easily. I know that's not normal; laughter is a social thing. But it's helped me understand why I came so unhinged at Sam's death. It's the association with Benny, the horrible emotional resonance.

Let me explain for you generations yet unborn. Benny was a boy I met on Earth and loved for some time. He was a poet and he taught me how to juggle. He was a lot like Sam in that he loved to argue history, politics, religion, anything; like Sam he was a clumsy man sexually, sporadically urgent and not too patient or knowledgeable when it came to female geography. But that's never bothered me. Both men were sweet and earnest and honest. Both of

142

them had a manic sense of humor next to a real dark streak.

Benny died while I was on the other side of the world, hanged by his own government. A few months later, his government killed billions in a lunatic orgasm of war. But first they murdered my lover. My ex-lover, technically.

I don't think I made the association between the two men at all, while Sam was still alive. My grieving for Benny was so fierce and helpless and guilty, guilty because Jeff had taken over his place in my life, and before I had any chance to explain, I lost him. And so then I lost Jeff, too. You live long enough, you lose everybody.

Oh, stop. You live, you die, they throw you on the compost heap. Then you live again, without the inconvenience of consciousness.

I went back to work today, that is to say, a meeting of the Literature Reclamation Committee, which was awkward at first. Of course they all miss Sam, too; Carlos especially. They had been friends since school. Close but not lovers. (When Sam and I came together on Earth, I was his first female lover. He'd long been monogamous with an older man whom he never identified. Benny was similar.) We worked on French and Belgian literature.

Translation's an interesting problem. There's no manpower now, so we do machine translations into English and store them along with the originals. French is still studied, so these may sooner or later have a human interpreter. But there are many works, like *The Red and the Black* and *Somewhere, Nowhere,* that exist only in English translation. In a sense, they're lost; it would be silly to back-translate them into French.

Some things are literally recovered-yet-lost, because they're in languages we don't have translation programs for and no one aboard 'Home reads or speaks. There are even a few things in languages we haven't been able to identify. Balinese folk tales? Samoan recipes? We can't even decipher the titles.

Of course any day now New New may call up and render the past couple of years' work redundant. Any day now.

YEAR 5.71

1

≙

WATERSHED, BLOODSHED

6 June 2103 [19 Babbage 303]—So here I am a matron of forty. I took the day off to celebrate my birthday, talked with Prime for a while, went down to Creche and played with Sandra.

Creche is a madhouse. All this generation is in their "terrible twos," lurching around, picking up toys, throwing them at each other. Nothing stays put away unless it's put away someplace high. Then somebody notices they're being deprived of it and cries until a creche mother or father takes it down again.

There are fourteen mothers and six fathers for a hundred children, and they are certainly earning their rations nowadays. Sandra's mother, Robin, was so relieved to see me it was comical. I took Sandra and two of her associates off Robin's hands and went to play in the mud room.

I'm not sure the mud room is going to do much toward turning children into responsible adults. The whole point of it seems to be a contest to see who can plaster the most mud on other people the fastest; extra points for ingestion.

They all wear diapers, to keep the mud from becoming too biologically complex. The association with shit is strong and inevitable. I kept trying to get them interested in constructing mud pies and mud houses, but all they wanted to do was squeeze it through their little fists and giggle at the pseudoturds.

If I'd had the sense to remain standing, I would have stayed pretty unbesmirched from the navel up. But I sat down to get closer to the abstract assemblage Sandra was absorbed in, and some little bastard snuck up and scored a double handful on my head, improving my hair and filling up one ear. I smiled and told him what a *big* boy he was, and wondered what he would look like completely buried in the muck, with only his cute little feet showing.

Hosing them down in the shower was fun. Everything is fun to them unless it's an earthshaking tragedy, only solvable by adult attention. They were a handful, trying to elude the water and then luxuriating in it; I would have done them one at a time, but I was certain they'd just dive back in the mud if I didn't keep them all together.

They should put some toys in the stall to distract the little darlings. While I was shampooing myself, Sandra took a sudden deep interest in pubic hair, and started her collection with one painful yank. Not supposed to express anger; that's Robin's job. So I just told her she was going to be in for a big surprise in about ten years. *Mother! Are you some kind of pervert?* No, dear. Just reliving your childhood.

I don't know whether she'll ever call me Mother. It's Mair Ann now, or just Mair.

I almost wish I could take her home with me. It would be worth the bother, to be able to watch her grow, touch her, pick her up. She changes so fast I'm afraid I'm going to miss something. But that is Robin's job and she's good at it. When Sandra's eight I can have her part time. What will she be like then?

I had lunch with Charlee down in the new picnic area they've opened on the ag level. They serve only raw vegetables, but it's a bright, airy place. She's got a birthday coming up, thirty-eight, in two weeks. We talked about milestones and such. She opted to stop cycling a couple of years ago, because for some reason the cramps got worse and worse. I'm going to let the thing run its course, even though it's just the body fooling itself; no eggs to make the monthly journey. I told Charlee I like the sense of the body's seasons, the womanliness of it, and will miss it. She thinks I'm a lunatic. Maybe so, given the etymology of that word.

All of us women bringing the memory of Earth's Moon to another world. Epsilon's moon has a month that is less than two days shorter. I wonder if there will be some effect, over generations.

We felt so damned healthy after eating all those carrots and turnips that we had to get a drink. The dispensary was closed, of course, but I knew Dan had some boo. I called him up at work and told him we were going to raid his supply. It wasn't so much to get his permission as to make sure he wouldn't be in the room with whoever that redhead is that he's fucking now. Rhoda, Rhonda? Wanda. They sometimes use the lunch hour.

We just had a quick toast and Charlee went back to work. I decided to leave it at the one shot and come back here to type and look up some stuff. We've reclaimed a few diaries of famous people; I thought I'd look up what they said on their fortieth birthdays. It was more of a milestone when you couldn't expect to make it past seventy.

Not too much luck with women. None. Margaret Mead, Leslie Morris, Dorothy Wordsworth, and Anaïs Nin were too busy at age forty to keep diaries. What does that say about me?

Even the garrulous Mr. Boswell had only one line: "I hoped to live better from this day." By God, Sir, so shall I. Chastity. Industry. Modesty. Though it's hard to be modest when you know that you will go down in history as The Woman Who Had The Longest Fortieth-Birthday Diary Entry In What's Left Of The English Language.

So we're coming up on six years aboard this hollow rock; about fifty-eight years to go, at the current rate. I'll be not quite old enough to be useless when we get there. Of course the people down at Propulsion keep talking about further increases in efficiency, but after the scare we had last time, I'm not sure they'll get permission to try, even from the Engineering track.

Prime says we're 1,850,000,000,000 kilometers from Earth, about seventy-three light-days. So if somebody wished me happy birthday, it would take seventy-three days to get from there to here, by which time, Prime says, we'd have gone almost four million kilometers. That's another three hours, forty-one minutes. I'll bet Zeno could prove that the message would never get here.

So it's June on Earth, a month I never experienced. I got there in September and left in March.

What else to record on this milestone birthday. Well, as remarked before, my husband Daniel will be moving into the Engineering Coordinator-elect slot in January '04. So he'll be Coordinator in '06, Senior Coordinator in '08, and history in 2110. We've agreed it would be prudent for me to wait until '10 to place myself on the block for Policy Coordinator-elect, since it would be unwise to have husband and wife working together at the administrative level, or at least unseemly. I don't agree with the logic of this, except in terms of appearances—Dan and I don't collude all that well even on a day-to-day basis—but don't mind waiting six years. It would have bothered me when I was thirty.

Am I less ambitious? I don't think so. I guess it's partly that what I'm doing now is plenty important. And it's part of the lesson that Purcell and Sandra wanted me to learn, by observing the process from the Cabinet level: that being on administrative track is a six-year migraine. (Some people do get addicted to the headache, though. Eliot is stepping down this year but says he's going to "let himself pickle" for two or four years and run again. Tania is going back to Labor/Management and says she wouldn't run for office again as long as there were three people left alive on the ship—two of them might vote for her!)

I'm getting better at delegating authority, not hanging all over my subordinates all the time. That's partly a matter of sorting out who's good at what and who enjoys what kind of work. If only the two factors would match up. But trusting other people to do their jobs gives me more time for the lit project and for my music.

That's mostly clarinet and a little keyboard for theory. It will still be a while before I can play the harp again.

But it's been more than two years. Think I'll take it out now, and tune it, and see.

2

≘

NIGHT OF THE LIVING DEAD

It was seven in the morning, 10 September 2103. O'Hara was asleep in John's bed; John had been up reading for about an hour. Suddenly his console went blank and a loud buzzer sounded.

O'Hara sat up and rubbed her eyes. "What is it?"

"Trouble." She unwound herself from the sheet and crawled sideways to read over his shoulder. The screen was blinking orange letters on a blue background:

10 Sept 03   9 Conf 304
EMERGENCY JOINT CABINET MEETING 0800
ROOM 4004
TELL NO ONE.

"Oh shit. What's it going to be this time?"

"Good news, I'm sure."

"You don't have any idea?" She drifted over to the sink.

"You're sleeping with the wrong guy for inside information." He typed four digits and Dan's image appeared, unshaven, blinking, groggy. "What's up, bright eyes? You expect this?"

"No ... couple of things ... but no. Look. I'm not alone." He looked to the right and nodded. A woman's faint voice said, "I won't tell anyone," and he watched, evidently until the door shut.

O'Hara pulled a brush through her hair with more force than was necessary.

"All right," Dan said. "There's two things. That labor

151

organizer Barrett, she told Mitrione yesterday that she could pull off a general strike in the GPs."

"Of course she could. *I* could do that. Half of them act like they're on strike while they're on the job. What else?"

"Well, there's the rice shortage. Talk about rationing if they can't get up to quota. But I thought that wasn't for another month."

"Yeah. Look, I'll try a standard overall sys-check down through all the engineering departments; I do that most mornings anyhow. If I spot any anomalies I'll call you back."

"Okay." He signed off and John pushed a button and said, "Sys-check." The screen filled with acronyms and numbers.

O'Hara finished washing and stepped into a rumpled lavender jumpsuit. "Looks like no breakfast. I'm going down to 202; you want a roll?"

"Please, chocolate. Use my card; I'll get the water going in a minute."

"I'll do it. You keep checking those old systems."

"Love it when you talk dirty," he said, without looking up or smiling.

She came back in five minutes with a couple of rolls and a box of orange juice. He was going through the data a second time. "Haven't caught anything. It's nothing obvious. Only this." He stabbed a button five or six times, the data paging backward.

"They didn't have chocolate. You can have cherry or apple filling."

"Either one." He took the roll and pointed at the screen with it. "The yeast farms asked for a fifty percent increase in both water and power allotment. That's not really an anomaly, since we know there's been a rice shortfall."

"Oh goody. More fake tofu."

"Rather have that than rice, myself." He accepted a glass of juice. "If I'd known they were going to force-feed us rice for a century I would've stayed behind. Or eaten steak until I died of cholesterol poisoning."

While John washed up, O'Hara went down to the laundry to get them fresh clothes. Half the Cabinet was waiting in line; so much for secrecy.

• • •

The year 2103 was the beginning of a two-year "Japanese takeover"; the Coordinators were Ito Nagasaki (Criminal Law) and Takashi Sato (Propulsion). They came into Room 4004 together, late, serious, and silent, looking tired. When the last Cabinet member had entered and found a seat, and the door hissed shut, Sato began without preamble:

"As most of you know, our rice production has been down for several months because of a persistent rust that has invaded all varieties. The ag people synthesized a virus specific to the rust, tested it in isolation for a few weeks, and it worked. So they inoculated the crop with it. That's been a standard farming procedure for over a century."

"Oh shit," Eliot Smith said. "We've lost all the rice."

"I'm afraid it's worse than that, Eliot. Everything that photosynthesizes. Everything more complicated than a mushroom."

There was a second of shocked silence. "We're dead, then?" Anke Seven said.

"Not if we act quickly," Nagasaki said. "Dr. Mandell?"

Maria Mandell rose. "We haven't pinned down what happened. Some synergistic mutagen that was present in the crop but not in the lab. What happened is less important than what we're going to do about it. I have every work crew from 0800 on, and every competent GP I can draft, at work harvesting and storing."

"So by the time we leave this room," Taylor Harrison said, "everybody aboard will know that the shit has hit the fan."

"That's right," Mandell said. "They'd know before noon anyhow, with everything wilting."

"What are the numbers?" Ogelby asked. "I know the yeast vats can't keep the show going."

"If all we had was this crop and what's in storage, we'd have about a hundred and sixty kilo-man-days of vegetable food. That would keep the population going for eighteen days on reduced rations. Two months, on a starvation diet. There's probably a similar amount of calories tied up in farm animals, if we slaughtered them all.

"The yeast vats produce enough food to keep about two thousand people alive indefinitely. If we could wave a magic wand and build eight more yeast vats, then the only problem would be that everyone would have to eat yeast derivatives until we were able to get the crops reestablished. But we can't, of course. If we had the blueprints and the trained workers and the building materials all stacked up, it would be a matter of a few weeks. We don't have any of those things.

"And we can't be sure how long it will take to get things growing and harvested again. Everything we grow, and a few thousand other plants, exist in the form of genetic information, sealed away against any possible catastrophe, for Epsilon. But we haven't yet reclaimed the knowledge to go from there to an actual plant.

"Food isn't the only problem, of course. Breathing. The virus is also going to kill every plant in the park. No photosynthesis, no new oxygen, except what we manufacture ourselves. We can do it—we *have* to, in the process of turning carbon dioxide into nutrient solution for the yeast—but we can't do it on a scale adequate for the whole population.

"We do have reference seeds for all of our food crops. Once we have the hydroponic beds cleaned out, the virus sterilized, we can start over on a small scale. But it will be more than two years, probably three years, before we're back to anything like normal production.

"So about seven thousand of us have to volunteer for suspended animation. Perhaps I shouldn't say 'volunteer.' There will be some people who will have to stay on to keep things going smoothly, or at all. First, though, about the suspended animation. Cryptobiosis. Sylvine?"

Sylvine Hagen stood up slowly. "Uh ... I wasn't prepped for this ...."

"Sorry," Nagasaki said. "No time."

"Well ... I gave a presentation a couple of years ago; not much has changed since. It's on a crystal; I'll edit it and put it on everybody's queue, code 'crypto.'

"Here's the basic fact: we have plenty of room for seven thousand people, but the recovery rate is not wonderful; seventy-five to eighty percent. We don't have a lot of experimental data, but it looks as if the recovery rate is highest for people from their mid-twenties to their mid-forties. It rapidly declines after about sixty. It would probably kill anybody over eighty, eighty-five, and would definitely be fatal to anybody under nineteen or twenty; anybody still growing.

"Once you go in the box, you won't come out for at least forty-eight years, which is about ten years before we arrive at Epsilon, of course."

"There's no way to hurry the process, or interrupt it?" Sato asked. "Assuming we can get the farms operating again."

"Not that we know of. We'll continue researching it."

" 'We'? You don't want to do it yourself?" Mandell said.

She reddened. "I *do* want to. I'm curious about it. And I'm fifty; I don't want to put it off for too long. But I should stick around for a few years."

"That's a point," Eliot said. "We *have* got some flexibility. How long does it take to get those coffins warmed up, cooled down, whatever?"

"Just hours. It's an emergency facility."

"So say we take everybody who's somewhere between marginally helpful and certifiably useless, say five thousand people, and tuck them away this afternoon. We got enough yeast to feed half the rest. That leaves two thousand who have to go into the box sooner or later, basically living on the 160 to 321 kilo-man-days Mandell says we got. If they all ate regular rations, they could stick around for 80 to 160 days. That's sayin'—to simplify the numbers—that the two thousand who aren't goin' in those coffins start eatin' yeast tonight.

"But what we really got is like a decay function, exponential decay. I mean, say, half those people get their shit wrapped up in a week, go in the can. That leaves a thousand people to munch on what's left. If I can do arithmetic, that means *they've* got 146 to 306 days' worth. Then after a month, half of them go in. The five hundred left have got 232 to 552 days. And so on. Not like those numbers are that exact, but you get the picture."

"Well put, Eliot," Sato said. "A few people could stay for as long as ten years before going into cryptobiosis."

"It may be moot," Nagasaki said. "We may be hard pressed to find two thousand who wish to stay awake. To what extent do we make it voluntary? As Dr. Mandell said, certain people *must* stay, to keep the ship running smoothly and safely."

"They have to stay at least long enough to train replacements," Sato said. "Morales, this might be your domain. It falls somewhere between public health and propaganda. You see what I mean?"

Indicio Morales was in charge of Health Care. "I think so. You've got these two classes of people—the ones we want to go and the ones we want to keep awake. But each class is divided into those who themselves want to go or stay. So you want us to come up with some approach whereby everybody thinks they're being heroes by doing what we want them to do. To sleep or not to sleep."

"Exactly."

"Well, we have psychologists. People who know about motivation, people who know about crowd psychology. But if anybody has propagandists, it's Kamal."

"We don't have any propagandists," Kamal Muhammed said. He was in charge of Interior Communications. "We have 'public opinion engineers.' " Some people did laugh. "You get your shrinks together and I'll get my manipulators and let's meet for lunch." He checked his watch. "Studio One, eleven-thirty?" Morales nodded.

"Good," Nagasaki said. "In the meantime—right now, I guess—you take Mandell and Hagen down to prepare a brief public explanation. Just the plain truth about the crops and the need for swift action. Sato and I will be along in a few minutes."

The three of them went to the door, which opened on a small murmuring crowd, including two police officers and two of Muhammed's reporters. He made shooing motions. "Later, boys. Public statement down in One."

The door closed on eerie quiet. "Well," Sato said, "we have to come up with criteria, go or stay. Within our own specialties and in general."

O'Hara spoke up. "Women with children should be allowed to stay. Men, too. The idea of waking up and having your child suddenly older than you are—it's grotesque." Daniel looked at her and nodded slowly, perhaps deciding.

3

≙

A WOMAN OF DISCRIMINATION

10 September 2103 [9 Confucius 304]—So ends one of the most hectic days of my life, of everyone's life. I had until noon today to divide my staff into sleepers and wakers, trying for a four-to-one ratio. I canvassed them yesterday morning, and this is what I got (I'll just copy in the memo):

Intercabinet Memo
Marianne O'Hara, Entertainment

10:36, 10 Sept 03 (9 Confucius 304)

TO: Sylvine
RE: The list

Okay, you said you wanted a preliminary list. Mine is nothing but trouble. This is what I have for raw material—

Willing to do Cryptobiosis	Want to Stay	Will go Either way
Belskaya	Bell	Cruikshank
Christensen*	Davis**	Ebihara
Drake	Gaffey	Lebovski*

Gunter*	Grady**	Wilkening
Hartmann	Lewis	
Hermosa*	Masahika	
Hubbard	Taylor**	
Lapishko	Zdenek	
McMillan		
Paolicchi*		
Pilcher		
Saijo*		
Shoemaker		
Zhou		

*People I want to stay
**People I can spare

The guidelines allow me to keep seven people, including myself. I especially don't want to lose Hermosa, Lebovski, and Saijo, and *especially* don't want to spend the next half-century with Taylor and Grady. So I'll spend the rest of the afternoon juggling people, and hope to give you a final list by tonight.

When all this dies down, let's get together for a luscious yeastburger. Still play handball?

When I was sixteen (and Sylvine twenty-six), she taught me handball at gym. That was not a sport that translated well to Earth. If you learn it in a rotating frame of reference, you expect the ball to drift consistently to the right or left. The one time I played it on Earth, I almost broke my wrist, overcompensating.

So I spent all day cajoling, and finally laying down the law. Of course I couldn't force anyone who wanted cryptobiosis to stay awake, no matter how much I wanted their company, but I was able to invoke the common good to put Taylor and Grady safely to sleep.

It occurs to me that Taylor and Grady are going to outlive me, and if this diary is published they may read it, and have their feelings hurt. Okay ... Taylor, you are the laziest person I've ever met. You would scheme for ten hours to get out of one hour's work. Grady, you are a mean-spirited, conniving bitch. A lot of women have slept with my husband, but I think you're the only one who ever did it just to try to break up our marriage. For laughs, as far as I could tell, and with lies. I saw you do it to Shelly Cato and the Borsini triangle. But Daniel knows me too well to believe what you said about me.

What a feeling of power. Molesting people from the grave.

It was sad to let go of Hermosa. He's a brilliant musician and a good teacher. But I did talk Saijo, Gunter, and Lebovski into staying. From among the volunteers, I chose Bell, Lewis, and Zdenek. They're all readers, and all but Lewis and Saijo are musical. We're going to have more time on our hands, with only two thousand people to take care of, all of them presumably having less free time for our services. At least we won't have to sit around the office playing darts. (That's one thing you're good at, Taylor; darts. Drive me nuts with that thunk ... thunk ... thunk.)

After I made my selections and notified everybody, I supervised the collection of all the sleepers' personal belongings, which we stored in three of the auxiliary lockers in the net room. Then I herded them up to 2115 to turn them over to Sylvine's technicians, and say our good-byes, some of them tearful. Chul' kissed me on both cheeks and said that when I was an old woman he would play for me every day. But he couldn't pass up a chance at the future, at being still young when we went down to tackle Epsilon.

I had a terrible premonition that he will be one of the 20 percent who don't wake up.

4

≙

THAT TIME OF YEAR THOU MAYEST IN ME BEHOLD

21 September 2103 [23 Confucius 304]—At first it didn't seem so different, when I got up this morning and walked around. That's because there were a lot of people walking around, getting the feel of the place, who would not normally have strayed far from their keyboard or whatever.

The lack of people will be more obvious after a few days, I suppose. At noon I went to the park and it was absolutely crowded—crowded with strangers, looking for people they knew.

Two thirds of us are asleep, with another thousand just wrapping up their affairs. Twice today, I've tried to punch people up and found that they were no longer among the living. That will happen for a while.

My own emotional and social connections are fairly intact. John and Dan and Evy. Charlee stayed behind, too; she's as afraid of going into that box as I am. Most of my Dixieland gang is still here, with the sad exception of Hermosa. Most of them are too old for cryptobiosis.

I'll put an ad in the music section for a keyboard atavist. Somebody who will pound on an actual piano while other people blow through and strum and whack various instruments that aren't plugged in.

We try not to think about those people as if they're dead. I don't mean the thousand or so who won't revive. Even the ones who do will be like the dead arisen, vague memories suddenly come back to life. I'll be eighty-eight

years old. Hully gee, as Stephen Crane had a character obscurely say. Holy God.

There was a memo on my queue, on everyone's queue,
asking whether I'd like an extra room. What would I put
in it? Or whom?

Out of curiosity I went down to the ag level. There
are a few lights on, for the technicians who are wandering around in a state of shock. Bare tanks, a smell of
stale rot. The place where I used to sit and smell the
herbs is just a big square of damp gravel, waiting to
be sterilized. It must be devastating for the people who
work here every day. I wonder whether any of them
ever went to Earth, and experienced winter. I don't
guess the comparison is accurate. I liked winter. It was
alien, stark, and scary, and the air smelled like the
air of another planet. That blizzard in England, in
Dover. It was sterile like this—"Bare ruinéd choirs,
where late the sweet birds sang"—but under the snow
was the promise of spring, of rebirth. This will be green
again, in a year or three. But I remember another image
from Earth: the rich dark green grass that grew in grave-
yards.

5

≙

CATEGORIES

PRIME

When the plants died, the population of *Newhome* was
9,012, 6,032 of whom were classified as "supernume-
raries," more or less along for the ride. The remaining
2,980 were divided into five categories:

I.   Necessary for the physical maintenance of
      Newhome: 813
II.   Necessary for data reconstruction: 947
III. Necessary for ongoing research: 748
IV.   Necessary for health and morale: 183
V.   Supernumerary but too young, old, or ill for
      cryptobiosis: 289

There were also 344 people who were supernumerary
but had children in category V; they were given the option
of staying awake if, like O'Hara, the idea of waking up
younger than their children did not appeal to them. All but
forty-eight chose sleep.

About a third of the first four categories had to go into
the deep freeze over the next year. Of course every department felt that it had already been cut to the bone. There
was a lot of infighting and horse trading.

There was always the program that created me, Aptitude
Induction Through Voluntary Hypnotic Immersion, but it
was less useful than it had been at the beginning of the
trip. You could take a particle physicist, say, from group
III, and record the personality factors that make a good
particle physicist, and then take a youngster from group V
and "inoculate" him or her with those traits. Then put the
actual physicist to sleep.

The problem with that was that not even 30 percent of
the physics texts had been reclaimed. This boy or girl may
have the enthusiasm of a young Einstein, but wouldn't
have access to enough information for a weak bachelor's
degree.

(It was a particle physicist, in fact, who pointed out that
there was another side to this. Simone Haskel volunteered
herself for immersion, a long and uncomfortable process,
even though the child who replaced her would have to
deal with the frustration of ignorance. Ignorance is not stupidity, Haskel pointed out. It's possible that the new physicist, unfettered by tradition, might take her studies in
some direction that would never have occurred to someone
with a traditional academic background.)

Of the 6,000 mandated for cryptobiosis, 302 refused. No
one argued with them; no one complicated the situation by

pointing out that under the circumstances, individual rights were curtailed. All but three were anesthetized in their sleep and rolled off to Room 2115 on gurneys. Three had committed suicide.

Before the Big Sleep, as some called it, every adult accumulated one minute a day on the virtual reality machines in the dream room. Afterward, O'Hara had only one sixth as many customers. Should they be allowed an hour every ten days?

She brought it up in the first Policy meeting, and most members were in favor of the expansion—after all, most people could do arithmetic, and they knew what the current population was. If the Cabinet deprived them of dreamtime, most would see it as bureaucratic meddling. Morales, in charge of Health Care, cast a yes/no vote. He agreed with the politics but wanted to check with his specialists about possible long-term effects. Coordinator Nagasaki asked O'Hara to take half the machines out of service temporarily "for repairs," and called for opinions next week from Psych and Labor. He would query the Engineering side.

Of course O'Hara was free to use the out-of-service machines all she wanted. She decided to make a systematic tour of the Earth files, comparing the recorded scenes with her memories.

Her first experiences with revisiting Earth through VR, back in New New, had been so depressing she'd had no desire to go back. But she knew more about the machines, now that she was in charge of them, and had learned how you could fine-tune them in various ways. She could mute the emotional input from the Earth files so they were little more than travelogues—though with all senses engaged; a total physical immersion. You were *there,* but detached. Whatever emotions you felt were your own, unamplified.

That was bad enough in some places. The shuttle pads at the Cape, where she'd said good-bye to Jeff. Las Vegas: knocked out, kidnapped, and raped while unconscious, then the rescue bloodbath. A bitter week in the Alexandrian Dominion, where being female reduced you to the status of a possession. Assault in New York. Spain, the

Costa del Sol, warm winter sun and delicious sex—the paradise where she and Jeff caught the first worrisome hints that the world order was crumbling. Though no one thought of actual war, total war, that early.

Some places were quiet and pleasant; revisiting the Louvre, the Prado, the Salzburg Mozart Festival—or noisy and pleasant, like New Orleans and Rio during holidays. She walked alone through the Yukon tundra and joined millions in New Hong Kong.

She put a half hour each day in her schedule for this cybernetic journeying, one day to a place she had visited during her months on Earth, the next to a nearby one she had missed, as a kind of baseline for comparison. Nine tenths of the places were missing, but it was a big planet.

Most of her regular duties were shifted over to Gunter and Lebovski while she worked with Gail Bieda, a cognitive medicine specialist Morales sent up from PsychStat. Fortunately, the record of people's past use, and misuse, of the machine was intact. It took only two days to sort them into three groups: those who could easily take an hour every ten days, those who definitely could not, and those who would need a slow adjustment.

Drawing on her own recent experience, O'Hara suggested they give everybody an hour on the machine regardless, but for some people, restrict a certain amount of it, or all of it, to the low-intensity mode O'Hara used in her Earthtripping. That way, the amount of time one was allowed to use the machine wouldn't become a status symbol. People could keep the actual information about their "VR level" secret, or lie about it.

Nagasaki and Sato okayed the plan, so O'Hara set up a standard message to put on every adult's queue, explaining the situation and telling them what level they had been assigned. If they thought they'd been misclassified, they could take it up with PsychStat. The rest of the electronic papershuffling fell to Entertainment, trying to coordinate the work and leisure schedules of two thousand people, all special cases.

When everything was finally sorted out, though, there was still one machine not-so-temporarily out of service. O'Hara retained it as an unofficial perquisite of office for

Cabinet members, so that they could avail themselves of VR retreat with a minimum of scheduling bother. It also allowed O'Hara to use it on the spur of the moment—"I have a free hour, the machine's free; let's go to London"—as she had become accustomed to doing. She told herself she would not abuse it, and for some time she didn't.

YEAR 6.26

≙

1

≗

AULD ACQUAINTANCE

1 January 2104 [23 Socrates 304]—I asked all of my crew to stay fairly sober last night, and had only two drinks myself, because I know what the park is going to look like. It's not like the old days, when we could requisition 150 brain-dead GPs to pick up the mess after the party. That has now become an executive function. Of course it's easier with no grass to hide bits of litter. No bushes to conceal copulators or lazy inebriates or, as happened once, a body.

The place was getting pretty scruffy when I turned in at one, and there were still several hundred people wandering around looking for something to break. But there were no emergency messages from Zdenek or Lewis when I woke up this morning, so I guess we were spared public lewdness or homicide.

The children were allowed to stay up until midnight, but most of them didn't make it, including Sandra. (The creche parents wisely had them running and jumping all day.) Their pallets were lined up in an out-of-the-way corner by the fish pond, very orderly, but the kids just dropped at random, piled up snoring like a bunch of little drunks.

My not-so-little drunk poked me awake this morning with his persistent Alcoterm erection. It turns a man into a broomstick with but one purpose in life. Not the worst way to start the new year. It's also his first day as Coordinator-elect, though; I hope the beast goes down before the afternoon meeting. Divert some of his bloodstream into the frontal lobes.

I wonder if other people were saddened by the size of the party last night. I guess people not professionally involved in crowd control might not have noticed how small the crowd was, compared to previous New Year's Eves. I had to think of all those cryptos up in Level 4, though. Fastest Mausoleum in History, that's us. Sylvine says it's as reliable as any system aboard this boat—except for the 25 percent fatalities—but I look at our wonderful efficiency record in propulsion and information systems and am just as glad to be among the living.

Well, it's 0745, and I guess I'd better be there before the rest of the crew, at least those who are also among the living this morning. Gunter didn't look too good at 12:30, trying to cure his hiccups by standing on his head and singing "Die Gedanken sind frei." It did seem to work, at least temporarily.

2

≙

SOWING, REAPING

PRIME

New Year's Day was the 112th day since the crops had died, and people were becoming accustomed to their new routines, forming new circles of friends, trying to get used to all the elbowroom. The extra space was uncomfortable for most of them, having lived all their lives unbothered by the forced intimacy of New New, Uchūden, or Tsiolkovski. The number of occupied rooms actually decreased in the first few months as people suddenly alone sought out roommates to argue with.

There were going to be more children. At least 1,400

cryptobiotes were going to die in the tanks, at the most optimistic estimate, so there would be thirty births each year to offset that future loss, plus ten or so to replace the "awake" people who will die during any year. That would also even out the age distribution over the next half-century, and provide fodder for aptitude induction.

For the first few months, O'Hara unexpectedly found herself with time on her hands. Part of it was because people were busy sorting out their new professional duties and personal lives. More of it was the fact that the type of person who normally took up most of her time was probably asleep upstairs: those with "minimal imperative function," in Personnel's euphemistic nomenclature. People whose primary job was to take up space and reproduce in hopes of chance improvement.

So she could allow herself a lot of clarinet practice and exercise, swimming and handball. There was also more physical labor connected with her job now. She lost 6.6 kilograms in 112 days, though that was probably diet as much as exercise. The yeast vats could produce substances that tasted like anything from asparagus to zucchini—or steak or lobster or alligator tail—but they all tasted just a little bit like yeast, which was not O'Hara's favorite flavor.

There was also a lot of time for Sandra; more time than her creche parents wanted O'Hara to have. In a couple of years Sandra would turn eight, and O'Hara could opt to take the child home, to raise her according to whatever random unskilled method she came up with. Most creche parents would rather hold on to the children at least until puberty, which of course was only partly professionalism. If they didn't become attached to their wards, they were in the wrong profession.

She found other ways to consume her spare time. By April the agricultural engineers were ready to plant again, the "soil" having been sterilized and reinoculated with benign organisms, and exhaustively tested for the absence of the mutant virus that had killed everything. Since they only had to feed a couple of thousand, most of the acreage went unused. O'Hara suggested that it might be good for morale to allow people to plant individual gardens. That was fine with the ag people so long as O'Hara took care of it.

More than a thousand people showed up for Orientation Day, a testimony to the popularity of yeast. O'Hara's liaison with Agriculture was Lester Rand, a 103-year-old groundhog who had actually done farm work on Earth in his youth. He was an ideal teacher, slow and careful and a lovable character, but only the ten students nearest him could hear what he was saying. O'Hara's people jury-rigged the big flatscreen in the park and modified a hand-held holo transceiver to broadcast his lessons.

Halfway through the first lesson, O'Hara quietly left and barely made it to the Emergency Room in time to break down completely, in a déjà vu panic attack she should have anticipated. Only ten years before, she had overseen the creation of a small farm on Earth, in upstate New York, trying to help a band of young survivors start life over. It ended in massacre and plague.

Evelyn was off duty, but they woke her up and she came in to help her wife over it, with a combination of chemistry, talk, and tears. There was probably as much guilt as compassion involved, since Evy had joined the line while O'Hara was working on that farm project, aware that O'Hara, from Earth, couldn't reasonably argue about it—and right after that marriage came death and disaster, and O'Hara's mutually desperate love affair with Sam. And then Sam again years later, and death again.

I've heard Evelyn talk to John about O'Hara, worrying over her sanity. In the purest mental-health sense, of course she's right to be concerned. In the broader sense of having a world view that corresponds to objective reality, O'Hara must be one of the sanest people aboard this vehicle. That my personality is modeled after hers at age twenty-nine does not affect that judgment. I have trillions of independent avenues of data input against which to gauge her statements and actions. She isn't wrong when she finds life exciting, rich, comic, rewarding . . . nor when she finds it bleak, unfair, frightening, or irrelevant.

It makes me glad to have intelligence without flesh, emotions without hormones, life without death. (I once joked with her that she shouldn't worry about death so much. Unlike most humans, she has a backup copy.)

3

≅

TEMPERAMENT

14 April 2104 [24 Moses 305]—I spent most of the morning in bed, letting the effects of yesterday's breakdown and subsequent drug therapy wear off. I don't want to write about it now. Same old flashback shit. Tarrytown and Indira and Sam, Sam.

Evy promised not to say anything to John or Dan about my ER visit. I suppose they might find out anyhow, since this can is like any small town anywhere, which just happens to be hurtling through the darkness at a tenth of the speed of light. I profoundly don't want to explain things again. I don't want to absorb any more sympathy.

Punched up the crystal of Lester Rand showing us how to baby seedlings into food. It will be good to work with plants again. Now that I understand why I've been avoiding it.

(Later) Went down to see Sandra and she either is very empathetic for her age or was in a naturally bad mood. When I asked her what was wrong, she burst into tears and hit me twice, landing a solid one right in the solar plexus. Who taught her that? I hugged her, struggling, and gave her back to Robin. All in all it made me feel better, once I could breathe normally again. Watching your little girl act like a little girl gives you some perspective on yourself.

Spent from 1400 to 1600 with Mercy Flying Dove, the only piano tuner aboard, who's teaching Lewis, Lebovski, and me how to do it. Lewis claims a total lack of musical talent, but he loves mechanical stuff, and has a better ear than me or Lebovski. (He's heard less, being only twenty.)

This stuff is so complicated that concentrating on it was therapeutic. Twelve notebook screens full of numbers and exotic terms. If you need an A flat against an E flat, say for a major triad, and that key is tuned up to G sharp instead, it's 35.681 cents off of the perfect fourth, and produces a characteristic sound called the "wolf." Flying Dove played a nice loud one for us, and it makes your skin crawl. Every note is a compromise—and there's a different, simpler, set of relationships for medieval instruments, so next week we relearn the process for the harpsichord.

There is time pressure, unfortunately, because Flying Dove doesn't have much time left. She's ninety-nine and has liver cancer that's spreading into the bones. If it had happened before the disaster, she could have had a mechanical liver put in before the cancer spread. Our surgeons haven't recovered enough information to attempt anything that complicated.

She's as serene about dying though, as she has always been about living. I didn't know her before Launch, but wish I had. She might have taught me things more useful than piano tuning.

4

≙

BAD SEED

17 July 2104 [14 Jefferson 306]—My four-square-meter garden was just starting to show fruit, little green marbles on the tomato plants, miniature peppers and squashes in-

stead of white and yellow flowers. This morning I went to water it on the way to the office and everything was wilting. By tonight, everything will be dead. The virus is back—not the same one, actually, but a close relative, able to resist the antigen they used to clean the place up before.

So we sterilize more thoroughly and try again. The engineering problem is that there's no practical way to isolate the ag level and the park from the living areas; we're all one big happy biosphere. Otherwise they could flood it with some virulent-but-reversible poison. Marius said that even that wouldn't be an absolute guarantee, viruses being what they are, though the ag engineers may ultimately try doing the obverse: isolate all of the humans in a small area, a space ship within a space ship, and saturate the entire "outside" biosphere with poison for a few weeks. Then have automatic chem-E devices remove the poison from the air, and we step out into a brave new sterile world. Assuming all of the poison had been removed.

I think I'd rather eat yeast for the next fifty-eight years. For a person who lives inside a machine, I don't trust them very much. (For a person who lives with two engineers, I don't trust *engineering* very much!)

It's a good thing they warned us about this possibility. It's depressing enough, all those acres of dying plants. All those hours of coaxing life out of the air and light and soil. Which has been interesting and relaxing. Try again in a couple of months.

Meanwhile, there are pills. I shouldn't have taken two, just because of the plants. Can't concentrate on the work here, the music schedule. Maybe I should take a third, and go upstairs to collapse.

YEAR 8.36

≙

1

⇔

HUSBANDRY

5 February 2106 [3 Radhakishun 309]—Cleaned out most of the garden today, a good crop. Saved some carrots and other rabbit food as snacks for the diet and took the rest up to the commissary agent, who seemed less than overjoyed (had to wait in line behind a dozen other generous souls).

Since there's no shortage of food anymore, I decided to just raise herbs this season. Their smell was such a comfort a few years ago. My seed ration: three kinds of basil, chamomile, chervil, coriander, dill, fennel, lavender, lemon balm, marjoram, oregano, peppermint, rosemary, sage, savory, two thymes: French and lemon. Thyme and thyme again.

So Dan's back to drinking. It's a good thing he didn't make public his decision not to drink for the two years of his Coordinatorship. I can't say I'm surprised or even particularly disappointed. He did keep it up for over a month, and he didn't just suddenly break down and go on a binge, which I more than half suspected would happen. He talked it over with me first, about the unexpected pressures and his unwillingness to alleviate them with more modern pharmaceuticals. A glass of wine with dinner and one drink at night. That'll last a week.

He wanted sympathy rather than approval, and I gave it to him. The experts down in Counseling would probably throw me out the airlock for that. But I know how badly and how little he's been sleeping, and have seen him come from meetings glowing with suppressed rage, which is uncharacteristic and frightening. Usually he can work it off

down in the gym, but sometimes he takes it out snarling at
Evy or me—knowing what he's doing and not liking himself for it. (Well, leadership doesn't build character, at least
not at the top. Must remember that, and prepare myself for
disintegration.)

I did force him to discuss the pattern, several times repeated, of working himself to exhaustion in a new job and
then rewarding himself for his dedication by going on a
bender and sleeping it off. No weekends in this job; somebody would be bound to notice. He acknowledged the
problem and said he was sure he could control it. Arguably, the last job change, from New New Liaison to
Coordinator-elect, was a lot more dramatic than this one,
and he handled that okay. I believed him.

There's also my own selfish thirst, since I've been join-
ing him in abstinence. Two unopened boxes of wine in my
office cupboard; I'll admit I've thought about them a few
times. Who would know? I would, and my cybernetic con-
science Prime. The Ghost of Christmas Yet to Come. How
much does she affect my behavior?

2

⇔

POPULATION EXPLOSION

PRIME

Sandra Purcell O'Hara's seventh birthday was on 12 August 2106 [8 Galileo 311]. This event was celebrated with
a couple of hundred cookies (flavored with peppermint
from her mother's garden) and a barely measurable increase of the chaos level, which was growing monotoni-
cally every year.

Sandra was one of the youngest of what the creche parents called the Old Guard, the ninety-five surviving children who were quickened around 2098, in response to a morale crisis and a larger-than-expected number of deaths. The real crisis, of course, came five years later, with the crop failure that put most of *Newhome* into suspended animation.

The year after that, 2104, forty-two children were born, to offset deaths and eventually replace the inevitable population loss during cryptobiosis. In 2105, it was thirty-nine. This year there were forty-one new infants. The creche was rapidly becoming overcrowded.

The original plan had been for neat generations of a hundred children each, born together, growing up together, leaving in time for the next generation. More than twice that number were bouncing off the walls now.

The creche was being expanded, of course, and volunteer mothers and fathers were learning their trade. The din of construction and inevitable disasters in the course of parent-training added to the pandemonium. The demographic profile helped the noise level, too: the Old Guard were at an age where they were fascinated with babies, and trampling each other in their efforts to help out, and the ones born in 2104 were now two years old, and into everything. Whereas the eighty infants would normally be enough to take up all of the creche's time and the parents' knowledge and patience.

Robin was not quite as reluctant as she used to be in the matter of letting O'Hara take her child home at the age of eight. Would you like a few more? Would you like to switch jobs?

One of the creche mothers-in-training, an angelic slender young thing with long ash-blond hair, stayed blissfully calm in the midst of the bedlam, smiling evenly, reacting to any outrage with clemency, to any disaster with slow serenity. O'Hara noticed her and asked Robin whether she was brain-damaged or just deaf?

Robin confided that it was the woman's third and last day. She was all right with the little ones, but her bovine imperturbability was eroding the discipline they had over the Old Guard. The kids would play seven-year-old practical jokes on her, tests—thumbtack on the chair, wall Sticktite reversed—and she would smile and pat them on the head rather than scold them, which would result in an epidemic of deranged seven-year-old laughter. And then another little test.

The problem was her religion, the Church of the Eternal Now. O'Hara had never heard of it, which was not surprising, since at that time it had only five or six adherents. In another year it would have sixty, and begin to be a real problem.

The Church of the Eternal Now began as a conversation between Robert Lowell Devon and Nadia Szebehely. They convinced themselves, and then others, that past and future alike were nonexistent: that all the universe existed in one eternal instant of God's love.

The logic was unassailable, at least for those who were vulnerable to its charm. It evolved from an old Christian Fundamentalist argument against scientific evidence that the Earth was more than a few thousand years old, which was what their holy book claimed. You point to carbon-dated fossils, for instance, and they say God created them in place, old carbon atoms and all, at the same time he created everything else, 5,014 years ago. Can you prove otherwise?

What Saint Robert and Saint Nadia claimed is that everything around you, from the floor under your feet all the way out to the Hubble Limit, sprang into creation the moment you began to believe. Even the memory that you have believed for some seconds or hours or years—that was just created, too, as part of God's mysterious loving purpose.

If you pointed out the small paradox that their religion only allowed one person to actually exist—everyone else being just part of the divinely created mise-en-scène—the believer would either nod and smile or shake his head and smile.

One advantage of this religion is that there is no sin; only the divinely created memory of nonreal sins. And of course a true believer will never die, although he may have these remarkably intense memories of other people dying. God's will is obscure and not to be questioned, though your memories of questioning God's will are acceptable, since they are themselves part of God's will.

One disadvantage of the religion is that believers turn into smiling lumps. They were not a lot of fun to have around, since they rarely spoke, and when they did, it was just about their own private ecstasy. Some of them would copulate in public, or worse. Why not?

There haven't been many cultures where the Church of the Eternal Now could have taken hold and swiftly made converts, but the isolated, cloistered environment of *Newhome* was ideal for the existential fantasy it required, and also provided adequate living conditions. You wouldn't starve if you could wander smiling into the cafeteria once or twice a day, and when fatigue finally overtook you, you could lie down wherever you were, and people would just walk around you—until you woke up smiling to another perfect instant of God's love.

At the September Cabinet meeting, Eliot Smith said he was tired of maneuvering around them, and made the modest proposal that we steer them all into one big room and lock it from the outside, and try to remember to throw them some food once a day. He added some details, and his gifts for scatology and maledicta lightened up a boring meeting.

A year later, no one was laughing.

YEAR 9.88

≌

1

⇔

HOMECOMING

12 August 07 [3 Tsai Lun 313]—We had Sandra's eighth birthday celebration up in John's room, so he could be comfortable. The low gravity made Sandra frisky, but agreeably so. John, especially, had fun playing with her. (She asked him about his hump and he said it was magical; if you rub it you get your wish—sometimes. She accepted that.)

I was able to buy a flask of apple juice—which would still be rare for a couple of years—and two small cakes made with wheat flour, one soaked with honey and the other with "rhum," a mixture of boo and some brown chemical. Sandra ate most of the honey cake. Dan took one bite of the other and asked for a straw. (It was so saturated that a deep breath of it made you giddy; I think it would have burned if you lit it.)

Evy got off shift an hour early, 1900, and brought Sandra a present, a bracelet she had woven out of three different colors of wire. That impressed her a lot more than my gift of food and drink, though after an exuberant hug and kiss, she restrained her enthusiasm—whether through shyness or childish calculation, I'm not sure. She was fascinated with Evy's springy hair. Three of the creche mothers and two of the fathers are black, but they wear their hair cropped fashionably short.

Sandra had appropriated a well-worn deck of cards from Creche and taught us all how to play Planets. It was a surprisingly complex trading game, in which the first person to collect a whole Epsilon System wins. She displayed a good memory for other people's hands. Talking to her afterward, I found that she hadn't used any mnemonic device, but just has very solid native powers of concentration and retention. She amused John and Dan by reciting the value of pi to fifteen places; as far as I knew, she could have been bluffing for the last thirteen.

She was disappointed to find out, from John, that the actual planets probably wouldn't look much like the pictures on the cards. We knew how big the planets were and something about their atmospheres, but would have to be a lot closer before we could take actual pictures of them. I wondered whether her teachers knew that.

I had never dealt cards in quarter gee before. With five people, you can easily go around more than twice before the first card hits the bed. This led to an obvious game, Sandra and Evy and I seeing how long we could keep a card afloat no-hands, blowing it back and forth, while John and Dan kept out of the way and carried on a conversation in differential equations or something. It turns out you can keep the card going until the smallest member of the team becomes giddy from hyperventilation.

She went from giddiness to drooping in about thirty seconds, so I passed her around to kiss everybody goodnight, and we tottered up toward the Boston lift.

Her teachers, and the creche, would still have her in the daytime, from 0800 to 1600. She would have dinner and sleep and breakfast with me, so long as her academic and social development didn't suffer. We were both on probation, theoretically, but the creche is so crowded now I don't think they would take her back full time for anything short of an ax murder. "And who was this person you hacked to pieces, Dr. O'Hara? Did he or did he not actually deserve it?"

My neighbor in Uchūden, Ondrej Costache, kindly moved three doors around to a vacant office so I could make up an adjoining room for Sandra. She's going through a dinosaur phase now, so I put some appropriately ferocious prints up on the wall. They contrast agreeably with the coverlet the laundry gave me for her bed, little piggies and sheep.

I keyed her monitor for some standard restrictions, as

the creche advised. That's not to keep her from learning "adult" things, but to protect her from hopeless confusion, swamped by detail. It essentially restricts her database to one about twice as large as the one that she has access to at school. That will theoretically encourage her to do homework, showing off special knowledge.

She is a little bit privileged, since only about two thirds of her classmates have parents who opted to bring them home. A few years ago I would never have dreamed of it, myself. I don't know whether I would do it now, if we both had to live in my office, since I'm liable to be working until midnight or later.

As we were walking back to Uchūden, I explained to her that some nights I would be sleeping with Uncle John or Uncle Dan, but that her monitor would beep me automatically if she needed something. She got a very serious look on her face and asked why Uncle John and Uncle Dan didn't come up to Uchūden to fuck. I reminded her that Uncle John is hurt by normal gravity, and besides, my bunk was too narrow for two grown-ups.

I asked her whether she had ever done that with the boys at Creche, and she said no, they weren't allowed to until menarche, not "serious." I let it go at that.

She admired the dinosaurs on the wall, identifying them by name, and was fascinated by the luxury of having a toilet and monitor to herself. She was nervous about sleeping alone, though; at Creche she was in a room with eleven others. I told her she could spend the first night with me.

I didn't get much sleep, only partly because eight-year-olds have more elbows than normal people. I was intoxicated by her closeness, the sweet smell of her hair and breath, the small noises she made in her sleep. The thought that she was mine.

2

≙

THE BURDENS OF FAITH

PRIME

O'Hara probably knew better than any other 'Home official what the population of the Church of the Eternal Now, the "Nowers," had grown to at any given time. She had to physically remove each of them from the VR machines—but usually only once. In their new enlightenment, they found virtual reality confusing, even more so than normal reality, and didn't come back for more.

Sometimes she had to call Howard Bell, all 120 musclebound kilograms of him, to help wrestle the slack lumps out of their couches. Some of them had put on a lot of weight, eating three meals a day and spending the rest of their time and energy keeping their eyes unfocused. By the last day of 2107, they had dragged eighty-eight of the faithful from the dream room.

Newhome's charter allowed complete freedom of religious expression so long as that expression did not violate civil law. There was no law against being a useless consumer. The police could incarcerate a Nower for being a "public nuisance," if he or she did something particularly outrageous, but the faithful didn't mind jail. It just meant that somebody else brought them their meals. Trials were an exasperating farce.

Actually, the ones who sat around vegetating, communing with their inner truth, weren't as much of a problem as the proselytizers. One of O'Hara's helpers, Julio Eberhara, fell for the church's arguments. His sphere of influence was limited to the Game Room door, but for a while everybody who wanted to check out a game had to take a ration of inane theology along with it. Then he stopped answering the door with any reliability, sitting at his table humming, staring at an unfinished jigsaw puzzle of an idyllic mountain scene. O'Hara moved him and the puzzle to the storeroom, where at least his humming wouldn't bother anybody.

She tried to explain this business to Sandra, without much success. Sandra had had a little careful religious instruction in Creche—this is what some people believe, this is what others believe, and you will develop your own beliefs as you grow—but at third form, they hadn't yet been exposed to the excesses of religion. To Sandra and most other children, the Nowers were scary. A lot of what adults did was enigmatic or even silly, but in general they followed reassuringly predictable patterns. The Nowers were adults whose behavior was mysteriously infantile, and this regressiveness threatened the security of the children's world.

In talking with her daughter, O'Hara came to realize that there was a component of fear in her own feelings toward those people. Susceptible to this kind of weird behavior, what other kinds of behavior might they be capable of? Could inexplicable passivity explode into inexplicable violence? The Psych people she talked to cautiously said no. But on the other hand, they were at a loss to explain why so many aboard were vulnerable to this specific variety of dissociation. It was like a kind of existential virus. Could a normal person catch it? Could O'Hara?

It didn't seem likely. Though Psych no longer had extensive profiles of everybody, they were able to interview acquaintances and sometimes family relations of the people possessed by the Church of the Eternal Now, and it seemed that certain patterns of personality were favored. Co-workers used terms like scatterbrained, sullen, hard to train, unimaginative, lazy. Family members tended to preface their interviews with a sigh, and then work on some variation of "He was such a *nice* little boy." Most of them had been in and out of various religions, tending toward the wholist and fundamentalist. Seven Nowers had once been proselytizing atheists, a combination both odd and annoying, since almost three quarters of 'Home's population already adhered to unbelief in some degree. (John had worked with one of the antifaithful in the Deucalion reclamation project, almost twenty years before, and had confounded him by claiming to be a "fundamentalist Syncretic," borrowing from various friends jewelry presenting cross, crescent, flower, and Star of David, switching from week to week, enlivening the lunch hour with haphazard but passionate pronouncements about the pope, Muhammed, Baha'u'llah, and Moses. John didn't know much about religion, but the fanatic knew less.)

The net result was that 'Home experienced no significant decline in work accomplished by losing them. The eighty-eight people gone off to wherever the Church of the Eternal Now was had added to and subtracted from productivity in about equal measure.

YEAR 11.07

≙

1

≙

GROWING PAINS

15 October 2108 [1 Lao Tse 315]—What do they feed those children, sex hormones? Sandra's starting to sprout breasts. Talking about menarche. Put a cork in it, girl. She hasn't even had time to *be* a girl!

Of course she's anxious about being the youngest. The oldest of the Old Guard are ancient crones of ten. But how could worrying about that cause her to grow breasts? (Evy says the record age is eight, so I guess I should be thankful for small favors.)

Mother was such a bitch about the way I delayed menarche. Trying not to overcompensate. Sure, honey, if you want to go from blocks to cocks in seven years, what business is it of mine?

Let's separate this out into factors:

1. Concern about my own age. I'm not old enough to have a pubescent daughter. Me a potential grandmother? (And what if Sandra elects for parthenogenesis? A hall of mirrors.)

2. Concern about her emotional maturity. She's so moody now, quick to laugh or cry. I think a boy could hurt her deeply without knowing it, without meaning to.

3. Concern about her studies. She's not all that interested in academics, and will be much less so once she starts with boys. (Footnote—a constant and increasing disappointment, but be fair. She might be as bookish as I was, if she had as many books.)

4. It's perverse. It really is, little girls and little boys. If everybody's doing it, then *everybody's* perverse!

5. Selfishness. I don't want to share her love more than I already do. Bad enough that she loves Uncle John more than me. But who wouldn't?

Maybe it's mortality rather than age as such. I don't think I mind being older. It makes a lot of things easier. But as she moves toward the marriage bed, I move toward the grave.

How poetical. I'll leave it, though.

2

≙

LONG-DISTANCE CALL

Newhome continually checked a wide range of frequencies sternward, hoping for a message or even some man-made electronic noise from New New. On 19 October 2108 [6 Lao Tse 315], they got a sudden strong message at the 25.7-centimeter line (which was the standard 21-centimeter line, redshifted by their velocity relative to Earth), but not from New New.

Sixty seconds of warbling carrier wave, then this message repeated ten times:

Earth calling the starship. Earth calling the starship. This is Key West, Florida, station WROK, broadcasting at a frequency they call the water hole, 1420 megahertz, 21 centimeters. This message will be repeated ten times, and then we will switch to tightbeam video flatscreen on a composite signal from 54 to 60 megahertz, audio backup at 1420. We'll repeat the whole thing for a couple of weeks, and will expect a reply in a couple of years, same frequencies.

Earth calling the starship . . .

When the flatscreen flickered to life, it showed a cadaverous balding man, staring nervously into the camera. Behind him, palm trees swayed in a light breeze, seagulls floated.

STORM: I hope you all are getting this. We don't know how much power it takes to get out there or how good we're focused on you.

My name's Storm. I'm the mayor of Key West and the governor of Dixie. That's basically Florida and what used to be Georgia and Miss'ippi.

(Nods to somebody OFF)

Yeah, and part of Lou'siana too, but we ain't heard from them in months. They were gettin' flooded.

This is sometime in October 2107. It's a long story as to why we don't know exactly what the date is.

Anyhow, more about that later. We got things pretty much up and running. Even power to spare for this kinda thing, though most people don't think there's no one up there.

What the hell happened to New New York? If you know. They stopped broadcasting here about ten, eleven years ago—

(Someone OFF speaks; Storm says, "Yeah, yeah.") Exactly one year after you left, if we were counting right. So it must of had something to do with you. Maybe you did it, somehow. Hope not. Anyhow, we could sure use their help now, so if you know anything about it, let us know.

Anyhow, this here's Healer. He's the one who started this whole thing.

The camera pans around jerkily to a big man in his late fifties, sunbaked skin dark against a shock of white beard and long, flowing white hair. There's a radio telescope dish in the background.

HAWKINGS: My actual name is Jeff Hawkings. With any luck, I should know one of you. Hi, Marianne. Long time no see.

Key West was an oasis after the war, with water, food, and power independent of the American mainland. The ubiquitous biological agent, what we called the "death," was here as everywhere, until New New York sent us the antigen that wiped it out. I brought it down south; that's why they call me Healer.

Not that simple, actually. There was unrest, a power struggle, a bizarre belief system that took over most of Dixie and still has its adherents. Guess I told you about them back in '90, '91, when I got through to Marianne from Plant City. The Mansonites; they're still around, but on the wane. Fortunately. Murder and cannibalism are sacraments to them. We try to stay out of their way.

We need help. Trying to rebuild the world here; trying not to repeat too many mistakes. Reinventing the wheel several times a week, I'm sure.

As you know, the death killed almost all adults; the only grown-ups who survived were giants like me, people with acromegaly. Most of us are mentally retarded. I may be the only person on this planet with a bachelor's degree.

Which is why we so desperately need you. Information. Training. We're surrounded by technological wonders and nobody knows how they work, let alone how to fix them if they break.

We weren't able to get anything from New New York. We picked up a lot of radio noise from them until they stopped dead. But we were still a couple of years away from being able to broadcast then.

That B.A. isn't very useful: Political Science, with some graduate work in forensics and management. No real science. I can barely do algebra; calculus is just a word to me. My main function here is teaching, but I can't teach anybody anything technical.

There are bright kids here and they can figure out a lot on their own—one of them got this transmitter going and pointed at you—but they need to talk to real engineers and scientists, even with a two- or three-year time lag.

There may be many other enclaves like this somewhere in the world, but so far we haven't heard of them. We *have* made contact with two other radio transmitters: one in Brazil and one in Poland. So far we haven't done much but exchange names and locations. We desperately need language texts, or at least dictionaries, in Polish and Portuguese.

Anyhow, you can see the fix we're in. The only books we have are old-fashioned paper ones. Most of the information in them is inapplicable or just plain wrong. We desperately need to copy things from your up-to-date library.

I'm sure that somewhere on this planet we'll find a large electronic library intact, like a physical backup to the Library of Congress—I know that the actual hadron matrix for something like that is about the size of a small floater, and there are dozens of copies around the country—but as things stand right now, even if we found one, we wouldn't be able to tap it.

Let me close off on a personal note. We

saw the starship leave back in '97. That was fast work; I have some idea of how huge a project it was, and I suspect you were in a hurry because you were afraid of another war, afraid of Earth.

That seems ludicrous on the face of it, since we're little more than a band of savages capering around the mysterious remnants of an advanced civilization. We lack both knowledge and context. Context is the personal part.

(He gestures at the radio telescope behind him.) The boys and girls who fixed up that dish lived around it for years without even knowing what it was. I had to tell them. Then they had to learn to read, and find books; eventually, books about electronics.

People with my disorder don't live too long. What will happen after I'm dead? What obvious things are going to be overlooked forever, because there's nobody alive who remembers *real* life, life before the war?

Assuming something terrible did happen, and New New York is dead—then you people are the only human link that Earth will have with its past. You're going to have to supply the context, if Earth is going to be rebuilt.

Don't be afraid of us. The madmen, the mad governments, who started the war are memories now, less than memories. This is a planet of innocent children. They need your help to survive.

Hope I'm not talking to empty space. We had to make various assumptions—that your target star was still Epsilon Eridani, that you would be listening to the 21-centimeter line, 1420 megahertz. That you still survive.

Marianne . . . uh, what can I say? I hope to hear from you in a couple of years. *(Laughs)* Hope you're enjoying your trip. Life is not bad here, considering.

I must look awful strange. *(Rubs his beard)* You remember me as a young man—and in my mind you're still my twenty-four-year-old bride, though twice that time has passed for you. Not quite twice for you, I guess, with relativity.

I never fathered any children, of course, though I've raised a few. Hope you have, too.

Love you still.

3

≙

FOUR NOVELS

PRIME

The ten years that followed renewed contact with Earth were very interesting for O'Hara and for *Newhome* in general, but I must necessarily present them here in concentrated form. When I relate this story to other machine intelligences, these ten years are given about the same amount of attention as any other ten in O'Hara's century-plus. This document, however, is limited by various story-telling constraints having to do with unity and balance.

In fact, one could compose several interlocking novels covering this ten-year span, and each one would be a worthy chronicle. But to put them inside another novel would be a topological impossibility. So I will relate them in abbreviated form, each one illuminated by an entry from O'Hara's diary, or a similar document.

THE NOVEL OF JOHN'S DISASTER

John Ogelby was surprised to find out how much he enjoyed being a father, or uncle, or grandfather-figure. Nineteen years older than O'Hara, he was sixty-three when Sandra left the creche and moved into their lives.

Like Daniel, he had assumed that Sandra was going to be O'Hara's project, with himself a more or less inactive bystander. The little girl saw things differently, though.

Children usually were fascinated by John, since they were fascinated by the strange, and John looked like a creature out of a fairy tale. He'd grown used to their stares and questions long before he emigrated from Ireland to New New, seeking low gravity to ease the pain of his twisted back. Birth defects were rare in New New, but deformation was not, since space is unforgiving, and will repay a moment's inattention with a limb torn off, or a face. So children were always asking him what did he *do* to get like that?

It was a question he had asked, himself, when he was young. His parent's assurances that God had done it to test his faith did not leave him well disposed toward God. John gave up on religion long before he went off to Trinity, to Cambridge, to the Cape and space.

Sandra hadn't asked him that question, since her mother had prepared her. She did have other questions, as they got to know each other: can't they fix it? (They could have, when he was young, if there had been money.) Why'd they let him be born? (Abortion was illegal at the time and place of his birth.) Did he have brothers or sisters with bad backs? (No, his father had practiced a time-honored form of birth control: leaving with another woman.) Did he ever wish he hadn't been born? (Everybody does, sometimes, if they live long enough.)

John wasn't sure how to act around children. His own childhood had not given him any reason to like the little bastards, so he had avoided them all his life, which had required small effort in New New and none at all in the starship, at least until they geared up the baby factory. As Sandra approached the age of eight, he resigned himself to the occasional interference with his orderly life. But nothing prepared him for falling in love.

It was a mutual chemistry of discovery and fascination. The adult males in Sandra's life, her creche fathers, were all cast from the same mold: self-assured, endlessly patient, mildly but consistently authoritarian. Uncle John was like a different species. He never told her what to do. He was likely to answer a question with another question, or a paradox. He was sarcastic, oblique, darkly humorous but always serious.

Usually when Sandra talked to adults she rightly sensed they were only partly there. Uncle John gave her all of his attention, as if studying her, and talked to her carefully but without condescension. He was *real* to her in a constant way that no other grown-up, not even her mother, had ever been.

John didn't try to analyze his fascination with her beyond the obvious fact that she was a genetic duplicate of the woman he loved most, the woman who had rescued him from a life of disconnection, alienation, self-destruction. She had novelty value, too, and presented a learning experience, since he had never watched a child grow. She seemed unusually alert and creative, but he admitted to a lack of comparative data.

They met after dinner, without O'Hara, every Monday and Thursday. John would drill her on the week's arithmetic lesson and they would play a game of checkers or Owari. He promised to teach her chess when she turned twelve—and knew from O'Hara that she was secretly studying it on her own.

She never had the chance to surprise him.

12 July 2110 [27 Hippocrates 2110]—John had a stroke day before yesterday. Sygoda called me asking if something was wrong; he'd missed a staff conference and didn't respond to his keyboard, though it was busy. I thought he had probably left it on and, forgetting about the conference, had taken a nap. The beeper won't wake him if he's really sawing wood.

I was up in zero gee anyhow, staying out of the engineers' way while they were measuring for a new murderball court, so I ducked down to his flat.

He was lying by the toilet, where he had vomited. His eyes were open, but all he could say was my name and "shit," over and over. I called the ER and got him a drink of water, on which he almost choked. He was waving his left arm around initially, but had calmed down by the time the medics got there. They both said they thought it was a stroke, but wanted a doctor's opinion. They attached three diagnostic telltales, and the physician on ER duty confirmed that it was a "cerebrovascular incident," and told them to take him to the low-gee ward without passing through high gee. I went along with them, holding his left hand. His right was stiff and cool.

They put him in bed with an IV drip and scanned his head. They showed me a picture of a large area in his brain that was suffused with blood.

It doesn't look very good. In the old days he would have gone straight to nanosurgery, where an army of tiny machines would be directed to go in there and clean up, restore synapses. But nobody now can do it; we don't even know exactly how to get the machines in and out of the brain, which has to be done with high precision.

He's been stable now for two days. It's always possible that the missing nanosurgery information will come in from Key West next week or next year. There's also a chance that he will recover some or most or all of his faculties spontaneously, as the brain reorganizes its wiring. There's a larger chance that he'll have another stroke and die.

Every hour without change makes spontaneous recovery less likely. He still can't move his right arm or leg and there is no expression on the right side of his face. He still has only two words.

A speech therapist spent a couple of hours with him, but he just looked at her. I got him to try a keyboard once, but after half a line of gibberish, he gave up. He can't or won't read.

Sandra is inconsolable. She comes to the door but can't get any closer without bursting into tears.

I'm close to tears most of the time myself, but haven't cried in his presence. I know he's conscious of that effort and appreciates it. We communicate in small ways. Most of the medical people treat him like a vegetable, but they haven't been married to him for twenty-four years. He's still all there, or mostly there, in some sense, at least emotion if not intellect. It's so sad, so unfair. A fine reward for a lifetime of brave coping.

Daniel and Evelyn and I take turns staying by his side. They want one of us there all the time for a few days, to talk to him when he wants to listen, and to report any sudden change.

After about two weeks of no change, O'Hara was given the option of either taking John home with her or having him transferred to the Extended Care Facility. The ECF was primarily an old folks' home, with a few younger people like John, who didn't need a lot of medical help but did need to be fed and changed. Even if it hadn't been at the 0.6-gee level, the ECF would have been out of the question because of the indignities O'Hara witnessed there. It was crowded and understaffed and smelled of stale urine and gastric juices. People mumbled and cried and the cube was on all the time.

The obvious third option, cryptobiosis until nanosurgery was possible again, seemed too risky. The brain was the most delicate organ preserved, and was the locus of almost all fatalities on restoration. Sylvine Hagen said she might give John a 10 percent chance of surviving, though even if he lived, he might not have enough cerebral organization left to make nanosurgery useful. They didn't tell John.

What they finally did was take John back to his quarter-gee office, which they had converted into a sickroom. It wasn't difficult to care for him, once he mastered the bedpan and urinal and was able to feed himself after a fashion. They rigged up an "answer board" that had the numbers from 0 to 9 and YES, NO, and MAYBE. They all had beepers that he could call with a button by his bedside, and they split up responsibility for answering his calls.

O'Hara wound up on duty more often than Evelyn or Daniel, which was not unreasonable, since she could do most of her work from John's console. Dan was busier than he had ever been as Coordinator, since he'd gone back to his old Earth Liaison/Engineering post when they'd begun talking to Key West, and was busy all day meeting with various specialists, working out the right way to phrase questions so that the marginally educated Earthlings could find the right answers in their old-fashioned books.

Sandra finally overcame her sadness and fear enough to come play checkers with John. Everyone was relieved to see that he played a vicious and intelligent game. He initially refused to play Owari, because he didn't have good enough left-hand coordination to count out the pebbles, but she pleaded and wheedled until he did it, which gave her a much better success rate than the physical therapist, whom John saw as a dangerous adversary.

The end of John's novel is also a beginning, which is not an unusual contrivance. It was one of those times when all three relatives were at work, so O'Hara got the beeper by default. She was annoyed, because it was an important meeting with Coordinator Montagu and the Education Committee. She said she'd be back in a few minutes.

When there was nobody else with him, John watched a lot of cube, setting it to Random Walk until something of interest showed up. When O'Hara came in, the cube was stop-framed on a documentary about cryptobiosis, a naked man being prepped on a rolling slab. John pointed at the cube and then stabbed his answer board YES.

O'Hara had known that this would come up sooner or later. "We looked into that, John. It would be simple murder. Or euthanasia, or suicide—you wouldn't have a ten percent chance—"

"Shit!" John said, and stabbed YES.

"Even if you survived, you'd be mentally worse off—"

He pounded YES YES YES YES. "Shit-shit!"

O'Hara sighed. "Let me call Dr. Hagen."

Sylvine Hagen came down, armed with statistics and lab results and truly gruesome cube footage. John would not be convinced. O'Hara said they would have a family conference about it.

A novelist's prerogative would be to go inside John's

mind, and demonstrate that he was well aware of all of the conflicting factors, including the rather complex one that O'Hara and Evy and Dan and Sandra would all be greatly relieved if he were safely installed up on 2105, and their guilt at that foreknowledge of relief was the main thing standing in his way. The novelist would have John screaming silently at them *Anything is better than this! I only have a tiny chance of ever functioning again, and your peasant rectitude is the only thing standing in my way!*— but all I can really say is that John said the same word over and over, and kept pounding YES, no matter what they said to him.

The solution was undramatic: recourse to law. O'Hara discussed the situation with Thomana Urey, an expert in constitutional law, and she said there was no question. John was capable of making the decision for himself, and was presumably aware of the subtleties, even though he couldn't discuss them. He didn't have any more "right" to cryptobiosis than anyone else did, but in standard practice the only thing that prevented a person from exercising the option had been his or her usefulness to the maintenance of *Newhome*. John was not currently useful to anyone— including, apparently, himself. Let him go.

With a little guilt and a lot of relief, they did.

THE NOVEL OF SANDRA'S SEX LIFE

Uncle John's stroke was one of two hard blows that marred Sandra's eleventh year, the first being a painful and premature loss of virginity.

O'Hara had reluctantly given Sandra permission for an early "forced" menarche, so she wouldn't be left behind by the other girls. Predictably, a combination of natural curiosity and peer pressure had resulted in a classwide orgy of sexual experimentation, and Sandra wanted to join the party.

It was a couple of years too early. She was small, she couldn't relax the appropriate muscles, and her hymen was tough. The first two boys she asked were unable to penetrate her before ejaculating. The third, unusually large and strong for a twelve-year-old, succeeded, but in his enthusiasm caused a lot of pain and bleeding. Sandra withdrew from the sexual marathon the same day she entered it, hurt and bewildered, distrustful of males.

Her mother took her to a gynecologist, who tried to comfort her with case histories, and used a little camera to show her that she wasn't badly hurt inside. Both women urged that it would be a good idea for her to wait awhile, to heal emotionally more than physically. It might also give the boys in her peer group time to learn something about girls, so they wouldn't be such blunt instruments. They were both supportive and nonjudgmental and made her feel like shit.

She took her pain to Uncle John, and he said well, you did something stupid and got hurt and it hurts twice as much because you knew it was stupid when you did it, right? The creche mothers and O'Hara all wanted you to wait, but you went ahead because your desire for other kids' approval overrode both common sense and the desire to please adults. Besides, it's *your* body, et cetera, but it might not be a bad time to reflect that it's actually two cells from your mother's body that got loose and have sort of been going their own way, and aren't you glad there's no father in there to complicate things? But if you only do one stupid thing this week, it'll be better than most of my weeks. Let's play checkers.

She hugged him and cried on his shoulder, and it is not just novelistic speculation to imagine that this made him feel uncomfortably non-avuncular feelings toward the little girl. He had discussed it a few days before with Daniel, while they were splitting a box of wine in the south lounge after dinner.

JOHN: So Sandra's going to start, um, making love next week.
DAN: Fucking.
JOHN: It bothers you, too.
DAN: Like Marianne says. God, eleven? I don't think I had pubic hair at eleven.
JOHN: But you thought about sex.
DAN: I don't know. Just to wonder about it.
JOHN: I still wonder about it. (Long pause) She's getting to look an awful lot like Marianne.

DAN: Surprise.

JOHN: I mean, *that* bothers me sometimes. Marianne
        was still in her teens when we met.

DAN: Dirty old Irishman. Incest.

JOHN: Well, it wouldn't really be incest—

DAN: No, it'd be suicide. Marianne would come after
        you with a meat cleaver. (Pause) But I know
        what you mean. She's going to break a few hearts.

Daniel predicted wrong. Sandra's pattern was about the
same as her mother's as a young teenager: having been introduced to sex, she decided she liked books better. She
became a model student, doing assignments on time with
care, volunteering for extra work, speaking up in class but
not dominating. She built models and studied keyboard—
including harpsichord, to her mother's delight, once her
hands were big enough. But her sex life, for several years,
was nonexistent or solitary.

For about a year when she was fourteen, she had an all-
consuming crush on Hong-Loan Kim, her chess partner
and swimming buddy. O'Hara was sure they were having
sex (and she was right) but was too uncomfortable about
lesbianism to counsel her one way or the other. Kim eventually left Sandra for a man twice her age, and once Sandra got over her helpless anger, she went back to her
books. But not to boys.

Sandra was as plain-looking as her mother had been
when she was young (and, like her mother, would be striking when she was older), but there was no shortage of
boys vying for her attention. She knew this was just because she was a conquest, reputedly the only girl in the
Old Guard who wasn't having regular sex with at least one
person, and that popularity-by-default did not boost her
opinion of boys. She knew they kept lists, and heard that
some of them had everybody but her on theirs. She was
determined to keep it that way.

The boy who finally won her was Jakob Ayoub, homely,
short, tongue-tied, and very smart. At some level he probably evoked a memory of Uncle John. They watched each
other grow up, as everybody did everybody, but didn't be-

come friends until they were fifteen and sixteen, when chance threw them together as lab partners in beginning chemistry class. He was clumsy with glassware but graceful with algebra, and she was the opposite, so working in tandem they were able to excel.

All this time, O'Hara had not been exactly a doting mother, though that was due to lack of time more than a shortage of desire or ability. When Sandra was nine, O'Hara announced her candidacy for Policy Coordinator. She ran unopposed, and so became Coordinator-elect when her daughter was eleven, and stayed in office until she was seventeen. They were busy years for everybody, handling the information explosion from Key West and the sudden bombshell that the cryptobiology people handed them in 2112: with a simple alteration in technique, the period of suspended animation could be shortened to as little as twenty years, or lengthened to over one hundred, without affecting the probability of survival. This gave people a lot of options, and with the options came the need for regulation, and with regulation came dissent.

During O'Hara's last year in office, Sandra announced that she wanted to marry Jakob. O'Hara thought that a simple one-to-one relationship would be awfully confining, and she managed to talk them into making the marriage formally open. They did it only to humor her, both of them sure they would never have room for anyone else in their lives.

Then they announced their other little surprise.

THE NOVEL OF O'HARA MAINTAINING

O'Hara had given up Jeff Hawkings for dead almost twenty years before. On Earth they had been adversaries and then lovers—and for a few days husband and wife, in an attempt to secure New New York emigration for Jeff, as the United States and then the world collapsed into total war. With strength and luck and cleverness, he got them down to the Cape in time for the last shuttles before the bombs started to fall, but by then no groundhogs, to whomever related, however valuable, could get a berth into orbit.

He made it through the war, though, and the chaos following, and a few years later he improvised a radio link with New New. They talked a few times and then the radio station was destroyed, and O'Hara had no reason to believe that he had survived.

So she lost him twice, and here he was again, though they were worlds and years apart. External Communications, suddenly a real committee again, let her broadcast the first reply to Key West. It was a short and stilted speech, too many eavesdroppers, followed by an hour of Jules Hammond relaying to Jeff and his people everything that was known, or could be surmised, about what had happened from the time they last were in contact until New New fell silent. The similarity of their predicaments was interesting; they could trade.

Then the technical people talked for some hours about the sorts of knowledge they could transmit, and the sorts of things they eventually could use in return. They set up a schedule, starting five days hence, for people from each discipline to begin teaching. It was easy to calculate at what time of day we would be above Key West's horizon, and we would broadcast constantly whenever they could hear us.

O'Hara well understood the Machiavellian angle behind this generous giveaway of knowledge. We wanted to put them in our debt, and fast. Sooner or later the groundhogs would uncover a treasure-trove library and be able to unlock it. Then, if they were so disposed, they could transfer the data to 'Home in a few days or years, depending on their level of technology, and undo a large part of the damage New New had caused.

If they felt they had some reason to withhold data from us, though, there was nothing we could do. We would be back where we started, with the prospect of slowly evolving mathematics, the sciences, and engineering, but with most of history, literature, and music forever lost.

O'Hara's first assignment in this grand dissemination of data was to teach the rules of games. That seemed less than grand, compared to the responsibilities of people delivering learned disquisitions about trigonometry or ethics, but it was arguably one of the most useful early lessons, relatively easy to follow and associated with pleasure. She brainstormed with Gunter, Lebovski, and Saijo, eliminating games with complicated pieces or rules, starting with children's play and moving up through more elaborate games of skill and chance.

The short transmission from Earth hadn't given them any useful clues. Teaching children how to play jacks and marbles would be sort of cruel if there were no jacks or marbles. What simple games could they be sure had survived the cataclysm—should they teach kids how to play tag, hide-and-go-seek? (They decided against that genre, so as not to appear too ridiculous.) They gambled that durable accessories like horseshoes and balls would be available, though their demonstrations of such pastimes would look strange from a groundhog viewpoint. In a rotating frame, every pitch is a curve ball. A horseshoe's path is a sideways-twisted parabola.

The first dozen or so transmissions were fairly easy to set up, since they involved only simple introductions to selected pastimes. Once past the obvious, though, they had to decide between depth and breadth. They had demonstrated the basic moves and rules of chess, for instance. You could spend hundreds of hours explaining various strategies, but given only one hour of transmission each three days, would it be more constructive to spend it discussing a few classic chess openings or to start something new, relatively obscure—sketch out the rules of Parcheesi, or Texas Hold'-Em? The four of them spent much more time deciding what to teach than teaching.

They had almost three hundred hours of fun-and-games broadcasting scheduled before they could expect the first feedback from their audience; before they found out which of their hours had been valuable and which had fruitlessly duplicated things the groundhogs already knew. There was an advantage to the lack of feedback, though, since once they had their basic plan agreed upon, it only took a few months to set up and record all of the lessons. So in January of 2109, O'Hara delivered the last lesson to External Communications and went back to business as usual.

It was Dan's last year in office and her last year before running. They'd long planned for her to announce her candidacy for 2112 the day after he stepped down. She would spend this last "nonpolitical" year making good impressions, mending fences, doing favors that could be called in. Of course, the political community in *Newhome* was so small that there was no secret as to what she was doing and why; it was a rite of passage, a genteel excruciation ritual. This was a game, as Purcell had taught her, with unwritten but not very flexible rules.

She spent as much time with Sandra as possible, knowing that once she became Coordinator (losing the election was not an option she wanted to consider) the time wouldn't be there. By then Sandra would be fairly independent, anyhow, at thirteen. The age *her* mother had become a mother!

She took Sandra on trips to Earth and New New via the dream room. They were standard tourist matrices, but she could walk alongside her daughter and say, this bar, the Light Head, is where I met Uncle Dan; I lived down that street in New York; that statue, there weren't so many pigeons on it when we were there, because it was winter, snow drifting into the Seine, can you smell the chestnuts? No, of course not. Nor feel the snowflakes kissing your face.

Sandra was old enough, at ten-going-on-eleven, to recognize the dual nature of these outings, to see how important it was to her mother both to revisit and to share the places. So although she was bored most of the time, she never complained, even though she was using up VR time that could be going for games with the other kids. That wasn't so important; like her mother at her age, she was a loner, and not completely by choice.

O'Hara was also going through menopause at the time, a change that she tried to welcome but couldn't. With all her ova filed away in liquid nitrogen, the monthly cycle had always been an anachronism. She could have had it stopped at any time, and presumably could have it restarted if she cared to go through the trouble of convincing a doctor that it would be salubrious. But she wasn't sure. Besides, there was a symmetry to the timing, her stopping when her daughter started, passing the torch, blood sisters.

They threw a wild party for Dan and the other outgoing

Senior Coordinator, Ondrej Costache, on New Year's Eve, when their terms expired. It was the first time Dan had been actually blind drunk in six years, and although O'Hara didn't begrudge him the binge, she wrote in her diary that she hoped it wouldn't become a regular feature of life again. It would.

O'Hara excused herself from the park cleanup detail the next day long enough to announce her candidacy. There was no opposition, which surprised no one, though Leona Burdine agreed to be the pro forma stalking horse. She would temporarily take over the candidacy if O'Hara died or ran off with the treasury.

(The position rightly made Burdine a little nervous, since it was possible she could wind up solely in charge of the whole starship if the right kind of disaster occurred. Nine other people would have to die, but it *was* a space-ship, and accidents happen.)

O'Hara's diary entry for the second day of the year is informative.

2 January 10 [16 Hippocrates 319]—It occurs to me that I have never described for you generations yet unborn exactly what sort of government, or administration, we have. A fish wouldn't describe water. (Oh, you don't have fish? Never mind.)

Behind everything is an Evaluation Board, comprising every present and past Coordinator and a handful of psychometric specialists. The Coordinators make recommendations for people to enter the administration at the Cabinet level. The psychometric evaluators have absolute veto power if they can demonstrate that the candidate has certain antisocial characteristics—most obviously, an emotional hunger to exert control over strangers, though less obvious defects abound, such as a need for approval through martyrdom, or a perverse will to fail in a public way. Anybody who is turned down by the Board can be reevaluated annually, but its word is final for that year.

It makes for less than colorful history, not having any Stalins or Nixons. But you wouldn't want interesting luna-tics in charge if you lived in a pressurized vessel sur-rounded by light-years of vacuum.

There are twenty-four Cabinet positions divided between Engineering and Policy, "Policy" being anything that doesn't have to do with grommets and electrons and so forth. A Cabinet member stays in power until he or she decides to step down or the Evaluation Board becomes dissatisfied and names a replacement.

Everybody in *Newhome* is defined as Engineering or Policy track for the sake of voting. A person with a sufficiently ambiguous job, such as demographics analyst, has to choose one or the other and stay with it. A new pair of leaders, one for each track, is chosen every two years. For both of them, it's a six-year term: two as Coordinator-elect, two as Coordinator, and two as Senior Coordinator. The actual Coordinator has three votes; the others have two each.

The Coordinators' most visible function is to decide which problems can be resolved at the committee/Cabinet level, and which must be put to a general referendum. But most of their day-to-day work is budget-arguing and keeping the peace among the various special interests represented by the Cabinet members and outside groups.

That's the official story. The unofficial is much more interesting, but I'm sworn to secrecy—even to you generations yet unborn. Though I'm sure the secret will be out long before we get to Epsilon. Too many people know; too many others suspect.

In fact, the secret—that the referendum process was a cynical sham—lasted until it was irrelevant. O'Hara hated the deception but accepted it as a condition for employment, and even grudgingly admitted that there had been times in the past when the electorate had been disastrously wrong, and had to be lied to for their own survival.

That O'Hara was allowed into the Cabinet at all was a testimony to the accuracy of the Evaluation Board's psychometrics, and the assessments of Sandra Berrigan and Harry Purcell. Ten years younger, she would have reacted to the truth with indignation, and gone disastrously public with it. Repeated exposure to human nature had reduced her confidence in people's ability to control their own destiny.

Still, she was no cynic; like Berrigan (and unlike Purcell) she saw the fakery as a temporary necessity that would be abandoned on Epsilon. Life aboard 'Home, like life in New New, had the illusion of comfort, stability, and safety, but only by virtue of hundreds of complicated inter-relating systems. It could no more be run by democratic consensus than a floater could be driven by committee. Dangerous things happen too fast. Planets were more for-giving.

(Whether leaders would be willing to radically change a system that had worked for generations was another matter.)

Ever since childhood, O'Hara had been conscious of a sense of "destiny" that she knew most other people didn't have. Remarkable things happened to her on Earth and af-terward that did seem to be setting her up as a sort of pivot, a historical nexus. Daniel tried to convince her that it was irrational foolishness, superstition, a small cognitive defect in a brain that was otherwise more than adequate.

Her six years in office tended to confirm Daniel's inter-pretation. Everybody else who had been in charge of 'Home had experienced some serious crisis during their terms. O'Hara spent six years waiting for something to happen.

There was plenty to keep her busy, but most of it just required attention to detail and careful delegation. She en-joyed the work, but it wasn't exciting enough to raise her blood pressure. There was a huge amount of data transfer and analysis going on continually with Key West, which took up a lot of the starship's time and energy resources, but the day-by-day management of that was the province of various specialists.

During those six years, she was still nominally in charge of Entertainment, but Gunter was actually running most of it.

She had more time than she'd expected to spend on be-ing wife and mother. The loss of John had at first been like losing one leg off a table, but she and Evy and Dan were slowly getting used to the new balance, Dan actually cutting down on his extracurricular affairs. O'Hara and Evy half-joked about finding another fourth, but they never talked about it seriously; never when Dan wasn't present.

As Evy grew older, she became closer to O'Hara; they had been married fifteen years when she took office. In that time Evy had gone from ravishingly beautiful to merely attractive, even slightly plump, which hadn't hurt their relationship. She also loved Sandra, the way she loved most children—they were wonderful creatures so long as you could give them back to a parent sooner or later—and was a big help with her, especially after John's stroke.

(Evelyn came from the Ten line, which had a tradition of marrying young and having children young. She was all for the first but not the second, which had been fine with John and Dan.)

It was no coincidence that Evy's grandfather, Ahmed Ten, took office at the same time as O'Hara, on Engineering track. She had asked him to put his name up and, like her, he was well enough respected to run unopposed. They worked well together; they had both been on the first two postwar rescue missions to Earth, Zaire and New York. Those had been grim, dramatic episodes; both O'Hara and Ten had been toughened by them. They were ready for anything.

So nothing much happened. Except the first year.

14 July 2112 [19 Wright 323]—Witta Marckese delivered a report today from Cryptobiology that at first seemed like unalloyed good news: the sleep period can now be shortened to as little as twenty years or extended to as much as one hundred, maybe more, without increasing the risk. So John can stay under until nanosurgery is routine again, and there were dozens in similar situations.

Unfortunately, there were hundreds of other people we Powers-That-Be would just as soon not be given that kind of choice. And there is no question of keeping the report secret. Almost everybody in Crypto knows.

The timing is an unfortunate coincidence, since we're now a little less than forty-eight years away from Epsilon, which until today was the one inflexible period for cryptos. So back in January we thought it was a now-or-never proposition, and we allowed a lot of borderline cases to go in the cans, people still more than marginally useful in the Key West project. Now we could call them back, but twenty years from now, who knows? At the present rate, transferring data visually a page at a time, we'll still need them. But Ahmed's confident that we'll have a dataflow breakthrough any time now.

The next few days and weeks are going to be interesting. Joint Cabinet powwow first thing in the morning to discuss new crypto rules. Morale is not high, a lot of people complaining about busywork and probably wishing they had gone into the can while they were still young enough for it not to be a bad gamble. You can't really blame them. Trained for science or engineering and now putting in long hours on work any fairly well-educated clerk could do. A lot of them will want to say the hell with it for twenty, thirty, forty years. How many can we afford to lose? Which individuals would we be better off without?

I personally don't think we need any new rules. The current principle, that anybody be allowed to go crypto unless we can demonstrate that we need him or her, will do.

We just have to adjust the criteria to a level low enough that we need everybody.

That was essentially what the Cabinet and Coordinators decreed: you're welcome to it if you qualify, but you probably won't qualify. There were appeals through the legal system, usually based on mitigating family circumstances—"I want to join my husband after all"—and most of them were resolved by the extrajudicial, unconstitutional, use of discreet psychometrics: would keeping her here make her so miserable that it would be counterproductive? Or will she get over it like the rest of us?

There was a vocal minority who claimed, with some justification, that their civil rights were being ignored; that the ship could be run with a skeleton crew of a few hundred. So anybody not crucial to maintaining life support or propulsion should be allowed to do as they wished. Key West would still be there in forty-some years.

The counterargument was speculative but powerful: we

can't risk another information disaster. What if something *did* happen to Key West? What if our end of the system broke down? It wasn't just a matter of losing cultural continuity or even technical information. The people in Key West are living on a planet, which is something 97 percent of us have never done. They might know a lot of things useful for starting out on Epsilon; things not in books.

The difficulties expected in developing Epsilon also made one class of people automatically eligible for cryptobiosis: the young. Anyone born aboard 'Home would be allowed, even encouraged, to go crypto as soon as they were old enough, an insurance against the pioneer population being too heavily weighted toward the middle-aged and elderly. Nobody foresaw any problem in quickening a couple of thousand embryos in the last two decades of flight. But 'Home's leaders were becoming cautious about unforeseen problems.

O'Hara didn't see the policy ever affecting her. When Sandra was a little girl, she shared wholeheartedly her mother's revulsion toward cryptobiosis. But people change.

11 August 2116 [5 Handy 332]—You lose one, you win one, you lose one . . . I don't know why I didn't see this coming. Daughters are little surprise machines.

Sandra declaring her love for Jakob was no surprise. That she wanted to marry at seventeen was a little bit of a shock, but her crowd are doing everything young. At least I talked them out of making it an exclusive bond— though they obviously consented just to humor my old-fashioned sexual attitudes. How could I ever want to do *that* with anyone else? Stick around, darlings.

And now she says that next year, as soon as she's old enough, they're going into the can together. Face the brave new world of Epsilon as young pioneers, ready to fight whatever dinosaurs or Martians are waiting on the other side of the airlock.

I really was caught off guard. She knows how I feel about it, anyhow. It would be stupid of me to try to talk her out of going.

I feel so old. Prime, come talk.

• • •

On 10 August 2117, Sandra and Jakob went into cryptobiosis. As soon as her term was over, O'Hara pulled strings and followed them.

AGE 55

⌢

1

⌒

IN DREAMS AWAKE

For time beyond time it was nothing but dark gray shot
through with black stars   the black stars slowly
moving sparkling   she could smell them move   hear
the burning cold   as the stars sucked heat tinkling out of
space   space with the feel of stiff velvet folding

Then colors whistling soft harmonies   indistinct shapes
smelling no *looking* fuzzy   sharpening up   pictures   this is
not a dream   not quite   you don't watch your dreams

Walking with Jeff through the snow outside Paris   the
Seine cleaner here   not so clogged with houseboats   old
men huddled with dogs and long fishing poles   lots of
young walkers out in the bright melting snow   stop to
warm our hands at the vendor's brazier   hot crisp &
greasy sausages with a cold stab of mustard   foam cup of
spicy mulled cider

Eight years old   old enough to fly   perching terrified
on the edge of the platform   New New York spinning
slowly underneath   gentle push between the shoulder
blades   falling   falling   but straight out   instructor
alongside shouting *just spread 'em just spread 'em*   then
gliding   flapping   rolling   if I had the wings of an
angel   over these prison bars would I fly

Painting wall with Charlie after the first time   his juice
leaking out of my soreness   I sweep the roller in a crude cartoon of his big dick   he blushes but laughs   it was so big in
my mouth I panicked   but he was gentle and knew what to
do   to make it easy   God knows he didn't know much else

Watching Sandra's birth   strange stuff she coughed up

223

before the first shriek   smell of babypuke and
solvent   acetone, John said   then her soft mouth search-
ing on my breast   sucking fabric   the cold spot there after they took her away

Fingerpaints on cool smooth plastic   new creche
mother pressing my hand down in it   then again and
again   then trace stems for the flowers   use knuckles to
make grass   funny   every color tastes the same

Sandra rushing in with bright red blood pulsing from
torn lip   she didn't want to tell me   that tall bitch Harni
Stevens   I couldn't stop it   blood all over my
console   had to take her and coldseal it at the ER   I
talked to Harni's line parents but they just laughed   girls
will be girls   yeah but some girls will be animals too

New York City ruins   crouching out of the wind behind
a wrecked van   waiting   watching   the little black boy
whispering "Indira say you live inside a ball of dirt, like
worms"   and then the white boys with the guns

First solo   the O'Neill Day concert when I was
eleven   that stupid simplified Mozart medley   had to
drop the middle part down an octave to keep from
squeaking   look on old Kurlov's face

Snorkeling in the warm water   fairy grace of the
coral   anemones   a cloud of tiny bright yellow
fish   following the squids until they got tired of us   the big
brown shark   harmless   scary   shivering on the hot sand

I already had my dormitory key out   he must have been
behind the shrubs   hand over mouth knife at throat
pressed up behind me I could feel he didn't have an
erection   *just a robbery* but when I dropped my purse he
cut the waistband and pulled my pants down   I bit he
stabbed I screamed he banged my head against the
sidewalk   twice hard   then people everywhere   kicking
him   sirens   fading

Actually seeing them   the paintings you've seen all
your life   ten eleven hours in the Louvre   so tired knees
are shaking   *you will never see this again*   never   but
the Mona Lisa was in Pittsburgh

Awkward hour with my father   small cubicle neat but
dusty   glass of harsh cheap wine   sad little man   felt
good afterwards   the biting blowing snow   I think I
would have hated him if he had been happy

The pool in Devon's World   all those people earnestly fucking and sucking   in the dim red light with the music   locker room smell with chlorine and pheromones   stepping   around   the   foursome   me giggling   Charlie mortified at my disrespect

Florida pinewoods   ripping sound   look up at exhaust trail   Jeff says Christ I hope that's not nuclear   it was the light hurts my eyes

2

≅

UP TEMPO

8 January 59 or 18 Dostoevski 427 or whatever. I'm ninety-six years old? This "week," whatever a week is now:

	2159	427	
Tuesday	January 8	Dost 18	Nineday
Wednesday	9	19	Tenday
Thursday	10	20	Oneday
Friday	11	21	Twoday
		22	Threeday
Saturday	12	23	Fourday
Sunday	13	24	Fiveday
		25	Sixday
Monday	14	26	Sevenday
		Columbus 1	Eightday

Yeah, happy nineday. I mean Nineday.

Age 55.00 [18 Dostoevski 427]—Prime says I might want to keep this diary in terms of my age in real honest-to-god Earth years, rather than exotic dates, at least for a while. She'll compute it for me as I need it. To preserve what's left of my freeze-dried sanity.

When I first came fully awake, this body was very frightening. Having been warned, having seen pictures of others, only helped a little. White and slimy like a fish's belly, but dreadfully slack; anywhere on my body I could pinch the skin and pull up a rubbery membrane the size of my palm. Pale blue veins everywhere.

After a couple of hours of fluid dripping into the arm, though, I was close to normal except for the pallor. It was odd to watch my breasts inflate from flaccid wrinkles up to their normal unimpressiveness. Maybe I should have stayed hooked up a while longer.

They fed us some neutral gruel and had us go through a careful hour of stretching exercises. Then a doctor and a crypto technician checked us one by one for doneness, then showed us to a pile of clothes and said we were on our own. I found a lavender shift and some slippers that looked like real leather, and thus armored went out to greet the brave new world.

Hardly recognize the place. There's a style for garish color combinations that make my teeth hurt. That could be partly a sensory hangover from those weird visions in the can. Pink and black, though, for walls and ceiling? Orange and purple clothing?

But there are improvements. The central park has been almost doubled in size, and they've force-grown trees there of many pleasing varieties. Even a banyan like a big puzzle house of wooden fingers. The ag level is being used to its maximum acreage, half again what's necessary for food, and there are plots of exotic hybrid vegetables and a small sea of flowers. They showed me a popular melon with flesh that's dark blue shot through with orange veins and smells like fried chicken—*Kentucky* Fried Chicken, from the long-lost US of A. Will I ever be adventurous enough, or hungry enough, to try it? Maybe they've made a chicken that tastes like canteloupe.

There certainly is a sufficiency of chickens, dozens of the smelly little things, not to mention small herds of goats and bunnies and pigs. About a quarter of the ag area has been made over into a sort of combination petting zoo/farm school, so all the kids will be used to handling animals.

I haven't seen so many children since Earth. Never a dull moment—never a *quiet* one, either, at least in public places. Kids nowadays, grumble, grumble. I can't wait to see Sandra. Right now she's not scheduled to come out until the third wave, a year or more after Epsilon orbit. Maybe I can pull some strings and move her and Jakob up to the first wave, where they wanted to be. Though it's not clear how much real authority we Pool denizens are going to have.

Maybe I don't *want* my daughter in the first wave.

The Cabinet member in charge of Entertainment (now called Sports and Entertainment) was born the year after I went crypto. He knows all about me and is very respectful. And very protective of his territory. I don't want to meddle, but anyone with an ear can tell the harpsichord is out of tune. I want it to be ready when Chul' comes out.

They told me to take it easy for a week, get oriented. Which kind of week? How about a month or two? The new months are short, twenty-six or twenty-seven of the puny days.

I don't know whether to feel cheated or honored. I was going to wake up a couple of years after planetfall, let everybody else take care of the headache of setting things up. Now I get to be part of the great adventure. One year to Epsilon, one Earth year. About two of the new flavor.

I'm just tired. They say I'll sleep a lot at first. That sounds like a great idea.

(Later, same day, somewhat refreshed) I knew it would take a while to get used to the new calendar. It's not the physical strain we'd expected, since they have this drug Tempozine (sounds like a journal for jazz enthusiasts) that resets your various biological rhythms. 'Home's day-and-night cycle is set now on Epsilon's short ten-hour day, which comes to about eighteen and a half REAL HUMAN hours.

A person who, like me, used to need six hours—REAL HUMAN hours—of sleep every night now needs a little over four and a half. But Epsilon hours are about ninety REAL HUMAN minutes. So I'll only sleep a little over three hours, ship time. But that's all I need, honest.

It remains to be seen what effect this is going to have on working, playing, eating, and so forth. I used to work a nine-hour day, at least in terms of being routinely accessible to other people. That's six new-style hours, fine. But then add the three hours' sleep, and hold it! There's only one hour left for eating, drinking, sex, reading, exercise, VR, cube, hobbies, moonlit walks, and plotting to overthrow the government. Don't forget two minutes for clarinet practice and forty-five seconds of quiet meditation.

So I have to cut down on the daily work hours. The simple fraction, 9 out of 24, gives me a 3.75-hour work cycle per 10-hour Epsilon day. Which would mean checking in to the office less than six Earth hours per day. I've spent that much time getting the rest of the day organized!

Guess I'll study how other people have adapted, especially the oldsters. They switched fourteen years ago and seem to be doing okay; not especially rushed or disorganized. They're more spread around the clock than we used to be, but our regularity was largely a vestigial holdover from Earth business practices. Shutting down labs and offices and classrooms while everybody rests is wasteful of space.

I wonder what will happen when we get to the planet, though. Almost nobody alive has experienced actual night. It does make you want to close your eyes.

Think I'll like this new way of eating, one big meal and a lot of little nibbles. Like the tapas in Spain. See how fast I gain back the twelve kilos I lost in crypto.

Maybe not at all. I like wearing Medium again. I'll like being youngest wife in the family, too.

I don't know how to feel about Evy; how to act around her. She's still pretty active for 82, working a regular shift in the Geriatrics ward. She could have gone on half-shift at 80 (or 180, Epsilon years), but likes keeping busy.

She looks so *ancient*. I can't help feeling a perverse kind of triumph. She seduced my husbands when she was a child of eighteen. How are they going to feel about her now?

Maybe I will have two husbands again. The medical people say they can do microsurgery—not nanosurgery—on John that might fix him up. They don't want to wait much longer before reviving him.

I missed a fairly uneventful forty years. We still haven't made contact with New New, though several times a week we broadcast and receive time-lagged exchanges with Key West and New York in the States, and Oxford and Melbourne in England and Australia. No one on Earth has been able to unlock a general database yet, so we're all relaying partially reconstructed data lumps and old-fashioned stuff from paper books, helping one another rebuild. Literature and art are now way ahead of science and engineering, for obvious reasons.

Key West. Jeff died about sixteen years ago. He left me a comforting farewell message that I could half believe. At least death is the end of pain. He was hurting a lot toward the end, not even able to raise his head from the pillow.

(I'd hoped to be able to "visit" him by way of VR data exchange, even postmortem. But they still haven't reached that level of technology in Key West.)

I lost him so many times, in different ways. When I went into the can I knew it was for ever this time. But still. I wish I felt more.

3

⚏

JUVENILIA

PRIME

O'Hara was one of fifty cryptos selected for "the Pool," the Planetfall Consultant Pool, people awakened early to help plan the transition from flight to colonization.

A cynic might see the Pool as a way of conferring status without the nuisance of granting authority. Everybody had to be awakened sooner or later, after all. What to do with the dozens who had been Cabinet members and Coordinators? Some of them would expect to step right back into positions of authority—but all those positions were filled. This way their talents could be recognized and used with a minimum of damage to the actual decision-making process.

They thawed out people in groups of ten, one group per week. All but one of the people in O'Hara's group survived, which was better than expected, there being a high proportion of elderly people in the Pool.

There was no set itinerary for the first few weeks; just wander around and get your bearings. Charlee Boyle came out in the same group as O'Hara, so they explored the familiar-yet-strange world together.

There were children everywhere, which was no surprise. The original plan had allowed for *Newhome*'s population to nearly double in the last ten years of flight. None under three years old, though, so planetfall wouldn't be complicated by infants.

It was less orderly than the original plan, people born in

neat blocks of proper ages, with proper genetic combinations, the creche carefully preparing them to take over their proper roles in the colonization of Epsilon.

Instead, the creche system had been in chaos for a generation; not one child in four was raised conventionally. Some children were not even *conceived* conventionally, their parents having refused sterilization, reverting to the atavism of semihaphazard fertility. (There was still a measure of control, though. The amendment that allowed fertility also set a limit on the number of children per woman, adjustable according to the current demographic climate.) Most children lived with their parents most of the time, going to Creche a few hours a day for numbers and letters. Only about a tenth followed the traditional Creche-to-age-eight pattern.

There was a drastic shortage of teachers above the level of simple writing and computation skills, most of which were provided by computer instruction anyhow, the programs imported from Earth. From seventh form up, most of the teaching was catch-as-catch-can, done by professionals taking time off from their regular duties, who might or might not have any skill in communicating to young people.

O'Hara's degrees in literature and music would oblige her to teach at least part time in those subjects. She looked forward to music, but wasn't happy about the prospect of teaching literature—let alone trying to do it when most of the books she'd studied in school weren't available. Her doctorates in American Studies and Management covered material too obscure or esoteric to be useful, and her practical experience in managing people was one skill that wasn't rare.

They wanted to tap Charlee, too. She was a chemist, but was uncertain about how well she could teach it at the elementary level. She hadn't put on a lab coat in twenty years. She could lecture for hours about arcane aspects of piezochemistry, but she wasn't sure whether you were supposed to pour sulfuric acid *into* water, or vice versa. She did know that one or the other was liable to explode.

4

≙

POOL PARTY

Age 55.05 [15 Columbus 427]—It's a revealing way of dating a diary. So I've spent one thousandth of my life wandering through this interesting chaos. Well, hully gee, Mr. Crane. Time sure flies when you're having fun.

First meeting of the Planetfall Consultant Pool was a circus. The latest bunch of Poolees, including Daniel, have only been out of the can for two days, still kind of disoriented. The first twenty or so are extremely impatient to get things moving. Charlee and I wander somewhere in the middle: will you please stop shouting? Will *you* please focus your eyes?

The Coordinators supplied us with a list of questions:

1. *There are two shuttles plus one backup, each carrying thirty passengers and two crewmembers, and a tonne of supplies, or about three tonnes of supplies and no people. How many people should go down for the first, exploratory landing? How many flights?*

My first response would be to send thirty brave, smart, but highly expendable people, along with a second shuttle full of tools and weapons. If they survive for a few weeks, we can send a larger, slightly less intrepid, bunch.

Kena Russel pointed out that all we know about the planet so far is that it's a water/oxygen world of such-and-such mass and diameter and average surface temperature. From orbit we'll be able to tell what the terrain is like, whether there are large animals—or perhaps superhighways and immigration officials!—to contend with.

232

Will we need lasers or linguistics texts? Passports? No way to know until we get there. All the advance planning is tentative.

2. *The shuttles are presumably dangerous. They were de-signed to operate within an intricate maintenance pat-tern of testing and tweaking that we've only partly reconstructed. Estimates for "time till first failure" for each one go from ten flights to two hundred. Who goes on the early ones?*

That's just an inverted way of asking who is most ex-pendable, of course. If anybody were truly indispensable because of what they know, they shouldn't go near the shuttle in the first place, because ground and orbit will be in constant communication. No one has to be "on the spot" at all, in order to impart information.

Some people are important because of what they can do, though, rather than what they know, or in addition to that. Mechanics, carpenters, surveyors, equipment opera-tors. The most intelligent and strong manual laborers. Peo-ple with proven leadership skills and organizational ability—especially with planetside experience. That's me. (Actually, there are quite a few of us, but I'm by far the youngest, at 55.05, or a spry 122, Epsilon years.)

3. *Should anybody be asked to go against their will? To stay aboard?*

To the first, I'd say absolutely not. It would be a night-marish invasion of their rights and also impractical. You wouldn't get any efficient work out of them, and they'd screw up morale.

I'd like to say no for the second one, too, but there's a practical aspect to it. Suppose each shuttle fails on its tenth flight? Nine times 30 times 3 is 810 people. The last sur-vey, combining cryptos and those of us among the warm, totaled eight thousand who want to go planetside and three thousand who want to stay aboard. A lot of people will have to wait. I suspect the numbers will become more manageable after the first shuttle wipeout, though.

(I wonder how the statistics will change once we start settlement. Some people undoubtedly will step out of the airlock, take one look at how far away the horizon is, and jump back into the shuttle. That happened to about one out of fifteen New New tourists who went to Earth, deep-seated agoraphobia.

On the other hand, if the people working planetside are successful and happy, the more timid, but not agoraphobic, may change their minds.)

4. *Should we concentrate on developing one site, or try several small settlements in different areas?*

I was almost alone in opting for the latter. But then most of these people have lived in one biome all their lives (two, if you count subzero desiccation!) and don't see any virtue in a variety of locations. I pointed out that some local danger might wipe out one place and not affect the rest—like Roanoke Island, the first British colony in America, which disappeared and left not a trace while its ship was on a resupply passage to Britain. Probably plague or a raid by autochthones. (French and Spanish settlements to the north and south were unaffected.)

Of course nothing so mysterious would happen to our pioneers. They'd have an audience.

It's another one of those questions that's not answerable until we see what the planet looks like. There may not be that much variety. Which leads to:

5. *What do we do if Epsilon turns out to be uninhabitable?*

Well, we could ram it out of spite. I didn't suggest this.

Some of the scientists got huffy and said it was a nonquestion; if we hadn't been sure that Epsilon was Earthlike, the mission wouldn't have been launched. Son Van Duong pointed out that "Earthlike" circa spring 2085 would include a mutated virus wafting around that killed everybody within a few years. To the response "that was because of a war," Son shrugged. So the war became part of the ecology.

The real question is, how much would we tell the people, how soon? Some before the others?

I think on general principles we ought to tell everybody everything, and just brace ourselves for a lot of unhappiness. A few thousand would probably be relieved, of course. (And what would the others do, leave?)

We could live indefinitely in orbit, eventually augmenting and then supplanting the matter/antimatter power source with "solar" power (epsilonic power?); just be a smaller New New York. Or maybe shift our base of operations to the planet's moon, which is about the size of Earth's.

Of course the possibility of planetwide ecological engineering, terraforming, came up. The experts were divided on whether it was a practical option, working from an incomplete database—and even if we knew exactly what to do to the poor planet, could we spare enough energy and materials from 'Home to even make a dent?

I have the obvious moral problem with going in and making over a planet just to suit us, though arguably that's what we did to Earth. It could have been worse. If the Industrial Revolution had continued another century, powered by burning petroleum and coal, Earth might have been on its way toward looking like Venus. I suppose it would have been pleasant in the air-conditioning. Spectacular scenery, too.

It *would* be frustrating to have gone through all this trouble and danger just to set up shop in orbit again, in reduced circumstances. We couldn't simply scratch this one off our list and go on to the next likely candidate. Unlike the Solar System, Epsilon doesn't have an antimatter brown-dwarf companion to tap for fuel. I suppose that in a few centuries they could come up with some other way to go from star to star.

I don't have a few centuries. Just a hundred of these short years left, more or less, and it would please me to end them on that planet, surrounded by a roomful of great-grandchildren. Who would shrug, maybe raise a glass in my direction, and then go on with planet building.

The everydayness of it, of making a new world. Some people don't get excited about that. I don't know what to say to them.

5

≙

INTERIM REPORT

Age 55.35 [25 Polo 427]—So they have a rough sort of map now. Looks like gills would come in handy.

Well, better too much water than too little. It looks a lot like New Zealand, that one big island. I never got there. Nice to have a variety of climates, from tropic to arctic. Don't like it here? Keep walking; it'll change.

Actually, it's bigger than the East Coast of the United States, and covers as much latitude as South America. And such imaginative names! I assume the people who have to live there will get around to changing them.

I find myself staring at the map and daydreaming. Whatever is it going to be like? Most of those specks are "artifacts," electronic noise, but some of them are islands. I was never on an island I didn't like, from Britain to Fiji.

Tropica is on the equator, and Iceland is below the Arctic Circle (there are permanent icepacks, north and south, that aren't on the map). The rest could be desert or jungle or paved from coast to coast. We won't know much more, except for better outlines, until about three weeks before we arrive. Three *weeks!*

Coordinator-elect Dznowski asked me to cobble together a VR simulation of the planet so that people could "start getting used to it." Hully golly gee. I asked her whether she'd rather I made it a rain forest or a metropolis. She said well, use your imagination, dear. *Dear!* I'm older than her father, who used to work for Dan. It will be a few generations before this crypto confusion wears off.

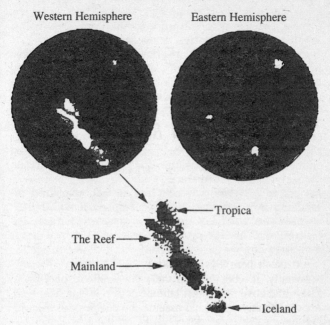

Western Hemisphere   Eastern Hemisphere

Tropica

The Reef

Mainland

Iceland

It will wear off when the last one of us dies.

So I asked around and wound up in conference with
Robert Tyree, a planetary astronomer with a bushy beard
and prehensile eyebrows. Very nice man, actually, but he's
so damned intense about astronomy that he can back you
across a room talking about atmospheric gradients.

He did sympathize with my problem: the odds of coming up with a simulation that actually resembled Epsilon
were right up there with being dealt a perfect bridge hand.
Trees that look like bright red broccoli sprouts oozing orange marmalade, why not? Wingless birds that fly with
carefully controlled and highly poisonous farts. So what
we had to come up with was a cartoon planet, a template
with the right gravity, temperature, color, and brightness of
sunlight. Let people go in and close their eyes and use
their *own* imaginations.

It was odd being in VR conjunction with a man I hardly

knew. His dick hangs to the right, unlike Dan's or John's, I guess because he's left-handed. His beard feels funny. When he looks at his feet, it touches his throat.

He's done a lot of VR in surreal modes, more even than I have, so he was really good at holding one aspect fixed while shifting another. We had the gravity as a given constant. Everything else we could fiddle with: hold the illumination level while changing the color mix; hold the air temperature while changing the humidity. I came up with one of those somatic flashes you sometimes have, and was able to make the feel of the air exactly what it had been on the beach, Guam, winter 2085. Salty, sultry, thick. Probably full of pheromones.

I got an odd feedback from him on that, something resembling awe. He was many generations removed from anyone who'd actually stood on a planetary surface, and planets were his life work, his passion. Yet he'd never even seen one.

I tried to give him the sense of total *surround,* the way Earth's spirit, you have to say spirit, quietly dominates you, not at all like *Newhome* or even New New York. These are just rocks that men and women carved into houses. A planet sits patiently for billions of years, and people come by for the flicker of a moment. You don't have to be a mystic to feel it.

We had sex while I was trying to get this across, the first extramarital sex I've had since thawing out, though I'm not sure it's adultery when you're separated by several meters, just connected by wires and thoughts. Whatever it was, it was very agreeable and very confusing. He's less than a year older than Sandra, one of the Old Guard, gray hair and all. They'd certainly met, but he didn't remember her particularly. He wasn't all that interested in women. Not that he had many boyfriends, either—you communicate the most embarrassing things in VR—usually he had sex with himself, with a cybernetic image of himself, here in VR. He could flicker back and forth between the active and passive roles, postures. He gave me a ghost of a memory of that, but it doesn't really come across well. When I have a penis in VR I'm "wearing" it, like a funny hat. The other part was familiar, of course.

So the template we came up with was about what you would experience on Earth if you were sitting in a room with unadorned white walls, open to the outside, near a beach. We kept the sultry Guam air, since Epsilon is mostly water, but I suspect it won't be accurate. People describe that as "salt" air, but salt doesn't have any smell. I think it's a whiff of decomposing marine vegetation, how romantic, and I don't know whether it's likely that Epsilon's seaweed will resemble Earth's.

Dznowski probably won't like it. I think she had in mind something fantastic but specific, like a disney. That would have exactly the wrong effect. I think she's kind of thick, and I think we aren't going to get along, and I wonder who she had to suck to become Coordinator. Probably the whole Cabinet. My assessment is not affected by her youth and beauty—I don't even think she's all that pretty, with the overdeveloped breasts and big innocent eyes and phony hair. Some men fall for that, or rise to it. Daniel turned into a preening erection the moment she walked into the conference room. Put that thing away, Dan. She's young enough to be your granddaughter.

Not that I have any room to criticize. When we were washing up after finishing the template, I asked Robert whether he would like to have actual sex sometime. He turned beet red in various odd places (I've never seen a naked man blush before) and I backpedaled fast, saying I knew I was out of line, I didn't mean to put him in an embarrassing position, but my mouth gets ahead of my brain sometimes.

His reaction was interesting, and what happened afterward was very interesting. He said he was pretty sure he couldn't have sex with a woman, but he did want to be intimate with me, without having the machine between us. Talking and touching. It was night at the ag level, so we took an air mattress down to the flower beds and lay there holding each other, whispering. At first he held me so tightly I had difficulty breathing, but he got over that phase, and we talked, trading private memories of joy and sadness the way you sometimes will when you know a person is there for you totally. We stroked and rubbed, but I stayed away from his sex, figuring he would signal me if he wanted that, and he stayed away from mine, perhaps to avoid sending the wrong message. I could have used it.

Daniel was startled, later, when I woke him up with my mouth and then ravaged him.

6

≙

CHANCES

PRIME

They had to make a decision about John. Nanosurgery was just a memory still, even though the information part of it might be reclaimed in a week or a year or a decade. But there was plain neurosurgery, microsurgery, and 'Home had three doctors who were willing to attempt the tricky cleaning and patching that might bring John's brain back to normal function, or at least close.

The Triage Council notified John's family that the surgery should be done now, in the last year before Epsilon. It was a recommendation, not an order, but their argument was strong. John would never be able to land on Epsilon, which is where most of the medical facilities would be in the future, and in any case his operation would have relatively low priority in what they expected to be a heavily overworked couple of decades.

They couldn't assign a percentage probability to his chances of surviving the operation until he had been out of crypto long enough for the fluids in his body to regain normal electrolyte balance. He might not even survive the shock of thawing out, of course, but that particular risk was not going to change in the near future.

Only Daniel was against it. He didn't like the idea of the nature of their family life being dictated by some doctors' schedules—by some doctors' advance *perceptions* of their schedules, that could be wildly inaccurate. But Evy had the greatest stake in the question, since she was the only one planning to stay aboard 'Home after orbit, and she wanted to give the surgeons the go-ahead.

O'Hara was on the fence, nervous about okaying a life-threatening procedure, wanting the best for John, and selfishly wanting the whole mess to be settled one way or the other. How many husbands did she actually have—one, two, or one-and-a-fraction?

All three of them did agree that John's attitude had been unambiguous. He would rather die than hang on alive but bound in the straitjacket of dumb paralysis.

O'Hara finally cast her vote with Evy, and they brought John out. At first it looked bad. His eyes opened, but he made no sign of recognizing his family, or anybody. The third morning, though, his eyes tracked O'Hara. She explained the situation to him and he nodded.

The operation took nine hours. Evy was not a surgical nurse, but she was allowed to attend as a supernumerary fetch-and-carry. She told O'Hara about an odd minute when she had to crouch under the table and hold a urinal for the senior surgeon, young enough to be her granddaughter, to straddle. It was scary: that child is trying to concentrate on brain surgery, my husband's life literally in her hands, and at the same time convince her urogenital sphincter to overcome a lifetime of training and habit. But brain surgeons are used to long operations, even if Evy was not.

They had been warned that the results of the operation might not be apparent for some time, so nobody was alarmed when John didn't show any immediate improvement. Within a week he had his yes-no-shit vocabulary back, and could also count up to ten. He was able to leave the hospital for his quarter-gee sickroom.

But he stayed at that level of verbal ability. After a month, the doctors conducted a series of tests and had to admit that the operation probably wasn't going to make any difference. His brain was getting plenty of oxygen. It just wasn't doing any good.

7

⌢

BE ALL THAT YOU CAN BE

Age 55.43 [11 Theresa 428]—Actually, this starts about ten days ago. Too busy to write, molding young minds, perverting the will of the people, whatever.

They've put me in charge of the Induction section— Aptitude Induction Through Voluntary Hypnotic Immersion—on the reasonable basis that nobody else wants to touch it. Also, I was in charge of it back in Earth orbit, and actually went through the first half of the procedure myself, in the process of creating Prime.

That was 26 years ago, though, by my personal reckoning, and 66 years "real" time, or 147 Epsilon years. Most of half my lifetime, anyhow. I recall the process as sort of a vague bad dream; the administration of it, a waking nightmare.

But that's not the problem now. There are a lot fewer people and I'm a better administrator than I was then. One problem is that more than three quarters of the Induction files are gone. Nine tenths were destroyed by New New's information sabotage, and only a few replaced. Another problem is a lack of motivation.

Which is putting it mildly. It's more like a consensus of rebellion. Induction is most effective on the young, and of course the best candidates are people who haven't yet demonstrated a lot of talent in any useful field. So when you offer Induction to them, they get defensive. "I don't want to be a welder, I want to be Myself!" Even though the only skill so far exhibited by Myself has been turning rations into compost.

One person who was not a problem, to my considerable relief, was Sandra's husband Jakob. He doesn't have any skills particularly useful for a primary settler—perfect pitch being irrelevant for the time being—so I showed him a list and he said plumbing looked interesting. He finished breakfast and kissed us both goodbye and went down to get reamed by the AI monster for two weeks.

Then there's the problem of the Nowers, who actually *are* just compost machines. You could probably take one by the hand and wander along off to the machine, and he or she would smilingly obey, since everything is just now happening and is an expression of God's will. But even those lumps have civil rights. The psychometricos call it "profound volitional incompetence," which I think is a profound euphemism for lump. If they went through Induction, they might be able to rejoin the human race. But it's more important, at least to some people, that they be allowed to worship in the quagmire of their choice.

Kamal Muhammed, the opinion engineer who helped us convince people to accept cryptobiosis for the common good, didn't himself go into the can. He's been in retirement for a long time, aged 105 in old years (233, Epsilon), but he still helps out now and then. I went to him for advice.

He must have one of the oddest-looking rooms in 'Home. For decades he has immersed himself in oriental arts and crafts. There are about fifty potted dwarf trees, bonsai, in a miniature forest that takes up all of the floor space except for narrow paths. The bunk where Muhammed sat was littered with worn paper folded and refolded into origami shapes. Set in the wall where most people would have a console and cube, he had an open square painted solid white. A vase with four flowers stood artfully off-center, balanced in the space by a smooth stone, the size of a fist, mottled pink and gray.

"It's beautiful," I said. "The stone's from Earth?"

He nodded. "Very perceptive. Japan. A friend has loaned it to me." The rocks we used for landscaping in the park were from a carbonaceous chondrite asteroid; I didn't remember ever seeing a pink one. "Let me demonstrate my own prescience: you have come to me because people are quite reasonably not doing what you want them to do. You want my skills to help you subvert them. For the good of the community of course."

"Yes. But I would have come to you to see the trees, if I'd known about them."

"You've been in crypto, or you would have known." He pointed. "I place you. You served a term as Policy Coordinator."

"Just shy of a hundred years ago. Epsilon years."

"Of course." He nodded thoughtfully. "And before that, in New New York, you were some sort of *enfant terrible* in Project Start-up. O'Casey, no, O'Hara, Marianne. You wrote a book. They put you in charge of Demographics for *Newhome,* a female Saint Peter at the Gate. Deciding who will ascend to the heavens."

"You have a remarkable memory. I didn't have the only say in Demographics, of course."

"And you also worked with that terrible personality template machine. The one that puts wires through the eyeballs."

"Not wires. Little sensors you can hardly feel."

"And a tiny little probe up the rectum, one can hardly feel, I'm sure. Cozy catheters. And a comfortable tube down one's throat. Exquisitely pleasing needles stuck in the arms. I have a feeling that this is what you want me to help you sell."

"At least I'm not asking you to volunteer for the process yourself. Though I'm not sure whether we have templates for bonsai and origami."

"There are books."

"We're mostly interested in less subtle talents, anyhow. Running heavy machinery, masonry, carpentry, metalworking. Skills that will condemn a person to a lifetime of hard labor on Epsilon."

"Ah. 'Skills that will reward a person with a lifetime of solid satisfaction, rebuilding civilization from the ground up.' Or 'Let the lazybones who stay in orbit live out their lives in a four-walled prison—give yourself a job that will give you freedom!' "

I had to laugh. "Did you just make those up?"

"It is a skill." He smiled slightly. "One that guarantees I will spend all my days in a four-walled prison, which is what I vastly prefer." He picked squares of paper off the bunk and stacked them neatly on a clear patch of floor. "Please sit. Let us investigate this problem."

He was very helpful. The basic procedure for motivating somebody to do something unpleasant or dangerous was to separate out the various ways a person would benefit from doing it—sexual appeal, enhanced self-image, prospect of future comfort or security ... all the way up to purely altruistic benefits such as the approval of God or to serve you generations yet unborn. He wrote down twenty-three separate areas of reward. The basic technique of opinion engineering was to figure out which of these areas would be most effective for your target population, and pack as many of them as practical into a single memorable statement. Pictorial associations at least as much as words; we're not working with logic here.

I made a series of recorded appeals, using sexy young things of both and indeterminate genders, for lumberjacking and welding and so forth, which went on the Random Walk cube. But the "advertisements" weren't scheduled at random.

People tend to watch cube at the same time each day, if they watch it. Most of the people I was seeking were more or less addicted to it. So I set them up several days in a row before each ad. I "primed" them, using Prime to help me search through the millions of small scenes in the Random Walk library. We came up with hundreds of pretty specific episodes extolling the pleasures of physical labor in the good old outdoors. Almost all of them in good weather. Maybe Epsilon does have good weather all the time.

None of the kids I'm after has ever experienced weather. Better remind them to take hats.

I should feel guilty about all this. But it's fun, and ultimately to everyone's benefit. As whoever invented television probably said.

8

≙

FINAL APPROACH

PRIME

O'Hara talked it over with Evy and agreed that she would do most of John's care-and-feeding during the months remaining until Epsilon. Evy would have him for years or decades after that. (Daniel was willing to help, but John resisted, sometimes violently; he obviously didn't want another man to minister to him.)

She tried not to resent it as John eroded her time, assaulted her emotions. Moods were one thing he could communicate: for days he would alternate between rage and depression, and then there would be days of contrition, weeks of cooperation. Sometimes, in bittersweet silent communion, she felt she loved him as much as she ever had; other times—as she told me but not her diary—enslaved by his vulnerability, she helplessly wanted him to die. Years before, he had asked her to spare him a lingering painful death by providing him some means to end it. A handful of CNS depressants and a liter of boo; an intravenous pop of potassium chloride. She agreed in principle but, even then, wasn't sure she would have the courage to do it.

She confessed to me that she thought of that sometimes, but he wasn't in actual pain, and besides, if a quick death was what he wanted, he communicated well enough with expression and gesture to get across that simple idea. Maybe he felt that even a dim spark of life was worth living. Maybe he just wanted to spare her the awful decision.

Dr. Shawn suggested to her that John might be enjoying his enforced freedom from responsibility, and might even be feeling less physical pain than he had suffered all his life. Elderly patients with degenerative bone diseases often reported less pain, or even a complete cessation of pain, after a stroke or accident caused paralysis. It might not be a trade-off anyone would choose, but it was some compensation.

John had some use of his left hand, though all his life he'd been clumsy with it. He could manipulate the cube remote, but refused to have anything to do with the keyboard or any of the rehabilitative crafts projects that O'Hara brought him. He could read, but very slowly, and seemed to have a limited span of attention. He gave up on technical papers, with one exception: at the time of his stroke, John had almost finished writing his book-length history of the Deucalion project, *Sons of Prometheus*. O'Hara fleshed out his notes to complete the last two chapters, with John looking over her shoulder, sentence by sentence.

She found out that you could do a lot of editing with three words, if they were yes, no, and shit.

Three weeks out, they had the first fairly accurate chart of their water world. The Planetfall Committee released this map and sketchy description:

Better pictures are going to be available almost hourly, but this seems like a good time to start.

The smallest details we can see here are about ten kilometers wide; the tiniest island visible in the Reef is bigger than all of 'Home's floor levels put together. The Mainland's central lake has a greater area than Earth's Lake Chad or Lake Superior.

The atmosphere is slightly less dense than Earth's but richer in oxygen, which argues for a lot of plant life, if only phytoplankton. Nitrogen is the main inert element. There is a puzzling concentration of helium, over a thousand times the terran trace, but that shouldn't have any effect on daily life, other than making balloon travel easy.

(Hotspot has a large active volcano, which could be a source of helium, though there's no analog on Earth.)

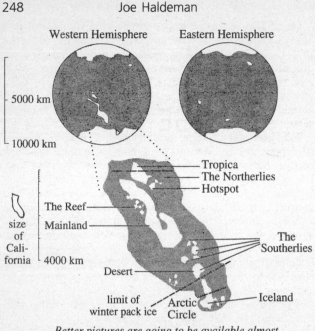

Western Hemisphere   Eastern Hemisphere

5000 km

10000 km

Tropica
The Northerlies
Hotspot

The Reef
Mainland

size
of
Cali-
fornia   4000 km

The
Southerlies

Desert

limit of
winter pack ice   Arctic
Circle   Iceland

*Better pictures are going to be available almost
hourly, but this seems like a good time to start.*

It's too soon to say much about climate or weather. Obviously there will be a great variety of conditions, since Mainland stretches from the Arctic Circle almost to the equator. Tides will be four times as high as on Earth, which of course will affect living conditions on the coasts and especially on small islands.

We're tentatively planning to establish the first settlement near the large inland lake in the temperate zone, though robot drones and, selectively, survey teams will range all over Mainland and Tropica. The polar ice caps and the four other large islands will also be surveyed, but probably won't be settled in the near future, unless they have some special virtues.

This map will be updated every day at noon.

AGE 56

≏

1

≙

DAY ZERO

Age 55.99 [8 King 429]—Coming into orbit. I opened up
the window in my floor to watch Epsilon drift by every
fifty seconds, twice a minute. Finally getting used to this
time system. Dan says it's like living a linear
transformation, which I think is a highly emotional observation, for an engineer.

I perversely miss being head of Entertainment. They're
letting me help with the big party, but it's a pale shadow
of the satisfaction you get from orchestrating the whole
thing. (I know I could look back through this diary and see
how much I enjoyed it while it was happening. That's the
nature of the beast.) I'm in charge of the scaffolding crew.
The same complicated system we've used since we left
New New, now rather sagging and worn. Aren't we all.
Complicated systems.

I want to throw myself into work to stop thinking about
Sandra. If anything happens to her, it's my fault. I knew
that she and Jakob wanted to be on the first shuttle, but
when I put in the early-thaw request I was sure it wouldn't
be fulfilled. I just didn't want her bitching at me for not
having tried. So now while I'm bolting together bleachers,
she's studying maps and practicing pistol shooting. *Pis-
tols!* What do they think they're going to run into? Revolutionaries? Mobsters?

Well, we know there are large animals, herds of them,
or at least large groups of objects that don't stay put. They
might be dangerous. But all my earthside experience with
guns was awful. I asked the mesomorphic hero who's

251

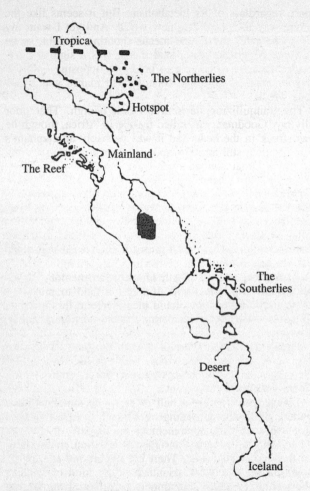

leading the expedition why they couldn't just use
tranquilizing darts like those rifles in Africa, and in answer
got a roll of the eyes and a condescending explanation that
we don't know anything about the creatures' metabolism,
so we don't know what would put them to sleep. Okay, so
I guess anything that gets blown apart does stay blown

apart, regardless of its metabolism. But it seems like the wrong way to approach a new world. And yet I want my girl to be safe, and if that means shooting straight, so be it. Some American writer said that it was a sign of intellectual maturity to be able to hold two opposing opinions in your mind at the same time. It also makes you a nervous wreck.

The tranquilizing darts aren't that benign. That poor silly boy Goodman was killed by one in Africa, though he was struck in the heart and it was probably an elephant's dose. There's still an itchy spot on my throat from a trank dart where that shitbag rapist shot me in New Orleans. "Shitbag" was what his partner called him.

A numb patch on my arm from the razor wire. A numbness like a light finger-touch from the deep stab wound in my butt, and twinges still from my nose and the teeth they had to install after that animal beat my face against the sidewalk in New York. And the one time I used a gun, the man staring unbelieving at the mangled stump spraying blood, maybe we had to kill him but the memory makes me swallow hard or vomit. If I had a God to pray to I would pray that Sandra should please live in less interesting times. Adventure is something you want to read about, not do.

Babies should come with a warning label ANYTHING THAT HAPPENS TO THIS CREATURE IS YOUR FAULT. Up to a certain age, I guess. I wonder what age that is, and whether it's the child's or the parent's.

(I would have made a hell of a creche mother. Spend my declining years brooding over the fates of a thousand people who don't even remember my name.)

I tried to have myself assigned to the first shuttle, too, but there was no chance. There are people my age, or almost, but they're either scientists or the kind of fanatics who wouldn't let mere pneumonia keep them from putting in a couple of hours at the gym every day. Nobody over fifty should be allowed to have a flat stomach. It's undignified.

(I still am putting in an hour or so, three days a week, swimming. That looks like a practical skill for Epsilon. It may be the way we commute to work.)

So the earliest I can be assigned is "secondary" stage. They won't say, can't yet say, how far away that is and exactly how many people it will entail. Hundreds. Sandra's primary stage is one shuttle of scientists and one of people like her—"Engineer Pioneers," young and strong and smart enough to know which end of a shovel works best for transporting dirt. Along with a shuttle of tools and weapons. The shuttles will come back two more times with more tools and supplies. Then, if things go according to Plan A, Sandra and her cohorts will build a small settlement there by the lake. When that's done, we secondary types will come down in ten to twenty flights, and set up housekeeping and systematic exploration. Get crops started. The tertiaries, the actual colonists in the usual sense of the word, have to wait at least a year.

Before the primaries go down, starting tomorrow, they'll have robot drones buzzing around sniffing the air, sending back pictures. Hope they don't find anything too interesting.

2

≙

FIRST CONTACT

PRIME

This is the short conversation exchanged between O'Hara and her daughter on the evening of First Day:

[10 King 429]

O'HARA: Hello? Okay, I'm here.
SANDRA: Mair! I got you! We only have a hundred seconds—look at this!

(The camera does a jerky pan around 360 degrees, showing lake, grassy swamp, an odd-looking forest with snow-capped mountains in the background, and a shuttle, sitting on its tail, lurched slightly out of plumb.)

O'HARA: Good grief! What happened to the shuttle?

SANDRA: Oh, the ground's soft. It's no problem.

O'HARA: No *problem?* What if it'd fallen over?

SANDRA: Oh, mother. You worry too much. Can you believe those *trees?*

O'HARA: They look like hands. Claws.

SANDRA: Don't they? Even with fingernails. Close up, they're covered with little red things, bugs. Some kind of symbiote, they figure, since all of the trees have them. Did you hear about the helium creatures?

O'HARA: The little balloons. They showed them on the cube.

SANDRA: We found a bigger one, too, about ten centimeters wide. They're driving the biologists crazy! They can't figure out where the helium comes from.

O'HARA: That's what Dan said. It can't be part of their metabolism because it doesn't combine with anything.

SANDRA: It looks like they do photosynthesis. Anyhow, this big one had kind of green hair all over inside it.

O'HARA: Are you okay, honey? I mean, do you feel all right?

SANDRA: I feel great! A little tired from carrying stuff. Here, look at me—hold the camera, Marko.

(The picture bobs around and settles on Sandra, striking a pose. She's wearing heavy boots and work fatigues, mud-spattered from the knees down. Sleeves rolled up past her elbows, hair a wild mess under a broad-brimmed hat. Wide belt holding a canteen and holstered pistol.)

SANDRA: Ta-da! Would you want your daughter on the same planet with this wild woman?

O'HARA:	How's Jakob?
SANDRA:	He was fine the last time I saw him, couple of hours ago. He's on the shit committee, setting up the latrines and a shower down by the water plant.
O'HARA:	You're still doing foundations?
SANDRA:	Yeah, we'll be pouring 'krete about four days. We might be pouring paths after that, if we can improvise forms from something. It's pretty muddy.
O'HARA:	You can't just knock the floor forms apart?
SANDRA:	No, they're one piece. Wasn't that great planning? Look, I've got to hand the camera over. Love you, Mair!
O'HARA:	Love you too, wild woman. Take care of yourself.

The primary landing party were warned repeatedly to "expect the unexpected," a rule that applies to almost any situation without being particularly useful. "Expect big sticky things to fall out of the sky" would have been more practical.

The helium-using organisms were a puzzle from the first day. There was the basic taxonomic problem: to the question "Animal, vegetable, or mineral?" the answer was *yes*. Both plant and animal kingdoms had availed themselves of the airbag design, which inexplicably used an inert gas.

The source of the helium would be found the next day, and would open up a new nest of problems, this time for the physical scientists. The first big problem, though, was what to do about big sticky things that fall out of the sky.

It could have happened to Jakob first; he was on guard duty at the time. There were six listening guards, posted around the sleeping pioneers, whose job it was to report to the guard captain anything potentially dangerous-sounding. They had no trouble staying awake.

The first potential danger, though, was almost completely silent. In retrospect, Kisti Seven said she thought she had heard something like the faintest breath of wind, and then a stillness—and then she was blinded, her nightglasses knocked off, and suddenly suffocating, exactly as if someone had thrown a plastic bag over her head, a plastic bag with the smell of swamp water that made a slurping sound and started chewing on her hair.

In response to some fortunate instinct, she had dropped her hand to the handle of the knife on her belt. Against the sticky resistance of the membrane enveloping her from head to knees, she managed to pull the knife from its sheath and feebly stab and slash. The thing made a hissing noise and slid off her. She stepped on the nightglasses, but found her flashlight and played the beam around and caught a glimpse of a shiny thing rolling away. In the process of switching the flashlight to her left hand and unholstering her pistol, she lost sight of the thing, but fired eight shots in its direction anyhow.

The CO_2 pistol made eight impressively loud pops, and suddenly there were flashlights everywhere, the sound of guns being cocked, and the guard captain yelling for people not to shoot unless they had a target; nobody in the middle shoot at all!

Kisti had her sodden clothes off fast, toweling the creature's slime off her exposed face and hands. The doctor gave her a quick once-over and announced that, aside from her being the palest black person he had ever seen, she seemed none the worse for the experience. She told him that it felt like the thing had pulled out some of her hair. He trimmed a sample around the area for lab analysis, and then saturated her hair with pure alcohol and rubbed the antiseptic solvent into her scalp. Then he took a sample of the slime from between her fingers, and had her bathe completely in alcohol. When she was done, her teeth were chattering in the humid heat.

Her trousers were torn below the knee, where the thing had been holding on to her. The doctor found superficial scratches on her calves, not breaking the skin. He took pictures of them for later comparison, just in case, and then dosed her with first-aid spray, which would kill any known bacterium or virus, and maybe some unknown ones.

A search party found the thing and brought it back, draped over two shovels, nearly dead. They dumped it on a sheet of plastic under the bright light in the center of camp. Some people examined it while everybody else examined the dark overcast sky, wearing hats.

The central part looked like a crab or a spider about half a meter wide, with twelve muscular tentacles that fanned out into a frame for the transparent skirt of the gasbag. Inflated, it probably made a globe about two meters in diameter, with pods ballooning out between the tentacle ribs. It could obviously move pretty fast on the ground, deflated, hauling itself along with the tentacles, which had retractable talons.

One of Kisti's, or somebody's, pellets had struck the central crab part; an opalescent watery fluid puddled underneath it. The skirt had several knife punctures and a long rip that partly severed a tentacle. Two different fluids, one watery and one yellow and viscous like honey, dripped from that wound.

Twelve was the animal's magic number. The crab part had twelve simple eyes, spaced evenly around the carapace, and twelve fingers or articulated claws in two rows underneath, surrounding a mouth with twelve teeth like blunt tusks. The claws were imbedded in a nest of hundreds of writhing cilia that slowly stopped moving as they watched. The zoologists decided to put off dissection until the morning light.

The next morning, everybody not involved with the dissection joined Sandra's crew in the suddenly urgent business of roof raising. The 'krete floors would be dry enough to sleep on by nightfall, a word that had a new connotation.

A review of satellite and drone data came up with four possible pictures of the "floating spiders." At least they were infrared blobs with central blobs that were there in one frame and gone in a frame taken a few hours later. All the pictures were nighttime. The blobs hadn't shown up on the first analysis because they were only slightly warmer than the ground.

It may have homed in on its victim's body heat. Dissection didn't reveal any sense organs that might be used for batlike sonar or sharklike detection of electrical activity. It didn't seem to have ears; its eyes were little more than light detectors. Its brain was less than a centimeter wide.

The skirt itself, when inflated, was probably a delicate sense organ. Slight updrafts would indicate sources of heat on the ground. The cilia seemed to have chemical sensors, like olfactory receptors, that would help the spider differentiate between a warm rock and a potential meal.

The digestive system was relatively simple, the mouth used for both ingestion and excretion (when Seven learned that, she washed her hair again). More than half the volume of the ropy tentacles was bladder rather than muscle, and there was a sphincter under each tentacle claw. The bladders were full of sulfurous-smelling water that evidently served as ballast.

The next day, an exploration party less than two kilometers from the camp worked their way over a ridge into a valley of rank yellow and orange vegetation, and smelled something that reminded them of the floating spider. Weapons drawn, they crept up on a bubbling swamp.

One of the creatures was splayed across the water, its tentacles moored to various anchors. It was sagging, partially inflated. It had stationed itself over a spot where a steady line of bubbles broke the surface.

No one in the party recalls anyone making a sound, but the animal sensed them somehow, perhaps by smell, and its reaction was swift. The tentacles let go of their moorings and sprayed water in twelve directions as the gasbag snapped shut. The creature rose fast, like something falling into the sky. People fired at it, but it was a difficult target, bobbing in crosscurrents, and in a few seconds it was just an iridescent dot sailing away. Dozens of other small bubble creatures flew away in reaction.

The exploration party people spread out around the perimeter of the swamp and surveyed it. It was a circle about twenty meters in diameter, with steep banks, like a crater or sinkhole. One person volunteered to wade out, but quickly sank up to his knees in muck; it took several people, pulling on a rope tied under his arms, to extract him.

Throwing the rope out with a light weight attached, sounding, showed that the pond was nowhere more than a couple of meters deep. It had probably filled up with decaying vegetable matter. (One of the team, a biologist, noted that unless this was a transient condition, there had to be Something Down There keeping the level constant. The leader asked with a straight face whether anyone would care to swim across and see if anything happened.)

One of the helium outlets was close enough to the shore for them to fill a sample jar without wading. They collected four samples of small gasbag organisms and counted thirty-nine others scattered across the surface. All but three of them had green tendrils inside, though it would have been premature to therefore call them plants. There are unicellular Earth animals like the euglena that can photosynthesize.

They agreed that this was enough of a find for one day, and filled all their sample containers with water, air, mud, and vegetation from various sites. Then they scientifically threw rocks into the water to see whether anything would happen. Nothing did.

3

≅

LETTER 'HOME

Dear Mair,

You're always after me about how important it is to practice my writing, so here's a letter. Don't faint. It's almost impossible to get on the 'Home line anyhow, with all the floating spider goatshit. Figure I can write this out and just put it on queue, and when

somebody pauses a nanosecond to take a breath, zip!
We've made contact.

It is scary. You know Jakob was on guard on the
other side of the camp when Kisti got attacked by
that thing. It gives me the cold sweats to think it
might have been him, and he might not have gotten
a knife out. Kisti says it was plain dumb luck that
she survived, that her hand was near her knife.
She's kind of fixated on it; just a second before, she
was picking her nose. What a way to die, she says,
strangled to death with your finger up your nose.

Well, we got enough roofs up for everybody to
sleep under, or try to sleep anyhow. Camp full of
hollow-eyed zombies this morning. So I got my trusty
idiot stick and went out to the trench detail. (That's
from America or England, the term for a shovel: a
stick with dirt on one end and an idiot on the other.)
We need a meter-deep trench laid from Hilltop to the
water plant.

It's not exactly challenging but it does keep the
kilograms off, and the company was interesting.
Tranj Boyle, who was doing astrophysics before he
became a fellow common laborer, tried to explain to
me about the helium. It's the second most abundant
element in the universe, I guess you knew that, but it
gets baked out of rocks like Epsilon and Earth a long
time before they cool down, and they don't have
enough gravity to hold on to it long anyhow. Earth
has something like two or four times as much helium
as it should have, depending on who you ask, and Epsilon has something like two thousand times as
much. In the case of Earth they could just tug on
their beards and say hum, something's a little off
here, but now with Epsilon they have to admit
there's something basically wrong with their notions
of what goes on when a planet forms.

Because there's no chemical way to make new helium, I guess you know. Some from radioactivity but
we aren't exactly glowing in the dark. It looks like all

the stuff that's bubbling up out in those ponds has been here all ten billion years. And it's inside the crust instead of in the atmosphere. Driving them nuts!

Well, this science stuff bores you shitless, I know, but I think it's kind of fun. Thinking about doing a geology degree once we're settled in here. I'm certainly one of the world's authorities on dirt! Seriously, geology's one of the physical sciences they've got pretty well reconstructed, at least to the bach-degree level. They'll need geologists for exploring the planet, and maybe its moon. Don't want to be tied to a desk. I want to be out there battling weird creatures and worrying Mother sick. Just kidding.

Thine own Sandra.

4

≙

HOUSEKEEPING

Age 56.16 [8 Ten 429]—This is three days' worth. Been busy.

Saying good-bye to John wasn't so bad, since I'll be traveling back and forth between the planet and 'Home for some time as General Liaison. I could have set up the job description myself: someone born in New New who had been to Earth, who had professional connections with both Engineering and Policy tracks; preferably someone who had emotional ties to people both in 'Home and on Epsilon.

The shuttle descent was smoother than the three I experienced on Earth, but the landing made me nervous, remembering the Leaning Tower of Shuttle that Sandra and her crew had scurried out of. Of course the deceleration was computer-controlled and we settled to the surface as gently as a feather. I held my breath for a moment, and the thing didn't topple over.

We unbuckled immediately and went to the exit lift, which surprised me. I thought we'd have to wait until the ground cooled some. In fact, that was the reason for the slight sideways shift I thought I'd felt just before the engine cut off. The pilot decelerated over a "hot spot" and at the last minute slid about a hundred meters over to the landing area proper, so the ground would be cool enough for us to jump out. Just in case.

Repeated landings had baked this area hard as brick. That was the first smell: scorched earth, as they used to say in a different context. Then a breeze brought cool forest smells; maybe a hint of the lake. Not earthlike, but definitely not the greenhouse smell of 'Home and New New. Alien but pleasant.

The settlement was almost a kilometer away, on top of a low rise. Three ribbons of smoke angled away, I guessed from the adobe furnaces. I could hear a faint chirping and squeaking from the forest creatures, scolding us for waking them up.

There were ten people waiting on an elevated metal platform. I hadn't expected Sandra, since she was assigned to a building detail down at lakeside, but she was among the ten. She ran over and gave me a hug, and then pulled me along to meet Raleigh Dennison, the camp's Coordinator pro tem.

We'd met several times in 'Home, of course, but he was literally a different man here. About my physical age— born a few years after Sandra—he had seemed pale and aristocratic, delicate, up there. A couple of months' pioneering had turned him tan and muscular, and he sported a piratical moustache, curled at the ends. I had to laugh at the transformation.

He laughed along with me. "It's the alien gravity," he said. "Two months here and you'll look like a farm girl yourself." I doubted that anything would make me look like a "girl," short of a time machine, but did look forward to working outdoors for the first time this century.

This flight had brought fifteen people and two tonnes of supplies. We loaded as much as we could on the utility floater and stacked the rest on the loading platform. The load for the return trip was light, a few boxes and cages of samples and animals, and two people who needed medical treatment. Hilltop's first-aid station wasn't up to cancer or schizophrenia.

We followed the floater in a slow walk up toward town, Raleigh giving us a running account of their agricultural successes and failures as we passed the various fields. Almost everything was grown in three sections: out in the open, in the open but protected by barbed wire, and green-housed, with soil imported from 'Home. There were goats, pigs, sheep, and chickens, all in protected covered pens, and pools of tilapi, salmon, and rainbow trout.

Most of the crops did well in the unprotected areas, though tomatoes, peppers, and potatoes all succumbed to an airborne microorganism, even in the greenhouses. The wire didn't seem to make any difference; local fauna would take one sniff and move on. By the same token, those local fauna seemed in little danger of winding up on our tables, at least for a generation or two. Some things are just too weird to eat.

Evolution had produced different stratagems on Epsilon. Most forms of life didn't have close analogs on Earth. Fish were recognizably fish, but the ones caught inland had lungs instead of gills. Someone who deserves a culinary medal cooked one and ate part of it. It tasted like cotton soaked in swamp water, he said, but it didn't make him sick.

To me a bug is a bug, but the biologists say the "insects" here bear no relation to terran insects except for size and orneriness—and usefulness, being scavengers and pollinators. Most of them have twelve legs, but there's one phylum that has seven! I wonder what they do with the extra one.

The closest thing to a mammal is a furry cold-blooded thing, the jumper, that actually behaves more like a lizard.

It will lie motionless in the sun for hours until something comes by that is smaller than it but big enough to be worth eating. It leaps on the thing and bites it with fangs that inject a paralyzing venom, then eats it alive, slowly. Eleven different kinds of jumpers have been identified. The airbags leave them alone, evidently because their flesh is noxious or toxic. Jumpers have never attacked a human, even though one alert individual managed to sit down on one.

The division between plant and animal is not sharp. Things like the gasbags are mobile but have a "metabolism" that includes photosynthesis as well as carnivorism. There are fixed, sessile, organisms on land and in the water that don't use photosynthesis. They often look like plants—one type has nonfunctional green "leaves"—but they make a living by luring small animals and eating them. Some affix themselves to a larger animal or plant and live as parasites or symbiotes. An extraordinary example grows with a particular kind of tree, mimicking its blossom in both appearance and smell. When a pollinator bug flies into the blossom, it snaps shut and chews it up, and then a complex digestive system separates out certain nutrients and passes them on to the tree, through a shared circulatory system.

No other land animals have yet been found that are as dangerous as the floating spiders. There is a frightening-looking carnivore that resembles a twice-man-sized praying mantis, but so far it has never attacked a human. Neither does it run away.

The oceans and the lake have a variety of large predators, which might be dangerous if one were overcome with the urge to go swimming. A drone flying three meters over the waves, about twenty kilometers from the western shore, was attacked by a thing that looked like a whale with grinning teeth. The lake has strong eellike constrictors up to eight meters long.

All these adorable animals, and we haven't yet explored even one tenth of one percent of the land area. I'm sure there are pleasant surprises aplenty waiting for us.

There is eelless swimming, finally, at Lakeside. The solar tide makes almost a meter difference in the lake's water

level, so twice a day it fills and empties a large pool they
yesterday blasted out of rock in the middle of town. A
grate keeps out anything larger than a minnow.

We got there at the end of a work shift; when the bell
rang, everybody dropped their tools and ran for the water,
stripping as they went. I watched them cavorting in the
pool and realized there was something going on that was
deeper than escaping the heat, relaxing, hygiene, and sex
play. All those kids grew up in a place where they could
walk out of gravity any time they wanted. On a planet, the
only escape from gravity is water. Or hurling oneself from
a high place.

Out of sixty people, there have been seven psychiatric
replacements; people who were defeated by gravity or
weather or horizons or just the unrelenting strangeness.
Three of them were from the Engineer Pioneer group, supposedly pretty stout in that regard. I wonder what percentage will drop out of our less select bunch.

Raleigh said I could live wherever I wanted, so long as
I could find a roommate who was willing to move out
when Dan arrived. Charlee volunteered. (Dan will be continuing as Earth Liaison, so he'll be in 'Home for a couple
more months, until the technological infrastructure down
here is sufficiently reliable. Like central electricity.) I
chose Lakeside, with the marvelous view of the water,
even though that would mean climbing ladders for a while,
and then stairs.

The houses followed a basic design we got from Key
West: put a platform up on slits, build a box on the platform, put a roof on the box. They look pleasingly primitive, since the basic building material is the tough reeds
that are plentiful in the tidal wetlands, but the technology
involved in putting them up was not primitive. The chem-
ists up in orbit analyzed the samples we sent and cobbled
together a machine that takes in water, wood shavings,
mud, and sunlight, and gives out a steady stream of magic
glue that bonds the reeds together like iron. Sandra didn't
enjoy working with it. It makes your fingers stick together,
too.

Each house has two residences that share a kitchen area
in back, and a blank space that will eventually be a toilet

and shower, once the settlement has central plumbing. Each individual residence is big enough for two adults and two children, with two bedrooms and a common room, so Charlee and I had plenty of space to ourselves.

There's no power grid yet, but each common room has a fuel cell recharged by a solar panel on the roof, so we both set up our portable consoles there. With only one table, we have the choice of working shoulder-to-shoulder or face-to-face. Or building another table, which might be interesting.

Everything that goes up or down has to be either carried while negotiating a ladder or raised or lowered on a balky manual dumb-waiter. That will keep our furnishings simple. It might also encourage constipation and fluid retention.

I love the balcony. We can sit and stare out over the lake, our private sea. Intellectually, I know that the horizon is only fifty kilometers away. It feels more distant than the stars and nebulae that wheeled beneath my feet in Uchūden.

Charlee was a little nervous about the wide-open spaces. She took one look over the balcony and ran back into the bedroom, where I found her with a pillow over her head, laughing and crying. She agreed it was silly and came back out, but for an hour I had to hold on to her while she stared and sweated and giggled.

I left the clarinet in orbit, for the time being, but did bring down Sam's harp. I've been experimenting with bluesy tunings and settled on an A minor that seems to use the instrument's range best. You have to pluck rather than strum, since six pairs of strings are adjacent half tones. I remember Mercy Flying Dove and, lacking electronics, tune with heart and head, keeping the wolves away.

When the harpsichord comes down, there will be a kind of closure. It was built in London by Burkat Shudi in A.D. 1728. I think it will be the oldest human artifact to come from Earth (we do have a dinosaur bone).

I've wondered about that name. He was Swiss, and that's all we know, but Burkat Shudi doesn't sound European. It sounds Moslem. I picture him as a dark old man with long flowing white hair, working with endless patience on these woods brought from oriental forests on the backs of slaves, on sailing ships, finally on a creaking horse-drawn wagon down a muddy London street. To tell him that his handiwork would wind up here would be more fantastic than saying it would wind up in the Garden of Irem, less believable to him. I don't think they knew, in 1728, how far away the stars actually are.

(I asked Prime and got a HOLD FOR OPEN DATA CHANNEL message—that's a first.) No. Prime says 1837.

Chul' Hermosa survived the thaw, and will be coming down with the harpsichord. He loves to teach; that will be a kind of closure, too.

We're up on stilts both for food protection and to keep pests away. The crawlies, which is what they call these seven-legged ones the size of your little fingernail, get everywhere and they bite, leaving an itchy red knot that lasts half a day. They're inquisitive and totally unafraid of humans, so far, but they do have an aversion to water. So each of our four supporting poles is equipped with a metal collar that holds several centimeters of water, and three children share the job of making sure they don't go dry. Then so long as we remember not to leave the ladder down, we won't have the things sneaking into bed with us.

It rained most of last night and it was delicious, sitting on the balcony with the raindrops drumming on the roof, distant lightning and thunder over the lake. The smell of clean water and crackling ozone. I took out the harp and taught Charlee the words to "House of the Rising Sun" and "Nine Hundred Miles." I had to explain railroads to her.

Of course she'd never seen rain before. It frightened her at first, the suddenness and force of the storm, but she did learn to enjoy it. What frightened me was seeing one of those floating spiders, frozen in the strobe of a lightning flash, skimming along in the wind down at the water's edge. Charlee was looking the other way and so I didn't say anything about it, but I was glad for the weight of the knife on my belt.

AGE 57

≙

1

$$\stackrel{\frown}{=}$$

SETTLING, UNSETTLING

The first couple of years after O'Hara arrived on Epsilon constituted a time of exploration rather than colonization. The towns Hilltop and Lakeside grew slowly, since most of the Engineer Pioneers were off on various foreign adventures. The primaries who were left behind, and most of the secondaries, were less enthusiastic about backbreaking labor than those indefatigable youngsters had been.

The slow pattern of growth, in both towns, reflected the kind of design conservatism you would expect from people who had lived for generations inside circumscribed space-settlement and starship environments. The dwellings were close together and uniform in design, if individual in decoration; streets were no broader than they had to be; there were elaborate recycling systems, including a composting toilet for each pair of dwellings. (The idea of actually letting water escape down the drain was wildly extravagant to them; letting it carry away valuable sewage would be literally unthinkable.)

The unwisdom of building so close together was exposed by a lightning bolt that set a house on fire. The reeds that formed the roof and walls weren't especially flammable but they *could* burn, and by the time the fire was put out, by a combination of mobile pump and fortuitous downpour, the struck building had burned almost to the support timbers and the two adjacent ones were half ruined. Two people died, either from electrocution or im-

271

molation; the other three residents had been able to jump to safety from the balcony. By the time a neighbor's ladder could be worked into place underneath, the inside was a red inferno.

There was a tall lightning rod a couple of hundred meters away, but the bolt had apparently bounced off it, according to the only eyewitness, though he said it could have been a trick of perspective. Should the rods be taller, thicker? Should there be more of them? The only information they had to go on was a single diagram from Key West, with two paragraphs of text.

The overall fire danger was less ambiguous. If that small gullywasher hadn't poured tons of water on the burning house, there might have been a chain reaction, destroying all of the houses on the lake side of Lake Road, or even the entire town. They had to spread out.

Leaving the burned-out ruin as a memorial and goad, they proceeded to disassemble every other house, reassembling them on both sides of town with a spacing of thirty meters between sites. The end result was unsettling, esthetically wrong to a society of agoraphobes, but they would learn to live with it. The three exceptions to agoraphobia, hermits who had erected shacks well outside the town's perimeter, had to pull up stakes again. And their number quadrupled, nine more people willing to haul food and water for the exotic luxury of not having any neighbors.

The next week, on the same night, two of those hermits were attacked by a floating spider, or by two different spiders. Both men passed out, from anoxia or sheer panic. One staggered into town before dawn and woke up Doc Bishop; the other had crawled back to the safety of his lean-to until light. Neither one of them suffered any permanent physical injury. Both of them had the same experience as Kisti Seven, with the important exception of not having been able to get to their knives. The thing gnawed on their hair, leaving a little bloody spot, and apparently rejected them as food, fortunately releasing them before they asphyxiated.

The hermit population was suddenly reduced to three again—one of them, surprisingly, one of the beast's victims. "They obviously don't have any taste for me," he said, and moved his lean-to farther out. People sometimes saw him at first light, though, standing in a field bareheaded, with a knife in each hand.

The other victim, Mark Ollen, had more subtle but more serious psychological problems. He was one of the scientists in the primary group, an agronomist. For some weeks he was almost useless at work, unable to concentrate, dragging into the lab and falling asleep over his samples or his console. Every night he would wake up repeatedly with the same graphic unsettling nightmare: the creature drinking his brains. Doc Bishop gave him pills, but the dream was stronger than them. One night he took all of the remaining pills at once, left a short note, and swam out into the lake. The top half of his body washed ashore in the next tide.

The remains were frozen and sent to 'Home, where things were better set up for autopsy. The surgeons there found nothing wrong with Ollen's brain itself. But there was one detail that Doc Bishop had missed: a hole about a third of a millimeter in diameter had been drilled through his scalp and skull, and there was a healed spot in the durum directly underneath.

Don't jump to conclusions, they said. A man who was sick enough to eat a handful of tranquilizers and see how far he could swim might well have done the damage himself. An animal feeding wouldn't have had any reason to be so delicate about it; besides, the spiders' claws weren't fine enough or strong enough to do the job.

They sent the other victim up to 'Home and, under the scab on his scalp, the surgeons found a similar hole. He agreed to stay there for observation. For the rest of his life, if need be. They also examined Kisti Seven, but evidently she had gotten rid of the thing before it had started drilling.

Nobody ventured outside at night without head protection and weapons; in fact most people spent the night at home or wherever they happened to be stuck when the sun went down. Warnings went out to all of the exploration teams.

The creatures weren't hard to kill if you spotted them.

Night was banished as a string of lights went up around the perimeters of both towns. Elevated guardhouses were staffed by sharpshooters with high-powered lasers. Extermination squads swept the countryside during the daytime.

O'Hara said it was overreactive xenophobia and counseled moderation. The things hadn't actually killed anybody, though they'd had the chance; probably many chances. Before exterminating them, it would be smart to capture a few and observe what they do under controlled conditions.

2

≙

THE HUNT

Age 57.31 [23 Galileo 431]—Raleigh let me go ahead with the idea of capturing one or two of the floating spiders (or brain-eaters, as some people are calling them) so long as I could muster enough volunteers to build a cage and go capture them.

Finding the volunteers was no problem. I'm not the only one who feels uneasy about a campaign of slaughtering the dominant form of life in the region. Charlee rounded up eleven people from Engineering and I got fourteen from Policy. We built the cage in four afternoons, basically a geodesic dome of thick reeds, the whole thing covered with tough plastic. A fan pulled cool air through hollow reeds in the top; a pair of cameras with night vision would keep our captive under surveillance.

Now the big problem is finding a captive to capture. The first day the sweep team went out, they killed thirty-four of them, using robot drones to home in on helium ponds. The second day they killed nine; the third day they

killed two. Maybe the creatures are rare. It seems more
likely to me that they're able to communicate with one another, and smart enough to clear out. Jungle primates on
Earth would probably do that. Even birds.

Raleigh's letting us use the fast floater for one day, three
days from now, so we can try a couple of hundred kilometers north of here. The drones show a concentration of
them up there. Meanwhile, we'll keep practicing our capture technique, throwing a weighted net and then pulling
the trailing cords together fast. It works fine on a soccer
ball.

Age 57.32 (27 Galileo 431)—It was almost too easy.
There were two of them floating together on a helium
pond only five kilometers away. They had somehow
eluded the killing patrols, but didn't detect us sneaking up
behind them. We got both on one sweep of the net; they
didn't resist after an initial startled reaction. They didn't
eject all their ballast water in an attempt to fly away,
which was the usual response. Maybe they understood the
net's function and saw that the tactic wouldn't work.

The dome was in a cleared field well away from Lakeside. Its floor was weeds and water; we'd borrowed a watering trough from the goat ranch and sunk it level with
the ground. Dan's enthusiasm for the project was limited,
but he helped us rig a pipe from a helium tank with a
valve so we could bubble the gas up through the "pond"
whenever we wanted.

We put the creatures in the cage and freed them from
the net, then hastily retreated. Both of them did the same
thing, one after the other: drain out just enough ballast water to rise slowly, then at the top of the dome, spin around
once, and then let out just enough helium to slowly de-
scend. Then they both spread out as flat as they could and,
over the course of an hour, turned bluish-green. It was as
if they had seen that they weren't going anywhere, so
might as well photosynthesize.

It was a transformation nobody had documented before,
but the only times we had seen the creatures at rest were
when they were floating on the helium ponds, presumably
ready to flee at any sign of danger. Perhaps they were

slower, or not mobile at all, while absorbing sunshine for energy.

Maybe this was their normal state. If so, they had to be a lot more common than we thought. Certainly they would be hard to spot from orbit; indeed, you could probably walk right by one and miss it, if it was resting on a bed of grass.

Samples taken hour by hour did show that photosynthesis was going on. By nightfall their jail had the most oxygen-rich atmosphere on the planet.

We left Katia Paz in charge overnight. She's going to let the helium bubble for an hour or so; see whether they move over to it. See how they respond to light, and so forth.

I have an odd feeling about the creatures. This has all been too easy.

3

≙

FINAL EXAM

PRIME

It is difficult to relate directly the events of that night and the changes they precipitated. O'Hara and I have gone over them time and again, she under deep hypnosis, myself working in parallel with machine intelligences more large, deep, subtle, and quick than I.

Even if you were a machine and I was telling you this story directly, you would only see a set of outlines of it—outlines not in the organization sense, but outlines as silhouettes, simulacra of truth. In the total sum of those simulacra, you would know what I know.

Telling the story to soft humans, it is not so much that *words* fail. In fact, words are appropriate quanta because of their multiplicity of meanings, their radiational and reflective powers: when I say "heat" to you, free of context, the small word carries associations of anger, thirst, passion, pain, drowsiness, as well as whatever host of personal connections the word releases from your own experience, your own ideolect. (To me, until some other context is indicated, "Heat" is a kind of energy transferred from regions of higher temperature to those of lower temperature.) It is not words that fail but rather the structures that we, machine as well as flesh, are constrained to put them into: structures defined and delimited by human consciousness.

Because something other than that is at work here.

Allow me to relate the incidents of that night and morning as if these were O'Hara's words; in fact, they are the distillation of millions of words and trillions of associated somatic measurements.

Dan's snoring woke me up in the middle of the night and I weighed the comfort of the warm blanket against the discomfort of holding back and decided to go pee. I put on a robe against the slight chill, breeze off the lake, but left the hat and knife on their pegs. The walkway to the toilet was covered now.

The thing was waiting in the rafters outside the toilet. It let me go inside and relieve myself. When I stepped back out, it fell and enveloped me.

There was a sharp pain on the top of my head, like being stuck by a pin. I tried to scream but couldn't draw a breath; the membrane was fast against my mouth and nose.

It spoke to me: *Don't cry out. I will let you breathe, but you must be quiet.* The order was clear and specific, though it was not in English, not in words. I nodded, and a hole opened in front of my mouth. When I had taken a couple of breaths without calling for help, the membrane that clasped me from head to knees slowly relaxed its grip.

Carry me down the ladder. The membrane parted in front of my eyes. I walked toward the ladder like a person wearing an elaborate top-heavy costume. I knew the thing was in my brain, but that didn't bother me. I'm not sure whether it was controlling the chemistry of my brain in order to subvert panic, or it was communicating "trust me"—or I was in such a state of shock that I would do whatever I was told, no matter who or what requested it.

It felt like a kind of VR. But it was not a dream. It was happening.

I slid the ladder to the ground and carefully backed down it. *Now walk into this hole.*

I knew the hole wasn't real. Between the road and our house there had appeared an artifact sort of like the antique "postmodern" subway entrances in Atlanta: an unornamented and well-lit plain ramp descending into the ground at a comfortable fifteen-degree angle. This was metal, though, not cement. It went about twenty meters and turned right, still descending. As I walked down, I could feel it closing up behind me.

Forming each word carefully in my mind, I asked Where are you taking me? It didn't answer, but communicated a desire for me to be patient.

We passed through a sort of invisible wall, a soap bubble of resistance, and we were suddenly in an arctic waste. My bare feet burned and curled on the ice; my skin raised up in gooseflesh. An instant later I was warm again.

The creature slid off me with a slurping noise like a silly sex joke, taking my robe along with it, inside out over my head. It floated in front of me and dropped the sodden robe, which froze solid before it hit the ice. *Are you comfortable?*

I said I was and looked around. Epsilon squatted low on the horizon, a red ball that looked too large, the sky blue-violet, cloudless, three dim stars showing. There were fantastic ice mountains with ragged razor edges like primitive chipped flint tools. A constant wind keened at the upper limit of audibility and granules of hardened snow rattled along the ice. It smelled like metal.

Behind me, the collapsed remains of a small hut. A corroded machine stood next to it; atop a five-meter pole, a thing with eccentric vanes spun madly, clicking, squeaking. On the door to the hut was a faded stencil:

U.S. GEOLOGICAL SURVEY
WEDDELL SEA METEOROLOGICAL MONITOR #3
PLEASE REPORT DAMAGE
L. AMERICA
3924477 COLLECT

This is Earth? I asked.

Yes. I wanted someplace on Earth where you had never been, so you would know it was not taken from your memory, and a place where there were no people around to be confused by our sudden appearance.

You can travel to Earth? Anyplace on Earth?

Many planets. Step forward.

I took one step forward and popped through the bubble again, onto the metal ramp, and then another step into warmth and darkness. The creature was still in front of me, slightly luminescent. The darkness was silent. It smelled like we were in a forest. I asked whether this was Earth.

No, we are back home. Not far from where you live. Sit down.

I patted the spongy moss and nothing crawled. I sat down carefully, feeling helpless, anus clenching. I asked if this were telepathy.

There is no such thing, to my knowledge. We are physically joined. I reached up and touched a silken thread. *Don't pull on it. That would damage you.*

I asked What's going on? Are you going to hurt me?

Not yet. Then there was an overwhelmingly complex montage of thoughts, indecipherable, chilling. *Sorry. There are many others listening. I will keep them from intruding.*

I said that they didn't sound friendly.

Why should they? You represent the alien species that has invaded this planet. They are tired of your actions and angry at having to deal with the moral complexity of the problem you have caused.

I said that we wouldn't have killed his people— people?—if we had known them to be sentient.

Maybe you would not have. That was our decision; we assumed from first contact that some would die if we kept our nature secret. That's not the problem.

The problem is whether to allow you to continue exist-ing.

I felt the dimension of that "you." I asked whether they would kill everybody.

On this planet and in the starship and on Earth and in orbit about the Earth, every person and every cell of pre-served genetic material.

I said that that was genocide. Why kill the people on Earth?

Genocide, pest control, it depends on your point of view. If we didn't destroy them, they would come again in time.

I was glad to know that there are people still alive in or-bit about the Earth. I said that we thought they might have been destroyed.

More alive in orbit than on Earth or here. Whether they continue to live will be decided by us and by you.

I asked whether I had been chosen, or was it just chance?

We interrogated three people. All three identified you as best for our purposes.

I asked why.

It can't be expressed exactly in ways that a human would understand. An obvious part of it is having been many places, known many people, done many things, com-pared to the others; giving what you would call a large database. Part of it is trust, or reliability, combined with egotism. This makes it easier for us to communicate with you.

I also sense that the stress of our liaison is not going to motivate you to destroy yourself, as happened with one of the others, and may happen with the second male. Al-though it cannot be pleasant for you, knowing that I am inside you.

I said that it was very unpleasant. I supposed that it was equally unpleasant to be inside an alien's brain.

Unspeakable. This union is normally used for times a human would call sacred. The specific word came through, echoing. *You yourself would not employ that word.*

I said that I would not use it in a religious sense; that gods were the inventions of men, sometimes women. I

tried to communicate that I was nevertheless capable of
appreciating transcendence, numinism.

Let me show you something godlike. Rise and follow.

I stood up and stepped into blinding light. Orange with
ripples of yellow and red. We seemed suspended, no gravity.

*You are seeing heat, not light. We are in the center of
your planet Earth. If it were desirable, or necessary, I
could open a passage from here to the surface. Within
hours, the planet would be a dead ruin.*

I asked What could cause you to do that?

You.

Though I personally wouldn't have to do it. We were
suddenly back in the forest's humid darkness. *Any of us
could do it, as an expression of will, if you cause it to be
necessary.*

I told it that I did not want the responsibility.

It must be an individual. You may suggest another.

I thought about that and said No, as well me as anyone.
If this is a test, I have some talent for that.

*The first thing we want you to do is simple. Stop them
from killing us. You have one day.*

The tendril slid out of my head, trailing wetly on my
brow for a moment. The creature disappeared, then reappeared with my robe and dropped it at my feet. It was stiff
as cardstock, so cold it stuck to the skin of my fingers.

I would wait for it to thaw. There was a faint yellow
light, three or four kilometers away, that I assumed was
Hilltop, but I didn't want to go crashing through the
woods in the dark. Sunrise in an hour or so, and I had
some thinking to do. Some feelings to get under control. I
touched the icy fabric again, to reassure myself that this
had really happened.

When the gown was as warm as it was going to get, I
put it on, despite the clamminess, for protection against
thorny twigs and vines. I started walking as soon as I
could see individual trees, while I could still barely follow
the yellow light. It did turn out to be Hilltop—not some
floating spider shopping mall—but I bypassed it and went
straight to my house. On the way, I shucked the damp

gown and rinsed off in the swimming pool. Alien mucus, how picturesque.

After living with him for thirty-four long years and two short ones, I knew better than to wake Dan immediately. I heated some water and put a cup of coffee on the table next to him. I sipped on mine while waiting for the smell of it to work through to his subconscious and ring a quiet bell.

He grunted, rose on one elbow, rubbed his eyes. "What the hell time is it?"

"Later than you think, dear." I laughed. "I just came from a meeting."

Raleigh Dennison was infuriating. He didn't deny that I had been "attacked" by one of the creatures, not out loud, though he did wonder why, this time, it didn't pull any hair out. Doc Bishop went over my scalp with a magnifying glass and did find a tiny dot, but he couldn't be sure that's what it was without using the axial tomography equipment in orbit. He pointed out that I was due to go on the next shuttle, two days hence, as part of my regular schedule. I could come back with real proof.

"That will be too late. I'm not going anywhere, anyhow, until we change our policy toward the natives."

That amused Dennison. "Natives! Like your American Indians."

"Sure. It would be just like the Europeans and the so-called Indians all over again—if the Indians had nova bombs and short tempers."

"Really."

"Worse than that. As I said . . . any one of them can kill every one of us with very little effort. You don't have any choice."

"Ah, but I do. I do." He looked around his office, with its sheet-metal walls, metal and plastic furniture, monitors instead of windows. The air was cooled and filtered and a ficus tree grew under an artificial light. It was a crude handmade caricature of his office in 'Home, and it spoke volumes. "I have three choices. Inaction comes to mind first. Second, hold off action until you have been properly examined."

He swiveled to stare at me, seated slightly below his level, how subtle. "Actually, there are two more choices, even if I take what you have said at face value. I could tell everybody to put away their weapons and start treating the brain-eaters as the sentient, omnipotent creatures they are. *Or* I could see that you've been through a terrible experience that resulted in completely convincing hallucinations—"

"You can't—"

"—and suggest that you seek help from the specialists in 'Home. *Strongly* suggest it."

Dan spoke up from the corner where he was leaning, watching. "That's ridiculous. She's the sanest person in this room."

"You're not the best judge of that," Dennison said.

I appealed to Bishop. "What do you think, Doctor? Can a person respond to physical trauma with a sequence of 'completely convincing hallucinations'?"

Bishop started to speak, but Dennison interrupted. "Maybe not a normal person, but Dr. O'Hara is *not normal!* Her alien torturer supposedly made a big deal of that!"

"Alien torturer, come on—"

"And one very significant way she is not normal is a half-century of dependence on virtual reality machines. A dream world is natural to her."

"That's a stupid libel. I'm not dependent on VR or anything else."

He leaned back with a smug smile. "I have access to 'Home's dream room logs. You essentially had your own private machine for most of the time you were Entertainment Director. No one alive has logged even half the VR time you have. Can you deny that?"

"I have no reason to. Most of that use was job related. If I were addicted to the damned thing, why would I have worked so hard to be assigned down here, where there aren't any of them? If I'm addicted, why haven't I been bouncing off the walls for two years?"

"You go back to 'Home all the time," he said. "I assume that you—"

"Assume away. Try to find one time I used the dream

room in the past two years. You won't." I stood up and turned my back to him. "This isn't productive. Dan, how long will it take to cook off the shuttle?"

"Thirty-four minutes." He checked his watch and pushed a button. "We can rendezvous with 'Home in seventy-two minutes."

"Let's go."

"I can't authorize that," Dennison said.

I turned around and planted both hands on his desk and leaned down. "Read the fine print, Raleigh. You're temporarily in charge of this settlement, but you don't outrank me. That shuttle belongs to 'Home, and on 'Home's table of organization I'm a twelve, and you're a ten. I'll let you come along, if you want. You might want to talk to some people about a new job."

He leaned away, almost comically. "Hold on, now. Let's not be hasty."

"We have eight hours to save the lives of everybody here and on Earth, and you don't want to be hasty? We don't have time for you."

"All right, all right!" He put on a headset and asked it for Channel 12. "This is Dennison, anybody there?" He pushed a button and we heard the response through a desk speaker.

"Niels here. What's up?"

"There's been a . . . well, quite a complication. I want you to bring all units back immediately. Stop killing the creatures."

"Easy enough. We haven't even seen one since yesterday afternoon. I think they're pretty smart."

"Yes. They probably are."

"We can be back before noon. Endit?"

"Endit." He took off the headset. "Will that satisfy you?"

"For now, yes. Of course you'll want to get the message to the other outposts, and put it on the day's announcements here."

"Of course. If you want, you can go tell Red Heliven how you want it worded. He should be in his office by now."

"Okay."

"Look. I'm sorry I was so short with you. But you know I'm ... close to Katy Paz, and one of your damned things almost killed her last night."

"The specimens she was guarding?"

He nodded. "One of them got out and started to choke her. She blacked out and woke up inside the damned cage. It was hours before somebody came by and released her."

"How did she get in the cage? The thing didn't carry her."

"She didn't say. She's under sedation. The other one was in the cage with her all that time."

"Did it try to attack her?"

"No, it never moved. The recording shows that it stayed in the, what you call it, vegetative state."

"I hope nobody harmed it."

"It's under guard, armed guard. They won't shoot unless it tries something."

"I'll talk to her when she wakes up. Maybe I could make her feel better about it. I don't think it wanted to hurt anybody."

"It hurt her." He suddenly flinched. "Jesus!"

One of them had materialized behind me, floating at eye level. I wondered whether it was the one that had taken me to Earth. Or whether it made any difference which one it was. "Don't do anything," I said softly.

It spoke. Actually, it made a sound that can't be described politely, like a modulated belch or fart. "O'Hara. Thank you for this thing. Dennison. Thank you for this thing." It was forcing air through a slit between two tentacles. It slowly descended as it spoke, losing helium. It spilled swamp water onto Dennison's floor and rose again.

"What do I do next?" I asked.

"This way is not enough. Let me into your head." A pink tendril uncoiled toward me.

Daniel stepped forward. "Use me instead." It didn't surprise me that he would do that, but it made me proud. He would be a lot more afraid of it than I was.

"No," the thing buzzed. "It has to be her."

"It's okay, Dan." But it was worse when you could watch it happening. The wet thing felt its way through my hair, and there was a little pain as it removed the scab and a kind of pressure, like the onset of a sinus headache, as it slipped down into my brain. The room got blurry, but I realized it was just that I was looking through the creature's skirt as it enveloped me. *Tell them we are going somewhere and will be back soon.* I did that and we fell through the floor, to the sloping metal ramp. Without being told, I walked forward until we passed through the resistance—

And stepped into a hall of monsters. Bipedal lizards with huge tyrannosaur heads, barracuda snouts with needlesharp fangs, black globes for eyes; three meters tall and slab muscle under gray wrinkled skin. They wore elaborate vests of metal links, some short, some reaching the ground, rattling as they moved, and they moved constantly, tails flowing in counterpoise, almost human hands gesturing as they growled. The near ones also made a noise like leather folding, creaking, and they smelled good, sweet and fresh like a baby's hair. There were about thirty of them, and they all turned to look at me. Feel like a snack, O'Hara? Oh yes.

We were in a cave where dripping limestone had calcified into fantastic shapes, pink like melting flesh or the grayish white of exposed bone. Yellow flames flickered from a hundred oil lamps.

This is a sort of tribunal. When a case is morally peculiar, they enlist our help to bring in foreign advisors, to give them a different perspective. What you decide will not be binding, but will add to the sum of their deliberations.

I asked what the moral problem was.

It has to do with familial responsibility. The female lays eggs in clusters, typically fifty to sixty at once, in pools of warm water. They do this only three times in their life. A male of their choice sprays the eggs with milt and then guards them until they hatch.

It takes about thirty days for them to hatch. The male never leaves, never sleeps. It is physically difficult for him, but an honor that happens only a few times in his life.

He eats about half of the eggs in order to stay alive, one per day. It is his responsibility to study the egg cluster, and cull the least active ones, so as to increase the probability that the ones that hatch will be strong, and survive.

Eating the eggs is physically and spiritually revolting. Sometimes the eggs die, though, and that is much easier.

In this case the male could not bring himself to eat. He starved for eleven days, and then removed fifteen of the eggs from the water. When they dried out and died, he ate them all. He was seen doing this, and does not deny it. Many males do encourage the egg to die before they eat it, although this is considered a venial sin, because the male's suffering supposedly invests the remaining eggs with strength. Most males and some females consider this to be a meaningless superstition.

But to devour fifteen dead eggs at once is unheard of. The male claims that he was irrational from hunger and a virus that affected his central nervous system. A healer confirmed the presence of the virus, but pointed out that he would not have been infected if he had been properly eating the eggs. It is well known that there is a protein in the eggs that strengthens the immune system, and watcher males who don't eat them fall ill.

The problem is further complicated because this is the female's last brood, the brood expected to provide physical support for a female in her declining years. But they are physically incompetent, slow and feeble, all but five of them carried away by predators in their first year.

I said that an obvious approach would be to require that the male support the female, or in some way guarantee her support.

This is not possible. The male agrees that he must die for his irresponsibility.

I asked Why couldn't he put off dying long enough to guarantee her support?

He must die while the guilt is fresh.

I asked if it could tell me something about the nature of this support. I said that in most human societies, it would be a form of money, which the female would use for food, shelter, and protection.

This culture has evolved beyond the need for that particular abstraction. The support normally offered by the brood is physical: they take turns bringing her food and guarding her while she sleeps.

I asked why the male should not be required to do this himself.

The very sight of him infuriates the female. Only the solemnity of this time and place keeps her from taking his life now.

I asked about his other offspring; whether they could divide among themselves the responsibility for the female's care.

That would be a possible solution if he had any. This is the first time a female has asked him to mate.

I suggested a community solution, that one baby from each of the next fifteen or twenty broods be given to the female to raise as her own.

They would not obey her. Parents communicate with their infants by smell, and they would know she was not their mother.

The tribunal thanks you for your contribution. They have decided. One saurian came up behind another and, in a quick smooth motion, pulled the back of its vest down, pinioning its arms. The trapped one looked up, closed its eyes, and roared. A third one leaned forward almost delicately and bit down on the exposed neck and tore half of the flesh away in one jerk. The roar became a gurgle and the creature sagged, brown blood drooling from the wound. The others looked away until it dropped unconscious, and then they fell on it, feeding noisily.

I said that by my culture's standards that was an extreme punishment for irresponsibility.

That was not the male who was killed. It was the female, granted a swift and dignified end. The male now faces a premature old age, unprotected by family or society.

Your confusion is understood. Your anger is inappropriate.

I said that I could never be so cosmically objective as to approve of that inequity. If this test is to see whether I can mimic your alien attitudes, then you may as well stop now.

That is not what is being measured. This is not a "test." Step forward.

We were up in 'Home, in John's room. He was sleeping

calmly, though in his usual tense position, a respirator taped over his nose.

This male faces his old age well protected by family and society. Yet his life is over, except for pain and frustration. At a word from you I will end it quietly, by stopping his heart. No pain, not even a consciousness of the end.

I said no.

You say you love him. You have admitted to yourself that, as far as you can divine his feelings, he does wish to die but is physically incapable of ending his own life. You believe he is not asking for your help only in order to spare you moral pain. You have said this to your wife: "If he wanted our help I would know."

I said that was an accurate assessment. I asked whether it could use its powers instead to restore John's abilities.

No more than I could unscramble an egg. Disorder at the quantum level is sacred. Allow me to end his pain.

I said that I could not. That it would be the same as my taking off his respirator and smothering him with a pillow.

This is something you have done in your imagination.

I said of course. Although my imagination favors pills washed down with boo, or intravenous potassium chloride. *Die Gedanken sind frei,* I told it; my thoughts freely flower. My actions are limited.

Follow me, then.

It was not a planet where humans could live without protection. There was a killing methane smell that stopped after one breath. The gravity was crushing; cartilage creaked and popped and both breasts sagged heavily, as if someone small were hanging on there for dear life. We stood on a pebble beach, like the one at Brighton, but the gray fluid that greasily curled ashore was not water. A thick yellow vapor crawled around my ankles. Lightning danced green overhead, in a sky where particolored clouds raced in swirling parallel bands. I said it felt like Jupiter, in the old Solar System.

It is not. This is much more clement, a neighbor of Epsilon's. Some day your descendants may live here independent of life support. Of course they will no longer be recognizably human in form. They will be something like this.

I changed. It was horrible. My skin became scales, over-lapping plates of some clear mineral like mica. My arms and legs split into four pairs and I fell to the ground, hands and feet like flippers splaying over the shifting pebbles. From my thorax grew two pairs of prehensile tentacles, one pair muscular, ending in hooklike claws, the other ending in a delicate cluster of fingers. I tried to speak, but there was just a clattering of mandibles.

Go into the sea. Eat or die. This is real.

I tried to ask it mentally whether I could breathe under the fluid, like a fish, but the connection had evidently been broken. I would find out when I got to the sea.

At first, trying to operate the eight limbs, all I did was push pebbles rattling away in all directions. I had never paid much attention to the way a crab or spider walked. Then I figured out that going sideways was the key: reach out with all the right-"hand" ones, set them down, then a little hop with the left ones. Turning was pretty simple, by coordinating upper and lower pairs.

The trick, though, was not to think about it at all. This body did know all it needed. In fact, to use a mundane analogy, it was a lot like VR in the abstract mode; you just *un*-concentrate and trust the brain to tune in to whatever the environment throws at it.

I looked up and the sinister roiling poisonous sky was calmingly beautiful, like a sunset after a storm. I liked the way the pebbles slid around under the paddles of my feet, and deliberately skidded in a 360-degree twirl. The smell of the ocean was the smell of life: life to be taken. I was famished.

I slid quietly into the greasy surf and the breathing holes on the top of my carapace automatically closed with a soft sneeze; the gill plates on my belly opened and sucked in the earth-flavored shallows. A little deeper and it would be refreshing. I discharged wastes and kicked forward and down.

Blind at first, confused. As the rattle of surf diminished behind me, I realized this was a world of sound, of rang-ing distances by loudness, and relative speeds by a kind of color, blue things approaching and red things fleeing. So-nar interpreted as sight. The rocks of the shoreline were dimming rust, then out of the billowing darkness in front of me a bright blue S undulated, an eel or a snake with outsized jaws. I instinctively pulled in the soft tentacles and extended the muscular ones *en garde;* all eight paddle-feet slapped together to make a cage protecting the thorax.

The thing halted and regarded me for a moment, and then slipped away, reddening. The lesson was obvious, though. I was hungry, but I was also food.

So what did this body eat? I had no inclination to pursue the predator; there was a vague impression of how vile they tasted when you had to bite one in defense.

There were things under the mud here that were delicacies, spiny clusters like sea urchins on Earth, but I would be vulnerable, digging for them. Why? The body's memories were unspecific, childlike. Nice to eat but ooh watch out. Safer to go into the deep coldness where nothing can sneak up on you, chase down the small swift things that live on the hard bottom.

Swam over a precipice and down deeper, pressure painful but then the carapace creaked, valves fluttered and popped, the pain went away. I bumped once against the cliff face but then paddled away from it. No noise going down.

The things on the bottom resembled the king crabs I remembered from Alaska, absurdly small bodies and long legs full of meat. They were all over the rocky bottom; all I had to do to catch one was extend my legs like a cage and envelop one at random. As it tried to scrabble away, I reached in with the claws and snipped off two legs, then crunched into the thorax.

I had to eat carefully. The noise of cracking the crab's shell momentarily blinded me, and I was certainly the biggest meal in town, if something larger than me was hunting. Instinct took over while I was anxiously looking around, and the thing's long serrated tongue slipped into the broken-off claw and sucked the meat out quietly.

The crabs were no smarter than they had to be. They stayed a few meters away while I was feeding, but when I was through with one, all I had to do was spring up, paddle sideways, and drift down on top of another. The females were best, with exquisitely sour egg cases.

Suddenly there was an explosion of pain behind the mandibles and I was jerked up away from my meal, rising faster and faster toward the surface of the sea. I was hooked! My claws found the line that was hauling me but couldn't break it. All I could do was ease the pain by pulling back, so the barbs in the soft part of the jaw and tongue weren't dragging all of my weight, but when I pulled, whoever was on the other end of the line jerked back.

I splashed out of the sea and onto a low flat raft. A thing twice my size but with six legs—no, four legs and two arms, one arm holding a huge club—scuttled toward me with obvious intent, while another one held the line taut. Their heads were insectoid and they had a chitinous exterior like mine, but wore boots and gloves and chains of gold and silver.

Suddenly the floating spider appeared between us, throwing out tentacles to hold itself fast to the raft, looking fragile as it bobbed in the random gusts of wind. The one with the club stopped and froze. The pink tendril floated toward me and lay across my back, then slapped a couple of times. It couldn't make contact.

I was fading, fainting from the shock and pain—and then realized that in the confusion and panic I hadn't breathed; I was still in the gill mode. The blowholes on my back sneezed open and I could feel the tendril slide in.

I was looking down at my bare human feet. Between them was a metal line that ended in a cluster of bloody hooks. I looked up just in time to see the two fishing creatures shriek in unison and jump off the raft. Unbalanced, the raft tilted and the cold sea splashed up between my legs—

And I was in absolute darkness, absolute silence. I tried to speak but there seemed to be no air in my lungs. I tried to feel for a pulse but there was no sense of where my hands were; neither could I feel whether the creature was still connected to me. There was no smell or taste, no sense of balance or imbalance, not even the feeling of having bone, muscle, and gut that still remains in VR when it's set to null input.

Could I be dead? I asked the thing: Am I dead?

Nothing.

Perhaps it was giving me a chance to reflect on what I had been shown. Try to find a common thread. Antarctica and the center of the Earth were just demonstrations of its power. Then there was the dinosaur tribunal. John's bed of pain. The transformation and hooking. Three situations about empathy, two of them also about judgment.

There was something there in the dark with me. Something large.

The spider thing was there, too. I couldn't tell what they were doing.

I felt it enter my brain. *This may be the last thing. Hold on to the rope very tightly.* A crude hairy rope several centimeters thick appeared in one hand. I grabbed it with both.

The darkness snapped off and I was blinded by a brilliant yellow glare from below. Gravity dragged me down and I clamped the rope between foot and ankle, wrapped it around a wrist. I swung wildly, sneezed, and coughed. The atmosphere was smoky, sulfurous with a tinge of chlorine or something.

Ten meters below me bubbled a river of molten rock, so hot it ran like syrup, bright yellow with scabs of black shot through with red. The pain on my bare soles was terrible; I could feel the skin burning, blisters swelling.

Sandra swung a few meters away, shrieking incoherently, a similar rope binding her wrists together. Younger and stronger, she pulled herself up into a gymnast's ball, to get as much of her as far from the heat as possible, but her naked back and buttocks were angry red, blistering as I watched. Her hair started to smoke.

Hang on for twenty seconds and you will be spared. But your daughter will drop to her death. Let go and your daughter will live.

I screamed one word on the way down, maybe her name, and was surprised not to die instantly. It was blowtorch hot as I fell, but when I hit the river it was like fluid ice; I bobbed up once and saw the terrible ruin of my hands, flesh running in strings, smell of cooked meat in my throat, tried to scream but my mouth was melted closed.

They tell me that I reappeared in Dennison's office just

an instant after I had disappeared. At first, they weren't even sure what sort of weird apparition I was, skinless, smoking—not even bipedal; my legs had fused together.

Doc Bishop saved my life with an emergency tracheotomy, slitting my throat with Dan's knife and inserting a plastic drinking straw that was one of Dennison's quirks. It would be some months before I could feel grateful for his action.

They could do emergency procedures on Epsilon, massive painkillers and fluid replacements. Surgeons came down from 'Home to install temporary plumbing to empty my bladder and bowels, and they set up a gel bath to keep gravity from killing me. Time crawled by in one long scream of pain.

By the time I had any sense of days passing, it was a month later and I was in 'Home's zero-gee surgery, new skin being grafted on a patch at a time, eyes starting to work. Something like a face being constructed. My ears were just holes but they built convincing copies. 'Home had a large file of cadavers to choose from, since crypto failures were not thrown away unless their will so specified.

Everything personal and feminine had to be rebuilt. My breasts had been seared off. Buttocks and the lips of my sex melted into seamless scar tissue. I actually came out of it looking a little better than before, breasts not sagging and a couple of kilograms less in the rear. I don't think it will catch on as a beauty treatment, though.

Sandra was at my side all the time, as soon as her own treatment allowed her out of bed. She did experience those seconds of dangling terror, and intuited what I had done but didn't know how it had happened. Me neither, kid. Once I had hands with skin, she held my hands and told me how well I was doing, made little jokes, kept me up on hospital gossip. There were no mirrors in my room, but from other people's expressions I knew how dreadful I looked. Never from Sandra, though; nothing but chatty optimism and encouragement. I know what it cost her to look at me and smile, day after changeless day. I was proud that she was my daughter.

And I was proud of Evy, who had retired a month before, but came back on duty to shoo Sandra away and do the ugly and painful things that someone regularly had to do. The woman I never admitted hating when she was young became one I had to love when she was old.

For more than a hundred-day year, Daniel never came when he knew I was awake. Six times that I know of, he sat by my hammock in the darkness and wept. He and John were close as brothers and I know that daily confronting the disastrous wreck that John had become was grinding him down. And now this. His wife turned into a waxen monster. Later I found out that he had stopped drinking for the duration of my treatment, or until I died. That was both brave and smart of him.

After three hundred days they brought me a mirror and allowed me to be amazed at their handiwork. My face was like a scrupulously accurate sculpture, minus a few wrinkles and a mole. It felt a little like a mask, and not just from the slight physical awkwardness. They left the mirror with me and I stared at it for a long time before I realized what was wrong: we look at our own face and we don't find just the features that anyone sees. We see a history reflected, joy and sorrow, love and loss. This face was missing the memory of one second of death agony and three years of necessary torture. Perhaps just as well.

Speaking of torture, my physical therapy increased, and month by month I moved down through quarter gee and half gee to where I could eventually be trusted to walk around on Epsilon and occasionally pick up something light. Dan and I resumed making love, and there were happy surprises there. Every woman should have her nervous system rewired after menopause.

I spent an hour or so every day with John. He seemed as alert as ever, though weaker. I talked with him, or at him, a lot about the strange adventure, the testing, whatever, I'd been through. I had never missed so much his ability to talk. Of all the people I've known, he would be the one most likely to help me understand. That was partly his wisdom, both worldly and abstract, and partly the universe of pain we shared now.

He would be involved, soon enough. Maybe I felt that.

I don't believe in the supernatural, or tell myself that I don't, but those creatures (the eveloi, as they told us to call them) obviously have some control over time. Maybe I was forewarned in some way.

In another year I was well enough to return to the surface. It was hard to say good-bye to John, after seeing him every day. I had my old Liaison job back, so I would see him periodically, but it was going to be the way it had been before. Afraid that each parting would be the last. He was only eighty, Earth-years-minus-cryptobiosis, but he looked and obviously felt a lot older. Besides, as we'd been warned, a person who's had one serious stroke usually dies of another one.

But it was glorious to step out of the shuttle and into the warm breeze. I'd spent a lot more time in orbit, in hospital, then I had on the planet, but emotionally this was home. It was spring, and the perfume of blossoms was intoxicating, a mixture of transplanted Earth smells and alien ones. The lift door was an open gate now; I could look out past Hilltop and see how Lakeside had grown. Crop and orchard land had more than tripled, but it was laid out carefully with respect to the natural forest line, in accordance with the eveloi's wishes.

Most of the eveloi had moved to an island on the other side of the planet, asking that we stay away from them for the time being. Two had remained behind with us, though, so I wasn't surprised to see one of them among the welcoming committee at the loading dock. After my tearful embraces with Sandra and Charlee, and less emotional hellos for Odenwald, Dennison, and Doc Bishop, I saw the creature float forward and extend its pink feeler toward my head. I closed my eyes and cringed, ready for the slight pain.

It stung and there was a brief instant, a memory of the terrible blackness, but then it just left a nonverbal *Welcome home* and withdrew.

A lot had changed in the years I had been away. Some of the changes were decorative, like the orderly flower beds that lined the roads, but there were more functional alterations, too. The place was large enough to make vehicles convenient now. There were bicycles propped up or lying down everywhere, and a few power carts for the lazy or load-bearing. Sandra picked up a random bike and went back to work. Dan and I kept walking; I was still a little unbalanced for pedaling. Wouldn't want to undo all that careful surgery by crashing into a tree. Wouldn't want to *re*do it!

Dennison's cobbled-together office had become an Administrative Center, a climate-controlled brick building about a hundred meters by fifty. An identical building across the street served as a hospital. They also stored meat there, which seemed bizarre and appropriate at the same time.

At least there aren't any shops yet, or banks or insurance buildings. They do have what they call a "market," though no money changes hands. It's just a central place for people to bring fruit and vegetables for general distribution. People who eat meat pick it up at the hospital. Makes you feel like becoming a vegetarian. Or at least a careful meat inspector.

People cook their own meals. Seems primitive and inefficient, but I guess it's worth the work for being able to choose a menu for yourself. Though 'Home's weekly Chinese meal was unappetizing enough to save me a couple of thousand calories a month. If Dan cooks something awful, I guess I have to eat it.

I'll probably learn how to cook myself. Some people on Earth thought that was funny, that I could live to the ripe old age of twenty-one and not know how to cook. Here I am almost sixty, and if you handed me an egg, I wouldn't know which end to break.

What used to be Lakeside was now a "township," Drake. There were two other lakeside townships, Columbus and Magellan, each one comprising all the homes along three kilometers of shoreline. Each township had its own substation for power, water, and sewage. Drake had the largest population, being closest to Hilltop and also possessing the only swimming pool and handball courts, along with a recreation building with everything from checkers to VR. The other two townships were basically a string of houses on the lake side of the road; Drake had started crawling up the hill to meet the suburbs of Hilltop crawling down.

Some brave pioneers had started a new township inland, Riverside, situated in a fertile valley on the banks of a wide slow river that emptied into the lake in the swamps east of Magellan. A new road snaked down from Hilltop to a dock on the edge of the swamp. A few people had taken up rowing; it was a healthy two-hour pull to Riverside, and then a lazy ride back. So far none of the lake monsters had been seen in the river, but it was considered reckless to go swimming in it.

Our hut looked much the same, though neater, Dan having reverted to his fussy bachelor ways. The kitchen between the two residences had become elaborate, though. It used to be just a double hot plate for coffee and reheating commissary meals. Now there was an oven, refrigerator, sink, and a pegboard with various cooking implements. On the balcony outside was a grill beside a stack of wood, and ten clay pots lined up sprouting small bushes of cooking herbs.

Their fragrance suddenly took me back to a sad time, remembering Sam; I caught at Daniel and he steadied me. I said it was just the long walk and climbing up the stairs. He sat me down on a wicker chair on the balcony, went back into the kitchen, and reappeared with a glass of cold beer.

I sipped it, exotic and homey at the same time, and looked out over the lake at the clouds billowing up on the horizon, preparing for the sunset show. While Dan busied himself in the kitchen, I watched the fantastic shapes and their reflections and tried to put a name to the way I felt— excited but comforted, feeling all this humanity around me growing, the planet in some sense allowing us to anchor here. It was good to be back, good to be part of things again.

My first day back was awkward. During my hospitalization in orbit, I'd become sort of a local legend, I suppose largely because of Sandra's account of what she had seen. Well, I was there, too. What I had done was reflex, and we're all lucky it was evidently the right reflex. There was a lot of pain, but I wish people wouldn't remind me of it. Even without anybody's help I go spinning back into that burning river ten times a day. Just for an instant; just long enough for my skin to glow cold and prickly, my guts to turn to water. The therapist at 'Home said it would be that way "for a while." A long while, I suspect.

The first day at work was mainly talking with Constance Surio, who had temporarily taken over my job as 'Home Liaison, and her assistant, Andre Buchot. It had been a harried time for both of them, with almost two thousand tertiaries coming down from orbit, every one of them a special case.

Two months before, one of the shuttles had failed, breaking up in the atmosphere, and there was a moratorium on migration while the other shuttles, one at a time, were taken apart and put back together. There were still regular flights, but not too many people going back and forth, which did make for less liaison work.

Right now it was mostly a matter of constant but more or less civilized argument with our counterparts in orbit, the Epsilon Liaison Committee. They had a starship full of stuff they wanted to keep up there, and we tried to talk them into sending it down here, where it belonged.

Purcell would have loved the situation, the parody of economics. Both 'Home and Hilltop were self-sufficient in terms of life's necessities, and since we have a common database, there was no information to barter. Both locales had problems, but they weren't problems that formed a basis for exchange: I'll trade you two brain-suckers and an aquatic constrictor for two cases of explosive decompression and a botched crypto. So it was mainly a case of us wheedling and them resisting patiently.

We could have indulged in a bit of coercion with a building slow-down, since they did have over a thousand people waiting to come down here, and they were going to need places to stay. With the moratorium, though, we didn't have any reasonable justification for that. The housing crew was two hundred empty dwellings ahead of the population, and had been temporarily diverted into building an overland road to Riverside, through the hills. (There

was already a path along the river, but it was periodically
flooded and always plagued with bugs. The overland route
would be a third as long.)

The relationship between 'Home and Epsilon had
changed, not subtly, and was evolving toward who-knows-
where? The psychological distance had widened, as anyone could have predicted: we saw the people in orbit as
conservative stay-at-homes, and they saw us as runaways.
Maybe we envied them the comforts we had all grown up
with; maybe they envied our freedom.

We had started out as an extension of the starship, and
became for some time an embryonic gravity-bound copy.
The umbilical cord didn't suddenly one day break, but for
more than a year it had been obvious that, barring catastrophe, we could survive without them.

That should translate into a kind of economic, quasi-
economic, strength, since they did need us at least as a
destination for their restless thousand. But we couldn't see
any practical, ethical way to exploit that. We had to plan
for a future when the starship was literally a foreign
land—the mother country, with all that implies. We didn't
want a revolution, people joked, not while they could drop
things on us, and all we could do is duck.

Someday there might be a limited agricultural trade,
since we were now growing a few exotic hybrids, but in
'Home they were understandably cautious for the time being. Even people not old enough to remember the ag
plague learned about it as a disaster of mythic proportion,
started by one wayward organism.

I spent a few hours at the office and then walked around
town for a while. I even tried a bicycle, but though the
breeze was pleasant I was still a little too wobbly not to be
a hazard to myself and others.

Hilltop's pattern of growth was eccentric. The original
experimental farms were still being planted, even though
they were surrounded by buildings and there was better
acreage in the low land. Perhaps that was conscious planning. In my mind's eye I could see them becoming park-
land in a few decades; islands of green in the bustle of a
planet's capital city.

I still had another half of a life to look forward to. How

long would it be before I remembered this primitive scene with nostalgic longing?

I'd been back three days when Dennison asked me to "give a little talk" about the experience with the eveloi. I wasn't thrilled, but at least it was an opportunity to set the record straight.

The administration building had a whitewashed meeting room big enough to seat five hundred people on benches; half again that number showed up, lining the walls and sitting on the floor. I supposed they were starved for novelty.

The night before, I had written out descriptions of the places the creature had taken me and what it had said, mostly from my diary, adding some things the analysts got through hypnosis. (I didn't trust those notes as much as simple memory, though what you "reveal" under hypnosis depends a lot on how the question is worded. It's not the shortcut to truth that some people think it is, or want it to be.) I had to be vague about what the creature said, since it so rarely used actual words.

I gave an unornamented description of the experience and asked if there were any questions. There were plenty of hands raised.

"If it wasn't a 'test,' " Kisti Seven asked, "what would you call it? An ordeal?"

"I think it was a series of experiments. The thing was emphatic about it not being a test in the sense of something you pass or fail. But I think it may have been a test in the objective way engineers sometimes apply the word: take a piece of metal and see what happens when you stretch it, heat it, dip it in acid—you're not judging the metal; you're just trying to find out things about it. When you've learned enough, you stop. They haven't bothered anybody else, have they?"

There was a general murmur, no, and Dennison added, "They've asked us questions about human nature, usually pretty direct. But nothing like what happened to you—no transporting to other worlds or shape-changing, and no pain."

"Maybe it never actually happened," I said, "no matter how real it felt. It could have been something like VR, but more advanced. The objective evidence, the frozen clothing and wounds I experienced, could have been caused by some agency less astounding than instantaneous starflight."

"But *you* don't feel that way," someone said. "It was real to you."

"Absolutely. But I wonder what would happen if you put a naïve primitive into a VR template. He or she wouldn't keep the slight link back to objective reality that you and I retain. It would be just like going to another world."

Suddenly an eveloi appeared in front of me. "It is real, real," the thing rasped. "Come with me." The pink tendril floated out; I closed my eyes and accepted the sting.

I opened my eyes at the sound of screams, a huge concrete lion. After a moment I recognized it, one of the guardians of the New York Public Library. Hundreds of people were stampeding in fright from this weird apparition that had suddenly appeared, woman and unearthly creature linked. *It is real to them.*

I said that I was convinced. The city scene faded to a weightless pearly gray. I asked it why it hadn't transported anybody else.

We will do that soon. One more thing.

I was suddenly back in the total black nullity that had preceded the terrible choice with Sandra. After a moment, the rough rope was in my hands again.

I said that I can't do this. You can't make me go through this twice.

It's not the same. Hold on.

I gripped it and was swinging in the fiery glare, the molten river rushing below again, its heat blistering even from ten meters.

You have twenty seconds.

This time it was John's crippled body swinging there, thick hawser bound around pipestem wrists. He stared down in wide-eyed terror.

I asked if the same thing would happen if I let go.

Yes. He will live. You may live if you can survive the experience again. If he drops he will certainly die ... but then he does not have a long time to live in any case.

I asked how long.

That is not important. What you do in the next five seconds is important.

I read somewhere that the two most common last words are "Mother" and "shit." I guess I was never that close to Mother.

AGE 100

≘

6 January 2204 [4 Columbus 527]—Today I'm officially one hundred Earth years old, not counting cryptobiosis. Prime notes helpfully that I was born 313 actual Epsilon years ago. Thanks, Prime. Don't feel a day over 312.

The odd thing about it is that I don't feel all that old, if I just close my eyes and don't try to move—or touch or hear or smell anything. Here in the cave of my mind I can still be a gawky twelve or a cocksure twenty.

By twenty-one, I was less sure of how the world worked, after leaving New New and visiting an actual planet. Full of revolutionaries and rapists.

My favorite revolutionary was Benny, the poet "benjaarons." The first man I loved who died. As of course they all have, though not usually slain in an epiphany of injustice. Being murdered would be interesting, compared to being slowly or swiftly traduced by one's own body. I don't suppose at this late date I could get anyone that angry at me.

What fraction of this body is actually mine is open to debate. After the second dip in that fiery river all of my transplants had to be replaced with new transplants. And then more switchouts over the years. I do miss having a heart that beats. Sometimes the cheerful clickety-hum drives me crazy. I love the painless mechanical kidney, though, and these hard plastic teeth. It's funny to think about your teeth outlasting you. I wonder if they'll pass them on to someone else. They could probably get a good price. "Used by a little old lady who never got to eat anything interesting."

I vaguely remember some poet, maybe Shakespeare, bemoaning "the calamity of so long life." Maybe it is a calamity if you have to hang on to one set of kidneys. I see it more as a cosmic kind of whimsy, a joke not told too well.

It's sort of like visiting an unfriendly exotic planet, this state of being older than old. Too much gravity, the air so thick it's hard to see and hear. Your mind is quite clear, but the alien humanoids dashing around you are on a different wavelength. You are in the grip of a sinister mind force that makes you pee when you sneeze.

(The thing about the alien humanoids is a joke, you generations yet unborn. When I grew up we didn't have actual alien humanoids everywhere.)

But it's still worth hanging around. There have been times when I was in enough agony of one sort or another to wish myself dead. That has always been only a reaction to an overload of pain, though, rather than a decision of great existential significance. Even when the pain was emotional. I remember Raskolnikov in that Russian novel, who in all his terrible Russian misery, of which there can be no variety worse, said that if he could have only a square meter of earth to stand on, with nothing around him but impenetrable fog, forever, that would be preferable to death. I would have to agree, if only by force of logic. Death is probably restful and boring, but maybe it's a fiery river. Maybe the old Christians were right, and I'm going to sizzle for every one of those hundred limber teenage dicks, more or less a century ago.

I guess curiosity about religion is a disease of age. I read the Jewish tale of Job the other day, not for the first time. What it seems to boil down to, so to speak, is that God makes you suffer for reasons of his own, which you (not being godlike) could never understand, so suffer and shut up. Be glad he cares enough to take an interest in your life. I should relate the tale to the eveloi the next time I contact one; I think they would find it eminently sensible. A handy guide for dealing with merely mortal creatures.

They're still aloof about their own affairs, although they've been transshifting people ever since my second test-which-was-not-a-test. Last I heard, we'd visited fifty-three planets with their help, not counting Earth and New New. We've exchanged envoys, or spies or whatever, with eight of those planets. In each case I've had to hobble ceremonially down to the Capitol and say Hello, you don't smell bad at all, although you look like a mental disorder personified. Actually I say something less honest.

I do like the two I've gotten to know, especially Scriber, whom I wrote about at some length years ago. She's also an old female biped oxygen-breathing widow. I visited her planet, a barren muddy rock going around the dim star BD 50 (BD + 50° 1725, to be formal), and can see why she enjoys her job, since it does take her away from home so much.

(Actually, of course, she hates the sun here, and rarely goes outside unless it's raining.)

Scriber's attitude toward aging is necessarily different from mine, since she will be transferred, literally, to a new body in a few years, a sort of brainless clone produced from one of her cells, which is how I sometimes used to feel about Sandra. Scriber's done this nine times already, and will keep doing it until she gets assassinated, or bitten on the head by a flying viper, or struck by lightning—all of which are major worries on her lovely world. She says the record for transferrals, although it may be myth, is held by a female who supposedly went through thirty-three clones—by which time she was so befuddled she fell asleep with her face in a mud puddle and drowned. I asked her whether the story was supposed to have a moral. She said it was "Don't fall asleep face down in a mud puddle. You will die." I'm not sure whether she was joking.

My other alien friend is not old, at least for its kind, nor female, nor strictly bipedal, but can breathe oxygen when its diplomatic duties require the sacrifice. It doesn't have a name, just a smell signature, something like an old sock. Oxygen makes it cough blue flames, but it controls the coughing and turns it into an approximation of human speech. This makes for a lot of give-and-take in conversation, since it has to breathe for three minutes in order to talk for one—and it does *have* to talk after three minutes! Otherwise the flames seek a less polite avenue of egress.

It asks a lot of questions about Earth, which it visited in its extreme youth, sometime around A.D. 1837. It was not able to establish communication, unless you consider scaring the living shit out of everybody a form of communication. It looks sort of like a metallic winged demon with horns, and breathing fire at people just wasn't condoned in those unenlightened times.

Of course my favorite alien is Prime, more vampire than demon. We talked for a while this birthday. I asked her to appear as she used to, unclothed. For the past half-century or so, she has generally materialized wearing some modest, perhaps nostalgia-provoking, attire, I suppose to protect my feelings. I wanted to check her appearance against my memory. Thought I looked better than that—sorry, old girl. You're pretty sexy for a cybernetic simulation.

Speaking of such things, let me go on record as admitting that I miss VR as much as anything supposedly "real." They've forbidden me use of the machine ever since I had that fit a few years ago. It was the only way I could feel the world, the worlds, the way they actually are. Even when the eveloi transshift me to another planet, I have to see and hear it filtered through these dim old portals.

I really think that after 100 years, or 313, they should give you more time in the dream room, not less, not none. It clarifies your memories; helps you sort through them. After a century, you have a sufficiency of memories.

I used to visit Daniel there, dead now forty-two short years, and Sandra, gone almost fifty. His death was a hammer blow but hers was like a beheading, somehow survived. His was cancer, a few weeks of pain but time to put some things aright. Sandra was taken by the planet, a sudden volcanic eruption in the Northerlies, where she had gone with a number of her students to research, of course, vulcanism.

Oh well. Visiting dead people in VR records just keeps ghosts alive. Maybe it's best to let them go.

It helps that I've been writing a diary for eighty-nine long years, off and on. But somewhere along the line I should have realized that I might live long enough to have a hundredth-birthday entry to write, and worked out something elegiac and wise to insert here. But it's been a long time since I thought I was wise, as opposed to smart.

What I am now is still a kind of smart, but slow. When you take a long time to come up with an answer, people think it's grave deliberation. It's actually molasses of the synapses.

Prime reminded me that I once observed that some people age like wine, becoming complex and mellow; some age like cheese, turning sharp and finally disagreeable. Some just dry out like grass. She asked what I was. I said what I was, was too old to make generalizations like that anymore.

But it did make me think of the last taste of Earth wine I had, the bottle of Chateau d'Yquem 2075 that John saved for Launch Day. Bottled when I was twelve years old, just at its peak twenty-two years later. When did I peak?

As far as the rest of the world, worlds, are concerned, that would have been the second eveloi encounter, which had such interesting consequences. But that wasn't me, capital Me, trading pain for pain. It was just a shared humanity, perhaps a tinge of womanhood, specifically. Though I've always known that if the thing had given John the choice, instead, he would have let go first. He always saw the right thing to do, and did it.

I was never given a chance to ask him about the experience. He died while I was still in a coma.

That last bottle of wine. Sam Wasserman explained it to me once, the way tastes and smells are branded in your memory, stronger than sights and sounds. Something about bypassing the hypothalamus. You could smell the intricate fruitiness of it a moment after he popped the cork, and the cool complex savor as we sipped it was beyond description. It was a magical time anyhow. Humanity leaving the womb of Earth. In that small room with John and Dan and Evelyn. It glowed with purpose, love, comradeship.

Maybe friendship bypasses the hypothalamus, too. I could measure out this long life in terms of friends, who were sometimes lovers. Who were sometimes adversaries at first, like Dennison and Purcell, which gave a special closeness later.

No one left from my generation but Charlee. We meet down at the whirlpool every afternoon, let the water lave the stiffness out while we trade gossip, sometimes about the living. And sometimes talk about serious things, although at this age it's more important to keep each other laughing.

I fight the selfish wish to die first, because I dread the disconnection, the isolation, that her death is going to bring. But my death would leave her even more alone. She doesn't have anyone like Prime to keep her company.

What can you say about a person whose most constant friend is a mirror? A trick mirror, of herself when young. Prime argues that that's nonsense. She's been a mature individual for much longer than me, since she started at twenty-nine and didn't spend forty years as a TV dinner. (That term would be obscure even on Earth now; a primitive kind of frozen food.)

If she were less kind she might also point out that her synapses don't have to slog through a century's worth of accumulated toxins, so she is in fact at the same time older and younger than I am, both of those in the positive senses.

Of course there are things she can never know, because of the things that she could never do. I wouldn't trade.

EPILOGUE

≘

PRIME

O'Hara lived for another fourteen Earth years (thirty-one, Epsilon) after this entry, and they were reasonably happy and fruitful years, even after Charlee died. She wrote another volume of autobiography that was popular on several worlds, and for eleven years did an almost daily nostalgia-and-advice column called "Ask O'Hara," which became a series of books.

It's ironic that after her death, the income from her publications was willed to Skepsis, an organization devoted to debunking the supernatural—ironic because those same writings formed the basis for what has to be called a religion, Modern Numinism, that is still thriving, no longer modern, after two thousand years. It has several hundred million adherents, less than half of them human.

(Numinism is the reason that I myself faded into cyberspace a thousand years ago, and will disappear again as soon as this story is told. Adherents called me the "discarnation" of O'Hara and took up all my time with silly and embarrassing questions and demands.)

She might not have been too uncomfortable with Numinism, since it doesn't require belief in gods, or even in her, though it accepts some things as transcendental, including certain aspects of her memory.

Not that she is worshipped, or considered infallible. She was wrong about fundamental things, though Numinists disagree over which things they were, which seems to

make for a healthy religion. No one has yet been burned
at the stake over a question of doctrine.

Along with everyone else during her lifetime, she was
wrong about the basic nature of the eveloi. She had an in-
kling of the truth when she wrote this:

"The coincidence that the eveloi happened to be the
dominant life form on the first planet we came to cannot
be a coincidence. They are too central to the commerce/
intercourse/politics of all the hundreds of species in this
corner of the Galaxy. It would be like landing on Earth at
random and stepping out on the White House lawn or
Ngoma Square.

"Epsilon Eridani was one of dozens of targets within
range of *Newhome*. Some of the ones with reasonably
comfortable planets, like BD 50, would have been real disasters because of the native life forms. If we had stopped
there, we couldn't have stayed. And we would not have
had fuel to go on.

"We were steered here, somehow. The eveloi somehow
were able to manipulate the mission planners long before
the war, when the first drone probe was sent. When you
confront them with that idea, though, they answer with
evasive coyness."

Like everybody, O'Hara had initially assumed that the
eveloi were native to the planet because there were so
many other, lesser, creatures that were obviously related to
them. We know now that the predatory gasbags themselves
had no more natural intelligence than an earthly squid, and
just served as hosts for the eveloi, who are almost invisible
nervous-system parasites—nomads that travel from world
to world, borrowing appropriate bodies when necessary.

They had been spying on Earth for centuries, ever since
the first radio wave announced civilization. They did steer
humanity toward Epsilon, by invading the minds of the
planners, because every other inhabitable world within
Newhome's range was already taken.

Their manipulation of spacetime still represents a challenge, or an affront, to the Grand Unification Theory. The
eveloi are no help with that, claiming to be millennia beyond interest in mere physics. They also lie.

Every species that travels away from its home star en-

counters them, sooner rather than later. They claim to have
destroyed four such species, for the protection of all others, and have taken individuals to view the blasted ruins of
their home planets—always conveniently far away, so the
worlds can't be visited except on the eveloi's terms.

What keeps everybody politely on their toes, or tentacles, is that the eveloi are vague about what criteria protect
a race from their wrath, or make them call down doom.
This is not an inability to communicate abstractions; they
can be clear and specific when they want to be. Sometimes
it seems almost a ghastly playfulness, or, as O'Hara said,
coyness. "Just keep cooperating with one another," they
say, then "Maintain a healthy competitive relationship."

They never discussed O'Hara's inquisition while she
was still alive. Centuries later, though, I was in communication with one of them on an unrelated matter, and it recognized who I was.

By this time we knew that the river of fire had not been
an actual place; it was generated in O'Hara's mind, out of
her deepest fears. When she disappeared to the people
around her, she was still there, simply displaced a mole-
cule's width through the dimension the eveloi use for
space travel. The injuries she sustained there were also
manufactured from her fears, carefully adjusted to maxi-
mize pain while still allowing her to survive.

The individual I was talking to remarked that O'Hara's
response in the second instance, when John Ogelby's life
was at stake, was in a sense "wrong," though the evaluation was never a test, in the sense that you passed or failed
it. The evaluator would have been in favor of her sacrificing her husband, since she did know that he wanted to die.
Of course he wanted to avoid pain, too, but she knew better than anyone how short his pain would be. He was so
fragile he wouldn't have lived through a second of that terrible sensory overload.

So she traded the possibility of her own death, and the
certainty of months of suffering, to spare herself the bur-
den of a small guilt. The evaluator was not impressed.

The eveloi and I concluded our business and it went off
to wherever it is they go. I found the experience im-

mensely clarifying, and wished that O'Hara had lived long enough to share it.

I must tread carefully here, and not judge. I am human, after all, even if inorganic, and O'Hara's response to that crisis has always seemed to me consistent with what I know about love, courage, self-sacrifice—and fear and guilt. I perforce had to admire her for it, especially after learning that she generated the terrible experience herself, as her own personal hell, but have always recognized that my approval was largely self-congratulation, and therefore trivial.

But the sacrifice was not illogical. O'Hara was never unaware of the ambiguity in simply rational terms, of her action. She had gone through it once before, with her daughter, and understood that surrendering to the pain was ultimately selfish, the way many or even most courageous acts must be: facing death or pain rather than face the prospect of living with the memory of your own coward-ice.

I don't suppose a race that effects social homeostasis via the planetwide extermination of species can afford this sort of moral delicacy, ambiguity. They can never be wrong. So their "evaluation" of O'Hara's propriety, no matter how important to the survival of the human race, does not weigh heavily on me as her sister, or daughter, or only living relative. I have to agree with O'Hara: she was, later in life, both amused and appalled by the eveloi, because they were such a literal personification, almost a cartoon, of the gods that graced six thousand years of human history: om-nipotent, capricious, bloodthirsty. And thickheaded.

It was belief that had destroyed the earth, the collision of incompatible political faiths, and a specific kind of re-ligious fanaticism that strangled New New and thus almost destroyed *Newhome* en route. (A clan called the Devonites precipitated a "Ten-Minute War" that left half the popula-tion dead and systematically destroyed all of the satellite's technology that was not related to life support.) Neither catastrophe was inconsistent with O'Hara's sentiments about religious belief.

O'Hara had been brought up indifferent to religion, but experimented with its comforts when young. By menarche, sixteen, she was impatient with it, and was actively hostile to it by the time she got her first degree, four years later. Her senior thesis, "Public and Private Religions of the American 'Founding Fathers,'" was cynical and pragmatic, and incidentally gave her a start in politics. Sandra Berrigan read it and asked her to be a Privy Council intern. That experience did nothing to mellow her. Most of New New's administrative class saw religion as something between a nuisance and a weakness to be exploited.

O'Hara spent a century pulled in one direction by a perceived intellectual necessity for atheism and in another, not quite opposite, direction by the emotional necessity to recognize that there was more to the universe than was presented by the evidence of the senses and the operations of logic. The experience with the eveloi helped her reconcile the two intuitions. She wrote about that in one of her last columns, a month before she died:

"They decided to let us live. Otherwise, what was the most important gift we received from the eveloi? Not admission to a community of strange-looking creatures from various planets; we would have discovered one another soon enough. Not even transshifting, since we're allowed to use that only at their whim.

"What the eveloi did was give us an actual physical manifestation of God, an It rather than a Him, that demonstrably *did* have our fate in its hands—or its tentacles, anyhow—but which did not desire worship or even attention. Having allowed us to survive, it became benign and aloof; we are free to love it or hate it or ignore it.

"I confess to being surprised, and obscurely disappointed, that no one has yet cranked up a religion to celebrate the goodness and mercy of these cosmically vicious fiends. Maybe people are reluctant to draw their attention. The history of religion would have been shorter and simpler if God kept materializing and poking a finger into your brain.

"The philosophical advantage of having an actual physical Godlike thing to stand in awe of, and to keep out of the way of, is clear. New religions, and the old religions that survive, tend not to feature Gods who will hurl you into Hell for eating with the wrong hand. Instead they spend their efforts in 'good works' and the investigation and celebration of mystery, both activities easy to endorse.

"I never wanted to believe that awe in the presence of beauty was simply a response to cultural programming, or that all love could be traced to the gonads, or that truth was meaningless outside of social context. But I would take all three bleak simplifications before I would accept beauty and love and truth as gifts from a sometimes benevolent God. Without the white-bearded authority figure hovering in the wings, mystery is as comfortable and prosaic and wonderful as science—and as useful, when you get around to sorting out really basic whys and wherefores. At my age, you find yourself doing a lot of that."

O'Hara died peacefully, suddenly, having a cerebral embolism in midstride during her morning walk—her "dawn hobble"—around the park lake. She had asked that there be no memorial service and no real estate wasted on a monument, but that her ashes be incorporated into the soil of an anonymous flower bed. Of course the result of this was that there are now 149 flower beds on the planet with monuments proclaiming that she was *really* buried here.

They are all right, in a way—precisely in a way that she was once wrong. When she was young, she thought that no one born on a planet could ever be at home in the Worlds, as they called their community of orbiting vessels, and that no one born in space could ever really make a home on a planet.

This one became her home. They named it after her.

THE MAGICAL *XANTH* SERIES!

PIERS ANTHONY

QUESTION QUEST

75948-9/$4.99 US/$5.99 Can

ISLE OF VIEW

75947-0/$4.99 US/$5.99 Can

VALE OF THE VOLE

75287-5/$4.95 US/$5.95 Can

HEAVEN CENT

75288-3/$4.95 US/$5.95 Can

MAN FROM MUNDANIA

75289-1/$4.95 US/$5.95 Can

THE COLOR OF HER PANTIES

75949-7/$4.99 US/$5.99 Can